March,

Dear Charles family,

You will perhaps remember two Dutch people who rented Parks Court, when one of them was already very, very ill.

My first novel is very inspired by my best friend passing away, but also the time we spent at your beautiful house. Although a difficult time, I wouldn't have missed it for the world.

Love,
Margot Rijkamp
aka Emma Flagard

Emma Flogard

All I've Got

Heroes on Socks
true creator support

First edition, November 2012

Cover design by André Pluimers

Cover art by Hanneke Wetzer

HEROES ON SOCKS
True Creator Support

ISBN: 978-90-818242-0-0

To my darling friend

That room in my heart

Belongs to you always

To my dear readers, my friends and maybe future friends,

I sincerely hope you will enjoy this book. The book was written with love, and that is exactly the message I wish to convey: the feeling of being loved, that comes in many shapes and sizes and more so with ups and downs.

Yours with love,

Emma

x

Prologue

Only few people would truly realize how much she would miss him. Not many people had known how much she'd really loved him for all those years. Oh, sure, everybody had known they were the very best of friends, soul mates even. They had shared everything, been part of each other's daily routines. But this is what she'd had to learn to value.

Chapter 1

"Come *on*, Dad, you can't be serious!" Sarah stomped through the living room in frustration. "You promised me I would be able to go abroad, and now you're telling me I can't! This is *so* unfair!"

Bill McFadden looked at his tall, headstrong daughter.

"Sarah, I don't recall we ever promised you that you could go after high school," he said with a calm voice.

"Nicky was allowed to go to Australia when she was my age!" Sarah argued, her green eyes spitting fire.

He inhaled slowly, buying himself some time.

"Sarah, you are *seventeen*," he said with emphasis. "Nicky went to Australia for her first job, after finishing her degree."

Sarah gave her father a cold glare.

"There's nothing wrong with staying in Halifax and going to Dal-U; it's a very good university," Bill said.

"There is nothing wrong with *Dal-U*; there is *everything* wrong with **You-U**!" Sarah yelled.

She gaged her father's reaction. His determined poise left no room for doubt; the decision was final.

"I am *not* staying here!" Sarah said fiercely, trying to hold back her tears.

"I'm sorry you feel that way, but it does not change our decision. You're going to Dalhousie and that's final." Bill turned away from Sarah considering the conversation over.

"No, I'm not!" Sarah shouted and ran up the stairs, now sobbing. Over her shoulder she cried out: "Even the *Amish* get their rumspringa period!!"

She bumped into her older brother Marc who roared with laughter.

"And wouldn't you just look adorable in a hand-stitched potato sack with a white cap," he teased her.

"Buzz off!" Sarah pushed him aside and slammed her bedroom door behind her.

"No, I mean it," Marc was still laughing and called after her, "you could totally make that work for you!"

"With a retard of a brother to match, you mean!" Sarah's muffled voice came through the door.

Bill McFadden walked into the kitchen shaking his head and looked at his wife Tracy.

"You know, Trace," he sighed deeply, "this youngest child of ours has always been a handful…"

Marc walked in after his father, still sniggering.

"Marc," Tracy looked at him reproachfully, "can you please not make the situation any harder than it already is?"

"I don't know, Mom," Marc smiled widely at his mother, "I'm not the one who raised the stand-up comedian – she's just too funny."

"Yes, very funny," Tracy said unsmiling. "You're the big brother, swallow your comments for a change!" She gave him a stern look.

Marc wasn't going to drop the subject yet. "Did you hear her just now? *Amish rumspringa*, I mean, where does she come up with that stuff?"

"Bill," Tracy tried to suppress a smile and quickly turned away, "we're doing the only thing we can." She rubbed her husband's shoulder briefly. "Goodness knows we've gone through enough getting her through high school."

"I know," Bill said as he poured himself a coffee. "She will not survive university if she doesn't have a strict schedule. Student life is even less organized than high school. She will always have more important things to do."

"It's going to be a long time before she sees this our way, sweetheart," Tracy said and added doubtfully: "*if* that day ever comes."

"Foolish, stubborn girl," Bill muttered and looked over at Tracy. "I wonder who she gets that from…"

Tracy laughed good-naturedly. "Don't you dare look at me, William McFadden," she said, "this runs in *your* family, not mine!"

"Yep," Marc added innocently, "and I did not inherit any of it either, Dad!"

"Sure, my dear boy, you go through life believing that."

Bill picked up his coffee mug and only said: "If you need me, I'll be in my study."

"Okay," Marc said ironically, "that's two sulking in their rooms… Two down, two-to-go!"

"Again, Marc, hardly helpful!" Tracy sighed.

Chapter 2

"Okay brother-mine, let's get you to Yarmouth and on to the *big citay*!" Paul Schmidt called out the window of his pick-up truck as he drove up to the front of the farmhouse.

"Matthew," Mary Schmidt hugged her youngest son, "will you please take care of yourself and let us know if you need anything?" She was having a hard time letting go.

"Where's Dad?" Matthew asked, looking around.

"Your father had to take the tractor back to the field," Mary said softly. "You know he never was very good at goodbyes," she smiled briefly. "He said to wish you a good journey."

"Oh," was all Matthew said.

"Did you pack everything?" Mary asked as she straightened the lapel on Matthew's worn jacket.

"I think so," Matthew looked at his mother. "Don't worry, Mom, I'll be fine."

"Come on, Matt, The Big Pear awaits!" Paul heaved the last bag onto the flatbed of the truck. "The city that always sleeps!"

"Okay, here I go – Halifax or bust!" Matthew hollered as he got into his brother's truck.

"Give us a call when you get there!" Mary called out.

Matthew stuck up his thumb in confirmation.

"So, my little brother is going to college," Paul patted his brother's chest.

"I feel so fortunate that I got in! I can hardly believe I'm actually going," Matthew smiled radiantly. He turned around to Paul.

"You could have gone if you wanted to," Matthew said. "Why didn't you? You're at least as smart if not smarter than I am."

"Rather you than me, Matt. College just isn't for me – besides, I didn't get the scholarship," Paul simply stated. "We couldn't afford for me to go!"

"You, my dear brother," Matthew challenged him, "did not get the scholarship, because you never applied for it."

"True, but that sounds less heroic. I didn't need the scholarship 'cause I'm taking over the farm."

"Well, no competition there, Paul," Matthew shrugged. "But what if Dad is going to stay on at the farm for the next 25 years?"

"Well, then I will just have to figure out somethin' else," Paul said nonchalantly.

"Will you tell Mom I'll be all right?" Matthew asked.

"Look at you, you old *mama's boy* – holding your bag of cup cakes," Paul teased him.

"And that makes you what? *Daddy's joy?*" Matthew teased back.

"Absolutely – who else does he have to go hunting with?" Paul sniggered. "Certainly not you!"

They both laughed as they arrived at Yarmouth bus station, where Paul unloaded Matthew's things.

As he gave his younger brother a bear hug, he said: "Take care, Matt, good luck."

"Thanks, Paul, see ya!" Matthew swallowed as he patted his brother on the back. "And take care of Tuffy for me, will you?"

"Takin' care of Scruffy-dog – *check*!" Paul mock-saluted as he got back in the truck.

The journey to Halifax took longer than Matthew had anticipated. He had tried to read on the train, but couldn't concentrate. His anxiety for what he would find overruled everything. Again he stared at the advertisement they had found in the local Yarmouth newspaper.

> **Halifax: Spacious, furnished room for rent**
>
> **with shared bath and kitchen facilities.**
>
> **Well suited for student.**

The landlord met up with Matthew at the house and showed him around. The furnished attic room was smaller than Matthew had imagined and the shared kitchen was messy and sticky. The temperature in the room was unbearable and the small windows hardly offered any fresh air. What a change from the farm!

Still, this was all they could afford, so he would have to make do with it. Matthew decided that feeling homesick would not help. He unpacked, made his bed and had an early night. Tomorrow he'd make an early start for the Campus. He heard unfamiliar noises coming from other parts of the large house and from the street below.

It was a long time before he fell asleep.

Chapter 3

On the first day after summer break there was the usual hustle and bustle of the new students' arrival at Dalhousie University. The nervous energy they generated would have been enough to power the lights at Dal-U for the rest of the year. Arriving from all over Nova Scotia - some even farther away – they felt lost on this large Campus.

Their introduction program started from the Dalplex Recreation Centre with a Campus Quest. Sarah had decided on her usual outfit: jeans, polo shirt and hi-top sneakers; her thick chestnut hair done up in a ponytail. She walked through the doors of the Dalplex feeling nothing but resentment for being there.

A senior student, Alvin, explained that 68 freshmen had enrolled for Design & Arts classes and he would be guiding them during the Quest. Sarah spotted a girl that she had been in high school with, Tanya Jensen. Although she did not really know Tanya all that well, there was something about her that made Sarah uneasy. Tanya saw Sarah and walked over.

"Hi Sarah, I did not know you were starting Design & Arts," Tanya said in an accusatory tone.

"Hi… Yep, here we are… Nice day for it," Sarah was clearly not in the mood for chitchat.

Seeing Tanya added to Sarah's frustration of being in Halifax and not somewhere more exciting.

As soon as Alvin started calling the names for the groups, Tanya poked Sarah in the arm.

"I hope I won't be in the same group as *hick boy* over there," she said snorting.

Tanya raised her voice slightly: "Our next model is John Denver and he shows us the straw hat look, adding some check pattern accessories."

Sarah looked over and saw a tall, slender, dark-haired boy

dressed in a plaid shirt, jeans and old-fashioned glasses. His dark hair covered his eyes as he stared down with an earnest expression.

"What's wrong with John Denver?" Sarah asked defiantly. "Personally, I'm a big fan!" she lied, leaving a baffled Tanya behind.

Sarah joined her group when she heard her name. There were six of them in the group and they made brief introductions. Among the six was the earnest boy, who introduced himself as Matthew. He was not much better looking on closer inspection, with his bad haircut. His shyness and dropped shoulders did not help.

The Campus Quest was okay. At least it was a lovely sunny day to explore the Campus. John was the clown of the group and they all laughed at the ridiculous answers he suggested. Sarah and Matthew were the most active in getting the answers right - Sarah because of her competitive attitude; Matthew because of his serious nature. Sarah was impressed by how much he knew, but Matthew did not feel comfortable with Sarah at all. Although he saw and admired the ease with which she talked to the others, he felt over-powered by her presence. She was far too good looking and sporty for his taste. He never had felt at ease with the popular crowd.

Somewhere towards the end of the afternoon, Sarah overheard some of the team making fun of Matthew. Here, too, John was the one mimicking Matthew.

"Come on, guys..." Sarah said. Not for a moment did it occur to her that Matthew might not want her help.

At the end of the afternoon it was time to go to the Studley part of the Campus for the big start-of-the-year barbeque party for all the Dalhousie students. Sarah asked Matthew if he was planning to go.

"I don't know," Matthew shrugged noncommittally, not looking at Sarah, "I have just moved into my student room and still have some things to do there."

Sarah noticed he was keeping his distance.

"I am *so* jealous you got to move into a student room," she said with a longing sigh, "I still live with my parents. *Boring!* Are you staying here in the dorms?"

"No," Matthew nodded, "the dorms were too expensive," he said honestly. "I came here on a scholarship."

"Oh, so where are you from?" Sarah asked. "I take it you couldn't commute?"

Matthew stared in the distance for a moment.

"I come from a small town Kemptville, near Yarmouth," he said. Pushing back his hair, he added drily: "My hair is from un-kempt-ville these days… barber broke his arm."

Sarah suppressed a smile and did not comment.

"Come on, let's go to the barbeque together," Sarah pleaded, "at least we will each know one person there between the masses. I'd hate to go alone."

Matthew looked at her in surprise.

"Yeah, maybe," Matthew said hesitantly, "I guess it couldn't hurt to get to know some more people before we start classes."

"Great!" Sarah said.

It was a warm summer evening, wonderful to linger and enjoy the music and the cold beers. For many of the new students this was baptism into student life away from home and they were thoroughly enjoying their newfound freedom. Matthew and Sarah had a good time. They wandered among the crowds and had a bite to eat. Sarah could not hide it. This shy young man from the South of Nova Scotia, with his warm dark-brown eyes, intrigued her. She asked him endless questions. Eventually, Matthew laughed at this; he sensed she meant well and her interest was genuine.

"So, Sarah, why did you choose Design & Arts?" Matthew decided to turn the conversation around.

"I guess it started in a place called Bath in the UK," Sarah said. "We always used to go there for our summer holidays. My father is a history teacher and he just loves Bath. He has infected us with that virus. The rich architecture there is what triggered me first, I think," Sarah said.

"Really, Bath?" Matthew turned towards her with clear interest.

"As in: Royal Crescent and the Roman Baths?"

"Yep, the very place!" she said.

"Oh, now *I* am the one who's jealous!" Matthew said. "Dyrham Park is near Bath, right?"

"Yes, you know it?" Sarah looked at him in surprise. Dyrham Park was not the first thing that would spring to Sarah's mind when talking about Bath.

"So far only from a book," Matthew's voice indicating regret.

"Beautiful 17th-century mansion, Dyrham Park, just big enough for my taste," Matthew said with appreciation.

"I used to be carried around Dyrham Park in one of those sedan chairs, you know, by two porters," Sarah haughtily stuck up her nose and then winked at him.

"Well, I'm just happy to see it didn't change your modest nature," he winked back.

"To be honest, I was only four or five at the time," Sarah smiled happily at Matthew.

Chapter 4

Matthew was slowly starting to get used to the differences between Kemptville and Halifax and was now seeing the possibilities that life in Halifax had to offer. They couldn't afford for him to go home every weekend and the first time he did, he was thrilled to go.

Paul had picked him up in Yarmouth. Matthew was very happy to see his big brother again. Despite the enormous differences between the two, they had always gotten along well. Paul was a real outdoorsman, a jock, who had not been able to pursue his dream of playing professional ice hockey. He had badly hurt his shoulder during a school football match, and had had to give up on the sports career. Now he often went hunting with the farmers in the area.

For Matthew going out hunting had been torture. He had tried, but could not bring himself to kill any animal.

His father and Paul always joked with him that he would be a vegetarian without them, and Matthew instantly agreed.

Matthew was happiest going to the library in Kemptville, always checking which new books had arrived.

Once a year the library sold their older stock and Matthew would spend all his savings there. One of his all-time favorites was a book about palaces and castles in England. He had bought it when he was eleven years old, and had gone through it so often, he would swear he knew it by heart. The house he liked the best was Castle Howard near York. The amazing pictures of the rich baroque house and the descriptions were engraved in his mind. He hoped he would be able to see it with his own eyes one day.

"So, have you made the Dalhousie Tigers team yet?" Paul asked teasingly, as Matthew got in the truck.

"No, not just yet. Actually, I did join a practice, but they said

I was too good for 'em," Matthew winked at Paul. "They felt threatened by me, I guess. Must be all that practice I got skating on the pond," Matthew said with the brightest of smiles. Paul only sniggered; Matthew's skating had been memorable to say the least, but not exactly because of his talent.

"So, how's the hunt been?" Matthew asked in return. "Did you hit anything after I left, or will I have to do it all myself again?" They laughed as Paul assured him that there would be a special treat on the table that evening.

Matthew had so much to tell, all these new impressions. His family couldn't wait to have him home again. His mother had been worried and wanted to know everything. How was the room? Did he like university? Had he made new friends yet? Had he found a church nearby? Did he clean his room from time to time?

John Schmidt took his wife's hand and pulled at it softly. "Give the boy a chance to walk in the door, dear," he smiled patiently at her.

Over a home-cooked roast Matthew told his family about his many new experiences, his progress at Dal-U, the neighborhood where he now lived, after which he couldn't wait to crawl in his own quiet bed again. Getting to sleep proved harder than he had imagined, though. One question of his mother's kept going round in his mind. *Had he found a church nearby yet?* The truth was, he *had* found a good catholic church not too far away. It was one of the first things on his list he had taken care of. But he hadn't gone to mass yet. He couldn't bring himself to go.

Even back in Kemptville he had often felt uneasy in church because some of the things they preached were so black and white, so intolerant. It had been impossible to discuss this with his parents. "Jesus gave us the example of tolerance and forgiveness, for all the sacrifices he had made," was the only reply he ever got. Since going to church was no longer a family thing in Halifax, he had felt less pressure to go. But he did feel guilty about this. He didn't want to start the discussion all over again, so he told his family of St. Patrick's Church on Brunswick Street, which was roughly halfway between his room and Dal-U.

Although Matthew had been very excited to go home for the weekend, he was also happy to return. His parents hardly ever drove, so Paul took him back to Yarmouth late Sunday afternoon. Matthew realized that the reason he was glad to be going back, was that the quiet atmosphere he had cherished so much before, had now become – it was difficult to say – oppressive. This probably had to do with all that was left unsaid.

Paul was trying to make casual conversation during the ride back, but Matthew was too deep in thought.

"I said, isn't it nice that Shelley agreed to *marry me*?" Paul raised his voice.

"What?" Matthew was stunned. "I am gone for a few weeks and you start proposing willy-nilly?"

"You mean, Shelley-Nilly? No, just kidding!" Paul laughed reassuringly. "We have been on a date together, but we haven't gotten to the aisle yet. I will let you know if we get closer."

"You do that, Paul!" Matthew said with emphasis. "If you need a best man, I'm getting better at giving speeches."

"No way," Paul teased him. "My shy brother, giving speeches?"

Matthew shrugged. "I guess that going to university is going to be good for something after all," he said soberly.

"And I still wouldn't trade you!" Paul shook his head, laughing.

They soon arrived at the bus terminal and Matthew jumped out. "Thanks for the ride, Paul," Matthew said. "It was nice to be home." He tapped the roof of the truck.

Paul waved briefly and drove off without looking over his shoulder.

Matthew stared at the truck until it disappeared. Much had changed over the past weeks, he thought, but the change wasn't in Kemptville.

Chapter 5

"Mom, can I bring a friend home for dinner tomorrow night?" Sarah poked her head around the kitchen door. Tracy McFadden looked at her daughter with slight bemusement. Sarah had been rebellious about having to go to Dal-U, but now that the first semester was well on its way, Tracy noticed Sarah's resistance was fading slowly.

"Of course you can invite a friend for dinner, Sarah," Tracy said.

"Well, I don't know if he will want to come," Sarah shrugged briefly. "He's moved out here all the way from near Yarmouth. I think he might be kind of lonely. I'll ask him today. Thanks, Mom."

Sarah's brother, Marc, sighed loudly. "Oh, please, haven't you had enough social youth projects in high school?" he asked, rolling his eyes. "For Pete's sake, a new 'stray puppy' to drag home?"

As much as Sarah wanted to ignore her brother, she said triumphantly: "Actually it's for Matthew's sake in this case." She put on her coat and called from the back door: "See you tonight, Mom, we will have classes till late in the afternoon."

In class they had now reached the Roman period and were learning about the improvements the Romans made to construction methods of the Greeks. A lot of this Matthew already knew, but he would never tire of it.

Sarah met up with Matthew in the hall.

"So, mine Herr *Sjjjmeet*, how was your weekend?" Sarah pronounced his surname, as Matthew had explained his German family did.

"It was okay," Matthew responded too blandly for Sarah's taste. She assumed he felt homesick after having been home. *Perfect timing then to invite him*, she thought to herself.

"I was thinking maybe tonight I could invite you for dinner at my house," Sarah said, checking out Matthew's reaction.

"My mom is a great cook and we'd love for you to come."
Matthew was slightly thrown by this. "Dinner… at your house?"
He looked at her with suspicion. "To what do I owe the honor of
this invitation? Do your parents know about this?"
"Do you think I would ask you if they didn't?" Sarah playfully
pushed him. "No, seriously, it would be great if you could come.
My parents are dying to meet you!"
"Dying to meet me, huh?" Matthew wondered what Sarah
could have told her parents about him. There wasn't so much to
meet as far as he could be the judge and he felt self-conscious
over the comment.
"Okay, I'll come," he smiled, "one evening of not cleaning up
after my roommates before I start cooking."
"Wounderbar!" Sarah laughed.
"Gives me a chance to check out your dad's humongous library
that you've been bragging about all this time!" Matthew teased her.
"Maybe we can find something for the assignment on the
Roman period in our *immense* library – something Bath-ian,
Bath-ish, from Bath anyway?" Sarah said dreamily. "Oh, it's
been too long since I've been!"

Late afternoon they met up and biked to Sarah's house on
Rosebank Avenue in the pouring rain. Autumn had arrived
early in Halifax.
Matthew couldn't help but be impressed by the widely spaced
residential area they had reached. In front of a large house
with an inviting bay window, Sarah stopped and got off her
bike. Matthew followed her and placed his bike next to hers.
"You realize I'm going to have to bike all the way back in this?"
Matthew pointed at the rainy clouds.
"At least you will have some decent food in you!" Sarah said,
refusing to feel sorry for him.
They went inside and took off their wet coats.

"Hi, mom, we're home!" Sarah yelled through to the kitchen
and Tracy opened the door to greet them.
"Hello, Matthew, how nice to meet you," Tracy said with a
warm smile.

Matthew felt more and more relaxed thanks to the calm welcome of Tracy McFadden. She was quite different from his own mother, much more stylish and elegant, but not overdone. "Thank you, Mrs. McFadden, for having me over for dinner," Matthew said politely.

After Sarah and Matthew had gone through the ideas for their assignment, they got down to the kitchen where Sarah's father and her brother Marc had already taken place at a large oak table.

"Wow, Mr. McFadden, I have been admiring your library," Matthew said, shaking Bill McFadden's hand. "That's an impressive collection of books you have here."

Marc whispered to Sarah: "I see you have met your Amish rumspringa boy at last!"

Sarah angrily glared at her brother and hoped Matthew hadn't heard.

"Well, thank you Matthew," Bill said, smiling, "I have been collecting books forever, mostly on history, of course."

"One day I hope to have a collection like yours on architecture," Matthew said.

Sarah saw that Matthew hadn't been quite as shy with her family as when they had first met and was happy about this. Matthew had such a great sense of humor, that it would be a shame if they didn't get to see that side of him. How refreshing to have a guy friend for a change. Sarah's girl friends in high school had been okay, but they could only talk about looks, clothes, shopping and dating – all highly overrated in her opinion. Her friends had often teased her because, out of school, Sarah mostly wore her tracksuit and was either on her way to or from the basketball court.

At the end of the evening Matthew thanked Tracy for the wonderful dinner and got ready to bike to his room.

"Where do you live now, Matthew?" Bill asked.

"North of here on Russell Street, Sir, just off Gottingen," Matthew said.

Marc wondered how a quiet farm boy like Matthew could live in a melting pot area like the north end of Halifax, but did not comment on it. Matthew was actually much nicer than the dorky types Sarah had brought home before. They'd had a good laugh at Matthew's impression of Professor Gellert at Dal-U, with his strong German accent and his rather forceful way of speaking.

After Matthew left, Sarah's parents commented that they had liked Matthew; he seemed polite and helpful.

Marc only gave a fake yawn.

Chapter 6

"Matthew, would you get your royal behind out of the canoe, so we can get it back to the rental dock?" Sarah called out, placing her hand over her eyes to block out the sun.

"I don't think I can, my darling Sarah," Matthew didn't move, "because I can't use my arms and my legs anymore."

The others couldn't help it; they were howling with laughter at the sight of Matthew returning upstream to the boat landing. He was sitting backwards and paddling backwards too.

They had wondered where he had disappeared.

"Matthew, what *on earth* are you…?" Beatrice wanted to ask him, but was laughing so loud, she couldn't finish her sentence and grabbed her camera instead.

"I have never seen anyone canoe like that before," Thierry stated drily. "Matt, what's your plan with that?"

"That's an interesting T-shirt, Thierry," Matthew tried to draw the attention away from himself. "Takes a very secure man to wear a Batman T-shirt."

"Well, I figured, if I wear shorts instead of tights, I could get away with it," Thierry laughed joyfully. "Now about your interesting afternoon, Matthew…"

"**Will** you stop laughing?" Matthew yelled at Sarah and Beatrice in dismay.

"Sorry, we're not even going to hide laughing at your expense!" Sarah said brightly.

"Nope, sorry…" Beatrice agreed, taking another picture.

"Can you believe it, Thierry?" Matthew's voice sounded highly irritated. "They forgot to tell me how to put it in reverse!"

"Reverse?" Thierry repeated in disbelief.

"No, honestly," Matthew said seriously. "As soon as I got to the middle of the lake, the wind caught the tip of the canoe and kept turning me the wrong way. I tried to turn around, but almost tipped over a few times with all my stuff on board. So I decided to be pragmatic."

"So this is you… being pragmatic?" Beatrice hiccupped.

Matthew moaned loudly as Thierry helped him out of the canoe. "Geez, I'm exhausted!" Matthew exclaimed as he gingerly sat down on the grass. "I don't think I can lift my arms anymore…"

"Don't worry, Matt, we will gladly feed you!" Sarah smiled at him sweetly.

After their second year at Dal-U, the group of friends had decided to go camping at Kejimkujik Park for the start of their summer break – they were ready to get out of the city. Being from Lockeport, Keji Park was a favorite get-away for Beatrice and her family. It didn't take her long to convince the others of the beautiful scenery, the peace, the quiet and the endless trails. They planned to do some hiking and had rented a canoe for the day.

"Did you guys see those *ginormous* turtles we passed as we paddled away from the landing?" Beatrice asked as they hoisted their gear out of the canoes.

"The slow long strikes as they swim," Beatrice said – sounding moved, "it's just amazing. I don't recall them being so big."

"Well, Bee, these dear turtles must have said the same thing about you as *they* got back this evening," Thierry teased her. With his hands on his hips, in a high pitch voice he lisped: "Did you zzee our little Beatrizze? I zzwear I almozzt didn't recognizze her in zzat big canoe," he stopped briefly to duck from Sarah, threatening to hit him over the head with a pan, only to continue undisturbed: "Boy zzhe'zz grown aftzer all thozze yearzz!"

"Yeah, yeah – first of all, turtles don't have that speech impediment that you do!" Beatrice chortled. "I mean, did you even *spot* the turtles? You should have stayed in Halifax, in your *blind-as-a-bat* cave!" Beatrice chased Thierry across the field but he was too fast for her.

"Oh, yes, …" Matthew sighed lazily. "Romance is in the air." He was still stretched out on the grass, totally exhausted.

Sometime later, the girls were preparing a meal in the cabin, while the guys were getting a fire started outside.

"What's going on with you and Thierry?" Sarah whispered to Beatrice.

"What do you mean?" Beatrice asked innocently.

"What do you mean: 'what do you mean'?" Sarah teased her. Beatrice looked pleadingly at Sarah. "I'm not sure..." she sighed, "I really like him..." she whispered the last part.

"Me-thinks he like you too!" Sarah nudged her and they giggled.

"Who's interested in a beer or a wine?" Thierry called out.

"I will have a glass of your finest Sauvignon Blanc, my good man," Matthew said in his to-the-manor-born voice. "And I will need a straw, because I cannot lift my glass anymore."

"I am happy to inform you, that we have a very nice bag-in-a-box under the cork," Thierry pretended to put a napkin over his arm, waiter-style. "Would you like to try it first?"

"You don't say, a bag-in-a-box is always a good choice, I'm sure it will be excellent," Matthew said approvingly.

They had a lovely evening, reminiscing over the fire about the first two years and planning what they would be doing after graduation.

As darkness fell, Matthew started scratching all over.

"Are you okay, Matt?" Sarah asked.

"Just a little itchy, and my skin feels a bit warm," Matthew pointed for Sarah to scratch between his shoulder blades where he couldn't reach. "All righty then, enough wine for me."

"Is it the light of the fire," Beatrice said as she looked closer at Matthew, "or do you look a very unhealthy red?"

Thierry and Sarah stared into the dark past the fire.

"No, not enough wine for you, but sun definitely," Thierry informed Matthew soberly.

Sarah teased Matthew: "You know for a farm boy, you do not deal with weather conditions well, do you?"

"My dear woman, don't be preposterous!" Matthew said in a snooty voice. "We Schmidts are of the high tech variety – we don't use the *weather* for our farming," he said in the most affronted tone he could muster, "that is so outdated!"

"Tomorrow, you'll have to wear a t-shirt while swimming,

so you don't burn too much more," Beatrice advised kindly. "Preferably a white shirt."
"Not to worry, Beatricci, I will dress for the occasion," Matthew winked.

The next day, while the others were going to one of the smaller beaches, Matthew decided to stay in the shade of the cabin and the trees. He took out his sketchbook and made small drawings of the cabin and the scenery around. In the evening they had another fire going, and were telling each other ghost stories. They made up so much nonsense that they howled with laughter.
Sarah walked into the cabin to find a sweater and found Matthew's sketchbook. She opened it and turned towards the light in the cabin. What she saw was stunning. She had seen Matthew draw buildings and structures, but she never realized how beautifully he could sketch. He had drawn a humming bird frantically hanging on to the feeder near the cabin. The level of detail was amazing.
He'd made funny cartoons of Thierry, Beatrice and herself. Thierry he had given a huge nose; most of Beatrice's face was covered with a smiling mouth and Sarah's own eyes were enlarged to looking glass size with lashes sticking out on all sides. Sarah chuckled; they were very well done.

As was so often the case, Sarah was surprised at the many talents Matthew had. What a great friend to have. Not only was he funny, they could have very serious conversations and heated debates about politics and religion.
Matthew and Sarah had agreed they would cook and eat together every Wednesday night, either at his room or at Sarah's house. This was an evening they both looked forward to.
Matthew regularly teased her that he would never forget the first exquisite meal of 'marble tiles and concrete' Sarah had prepared for him. She had tried to make cod filets, that were still *'somewhat frozen solid'* on the inside. Not to mention the dessert that did take on an *'ever so slightly more solid texture'* than she had planned.

In return, Sarah would express her amazement about him magically whipping up meals from the filthy kitchen at his house and the disbelief that he cooked these meals himself. His love for blue cheese was often too obvious in his recipes. From time to time Beatrice, Thierry or other classmates would join, bringing in new influences for recipes and topics for discussion.

Sarah walked out of the cabin with the sketches and the remainder of the wine.

"Matt, anything you would like to share with us??" she asked, holding up the cartoons.

Matthew didn't flinch.

"Well, what can I say that you don't already grasp?" he said happily. "We all know about Thierry's extreme nosiness. Don't we?"

"Of course!" Beatrice was the first to confirm and stuck her tongue out to Thierry.

"Common knowledge," Sarah added.

"Then we have our dear, darling, Beatrice," Matthew continued, "who is way too sweet for this world with her wide smile," he looked around expectantly. "Always the pleaser..."

"Nope, can't say I recognize that!" Thierry said, raising his hands in bewilderment.

"As for Sarah..." Matthew turned towards her as he said: "You have a problem that you suffer from a big mouth, sticking your nose in other people's affairs and eyes that look right through you," he smiled teasingly. "It didn't work to enlarge all of it on you, so for you I had to go with the eyes." He looked up at her flashing his own lashes.

Sarah pushed him playfully. "Don't give me that look!!" she said. "You're just lucky I can't draw, otherwise those big, whopping ears of yours would get a starring role!"

"Big ears? Me?" Matthew looked at Beatrice for support, who only pointed at her own mouth, making her 'wide smile' stretch almost from ear to ear.

"Extreme nosiness?!" Thierry tried to sound wounded, but failed completely.

"Who's gonna help me empty this?" Sarah held up the bag-in a box. "No good taking it back to Halifax. Matthew is already talking gibberish so he's had enough by the sound of it."

Chapter 7

Sarah arrived home in her apartment. She hadn't been there for some time and saw that the plants had given up in the meantime. She put her purse on the table and picked up the phone to call her mother.

"Hi Mom, it's me," she said in a croaky voice, "I'm back."

"Hi sweetheart, are you home?" Tracy asked softly.

Sarah broke into tears at hearing the calm, familiar voice. She nodded but couldn't speak for a moment. Tracy's heart broke as she heard Sarah sobbing.

"Do you want me to come over, Sarah?" Tracy offered. "I would have come but didn't know what time you'd get there."

Sarah swallowed hard and answered: "No, thanks, Mom, I should try to get some sleep."

"All right, sweetheart, let me know if there's anything I can do."

"I still can't believe it, Mom… 38 years old."

"I know…"

Sarah sat down in her favorite big chair and pulled up her feet.

Sarah had spent a number of weeks by Matthew's side in his splendid waterfront house in Dartmouth. The initial diagnosis of lung cancer – almost a year ago to this day – had come as a total devastating shock. How was it possible that someone so young, with just a persistent cough, could be so seriously ill so suddenly? The doctor had told him that both his lungs were full of tumors. There really was not much they could do for him.

"You know how much I admire you?" Sarah asked, looking at him.

"There's not that much to admire. It is what it is," was Matthew's reply.

"Well, all I can tell you is, we're totally going to beat this thing!" Sarah said bravely.

"*We*, Sarah?"

"Yes, *we*, Mr. Sjjjmeet!" Sarah said with emphasis.

The tumors were inoperable, so Matthew had been given a choice: take the one proven treatment with a 50-50 % chance that it would work – if it didn't, it would give him 6 to 8 weeks to live at most. Matthew had chosen to go with the experimental track of 6 different stages of chemo, which could potentially give him an extension of a few years, depending on how the lung tumors would respond to the chemicals.

His body had cheated him time and again. With each phase they were hopeful that the situation would stabilize or possibly even show a recline in the number of tumors. Every scan was a potential disaster. Only one of the phases had shown a good result, which had lasted exactly one extra scan-period before there was another increase in tumor activity. Once they heard that the cancer had spread to his liver, what they had feared for all that time became their reality.

Together with Matthew's mother Sarah had nursed him. Matthew had refused to be admitted to hospital. He had known that his time was limited in the end and he did not want his last impressions to be of a hospital room. The oncologist had given them advice on how to deal with a patient who had reached the terminal stage. They had tried to follow the instructions, although sometimes counterintuitive. They needed to give Matthew space.

The feeling of time slipping away was more than Sarah could bear. She wanted to say so much, knowing full well it had all been said a hundred times already. Somehow it never seemed enough. Sarah couldn't cope with the fact that there was nothing she could do. Sarah was always the practical one, getting things done, but in these months she'd felt totally useless. Matthew had told her time and again that the fact that she was there was the best thing he could wish for.

"You're all I've got and I need nothing more," he used to say. Sarah, almost as much as Matthew, felt betrayed by his disease. They'd had so many plans. It was like trying to anchor in just water, the fluidity of it rendered them powerless.

Matthew had given Sarah specific instructions about the cremation ceremony. He wanted just intimate family there. Sarah had discussed with Matthew to let his family take care of these matters. Not because she didn't want to – she would do anything for Matthew – but out of respect for his mother and brother. Whenever his family was mentioned in relation to his illness, Sarah saw the frustration in him.

"Sarah," he responded, "you of all people know why I cannot have them handle this."

Every time his voice sounded angrier. And Sarah, for the millionth time, pleaded with him to go home and talk to his family. This, however, was the one conversation Matthew refused to have with her.

"Hi Bee, it's me," Sarah sobbed into the phone.

"Hey Sarah, how did it go?" Beatrice said in a croaky voice.

"Bee, this is so unfair," Sarah said softly. "You guys should have been there."

"Don't worry, Sarah, you did what Matthew asked you to do," Beatrice reassured her.

"He wasn't well in the end, Bee," Sarah said in a strangled voice.

"I know, sweet pea, I know."

"You know, Bee, this small cremation ceremony was not befitting someone so young; so loved by his friends and his colleagues. None of them had a chance to pay their last respects," Sarah choked after every few words.

"Where are you now, Sarah?" Beatrice sounded worried. "Is there anything we can do?"

Sarah had not been prepared for the blow that would hit her after the ceremony. She was back in her own home, a place where Matthew hadn't been for such a long time. All of a sudden, all was said and all was done and the gaping emptiness in front of her was too much to handle. She just sat there, staring out of the window not registering anything.

The city was being decorated for the holidays - she saw none of it. Sarah and Matthew had always loved their preparations for Christmas. Every year they battled for finding the best tree and decorating it as lushly as possible. Matthew had the most colorful handmade glass ornaments he had brought from his travels all over the world. Sarah's tree was always too immense for her apartment and completely filled with wooden carved animals and figurines. Decorating both of the trees was something they hadn't missed since the first year Sarah had had her own place.

When two people were so closely connected, how could one be without the other – forever?

Panic-stricken with all the questions that kept flooding her mind, she remained seated in her chair until well after dark. In the distance she heard the phone ring a few times, but she couldn't bring herself to finding it. She didn't feel like talking to anyone just now. She thought of Matthew's mother, Paul and Helen and their two girls, who would now be on their way back home. It was less than two years ago that Matthew's father had passed away. He, too, had fought a losing battle against cancer. Even during the time of his father's illness Matthew had refused to consider having their differences out in the open. Sarah knew that Matthew loved his family more than anything. Maybe it was for just that reason he couldn't talk to them. It would hurt all of them too much. But Sarah, who strongly believed in openness and honesty, felt very sad that he wouldn't. She knew he would never get another opportunity to make things right after his father passed away.

Marc unlocked Sarah's apartment and walked in. It was pitch black, except for the streetlights shining through the big window. He found Sarah asleep, all curled up under a small blanket. She still wore the black suit she had worn to the cremation and hadn't even bothered to take off her boots. Marc's heart broke for Sarah. She had lost the most constant factor in her life, a man they had all come to know and love like a son and brother, since Matthew had spent so much time at their house.

Sarah looked so pale and vulnerable just now, lying there – something he had not seen in her before, ever. Marc decided to carefully wake her up.

"Sarah… Sarah, come on sweetheart," Marc whispered, "we need to get you to bed."

Sarah woke slowly and looked up at Marc.

"Hi, what time is it?" Sarah yawned. "What are you doing here?"

Marc helped her up and guided her towards her bedroom.

"Where can we find you something to sleep in?" he asked.

Sarah staggered alongside him and pointed towards the closet.

"Did you eat anything today?" Marc looked at her with deep concern. "Do you want something, Sarah, before you go back to sleep? I can make you a sandwich or a soup maybe?"

Sarah started crying – how sweet of him to come over. They had fought like cat and dog when they were children, but adulthood had made them solid friends and nobody ever had a better brother than she.

"I don't think I can eat just now, but I'll make something in the morning, okay?" her voice unstable.

"As long as you promise me that, I will call you in the morning to see if you need anything."

"Okay," Sarah couldn't help yawning.

"Good night, Sarah, I'm so sorry that Matt is no longer with us. You know he will always be there in your heart."

Sarah pulled the duvet over her eyes to cover her tears, but immediately turned back towards her brother.

"Marc, will we always be friends now?" Sarah asked, choking.

Marc's eyes went watery as he said: "We will *always* be friends, except on the basketball court. Now go to sleep. I'll call you in the morning."

He walked out of the apartment, deep in thought. Despite her 'go-getter' attitude, Sarah would always be his little sister and for once she was the one needing support.

The next morning Sarah felt like she had been hit by a freight train. She got up and made herself a cup of tea. She would decide what to do next and make a plan for the day. She would do only what strictly needed doing, not ready to think about work just yet.

Chapter 8

Sarah couldn't remember when it was exactly that she realized she had slowly fallen in love with Matthew. It had been such a gradual process. She also never could point out what it was that she loved about him most. She had sometimes wondered if she wasn't mistaking the comfortable deep friendship – having someone who knows all about you – for love. The moments that Matthew had been more than obnoxious and trying, she knew she would always forgive him.

"Matt, why are you so wonderful?" Sarah asked him during one of their Wednesday dinners in the third year of college. "I cannot imagine what I would do without you," she looked over at him. She had decided to try to tell him how she felt. Although they hugged on every occasion they saw each other, Sarah longed to be closer to him still.

"Why, fair maiden Sarah, I am not more wonderful than thou," Matthew said, getting up. "I would be completely lost without you keeping me sane in this big metropolis," he said, beaming at her.

Sarah tried to catch his expression across the table.

"You know, Matt, I am actually being serious – this is so much more than a joke to me." She sensed that Matthew was uncomfortable with the situation and didn't understand why.

She continued, her heart racing.

"We share everything, we see each other every day, you are so important in my life," she endeavored.

Matt picked up the water glasses from the table but didn't look at her before he turned around and walked over to the kitchen. It was a few moments before he returned, still avoiding her eyes. Sarah tried to swallow.

"What I'm trying to tell you is that I have fallen in love with you and want nothing more than to be with you," Sarah's voice sounded uncertain.

Matthew inhaled sharply and slowly walked over to her and took her hand.

"Sarah, my love, let me start by saying that I truly love you as a friend," Matthew said softly. He paused before he added: "I mean I honestly wouldn't know how to cope without you. But I can never be the one you love-love, because I can never return those feelings of being in love."

Sarah's eyes filled with tears. "Matt, what are you saying?"

Matthew let go of Sarah's hand and sat down on his couch, leaving Sarah behind at the other end of the room. He pulled up his knees and folded his arms around them. He sat like that for a few moments, deep in thought. Sarah felt tears running down her cheeks. She did not know what to do, whether to stay there until she had calmed down, or to run away as fast as she could.

But running away wouldn't help; now she had to know. Sarah inhaled deeply before she sat down next to Matthew, staring into space.

"Sarah, sweetheart, there is so much about me that you don't and probably don't *want* to know," Matthew finally said.

Sarah did not have the courage to look at him.

"You have no idea how much I wish I could tell you I love you in the same way, too," Matthew's voice sounded sincere.

Sarah turned toward him with an astonished look.

"Matt, what's wrong, what is it that I don't know?" she asked him and kept looking at him.

An eerie feeling swept over Sarah and she couldn't help shivering.

"I am so afraid of losing you if I tell you," Matthew said, his voice sounding unsteady.

"But Matt, how could you lose me?" she asked softly, "I don't understand…"

"Sarah, this is something I have been struggling with for such a long time," Matthew swallowed hard. "It is something that I've tried to push away and I've failed again and again."

"Matt, you're starting to scare me," Sarah now shivering all over. "What could you possibly be struggling with that I don't know about?"

"I know Sarah, that I owe you an honest explanation," Matthew cleared his throat. "Sarah… God, how do I say this… since high school I have known that I am gay…"
He paused to look at her.
"It is something I have literally never, *ever*, told anyone before," he said uncertainly.
Sarah bowed her head as she tried to process this information. Her thoughts went from *'Is that all?'* to *'Wow, this is big!'*.
She did grasp the situation immediately, but was deeply, deeply hurt. She hoped that it would eventually offer her comfort to know that this was beyond their control. For the moment, however, she felt so very lonely.
"Nobody knows this about me and it is a part of me that I have been struggling with ever since I was confronted with these feelings," Matthew told Sarah. Now that he had started, he did not know how to stop. He was so relieved he was able to share his feelings and his doubts. He was so happy that Sarah had not run out after hearing his big secret. In that instant it didn't cross his mind how badly Sarah must be hurting.
"I don't know what to do, I sometimes don't know who to *be*," the words were now racing out of Matthew's mouth. "I have real issues going out. I always think when people look at me in the street, they instantly see through me – that they see on the outside what I am trying to hide from myself on the inside."

    Sarah had gone completely silent.
"Oh, Sarah, please say something," Matthew pleaded.
"Matthew," Sarah swallowed before she could continue, "I really don't know what to say. I just want you to know that I have never had issues with people being gay. It's just that…"
Matthew interrupted her bluntly. "We had great girls in high school and my friends would brag about them, compare them and compete over them. I never recognized this. Until one day I met up with an old mate from school and didn't know what happened to me…" he stopped talking as he saw her look.
 "No, I mean, nothing so much as happened," he explained hurriedly, "but my head was in turmoil. I had never felt the same way about a girl before. I was so ashamed and tried over

and over to explain it to myself. There was nothing to explain. Although I have never been involved with anyone, I have been in love several times and they were never great girls like you."

Sarah was so confused; she was sad he didn't feel the same way about her; glad that he trusted her enough to share his innermost secret; angry that it had taken him so long to share it; hurt that he kept talking about himself.

There was a long pause before Matthew picked up on Sarah's silence.

"Sarah, I'm so sorry!" Matthew apologized. "The last thing I would ever want to happen is for you to get hurt. I really do love you on so many levels."

He added softly: "I mean it, you're all I've got!"

Sarah dried her eyes with her sleeve and looked at him intensely. "Matt, sorry, me and my big mouth… now I'm lost for words. Don't think that your secret makes you different from who you were before. It just means that I have to deal with my feelings, because you are still just as special to me," she cried softly. "I do understand, honestly, I do."

Matthew started to wrap his arms around her and said: "Thank you."

Sarah immediately broke free from his embrace and fled from the room. She cried the whole way home.

Matthew was left behind and started crying too, out of sadness for Sarah, but mostly he felt relieved; he was no longer alone with his secret.

Matthew did not see Sarah for a few days. The first thing he saw of her was a card she had pushed through the slot in his locker.

Hi Matt,
I hope you will excuse me for dinner next Wednesday,
and probably the one after that.
I am going to need some time to clear my head.
And my heart.

I want you to know this has nothing to do with you – strictly
with me and my own feelings.
Your friendship will always be important to me.
I will talk to you soon, for now: take care.
Sarah, x

Matthew read the loneliness in Sarah's card. He hated that he
was the cause of it. He did not actively look her up at Dal-U.
He knew he would have to give her time.

Chapter 9

On a Wednesday a number of weeks later, Matthew dropped a little card in her locker, which stated in his regular handwriting:

> Hi Sarah,
>
> I know that you said you needed some time; and I want to give you all the time in the world. But there is something that you should really know:
>
> I miss you!!
>
> Matt, x

He ran into Sarah some days later and saw a shy smile on her face. After classes she caught up with him.

"So, Sjjjmeet, have you thought of a recipe for this evening?" Sarah challenged him. "I am ready to be swept off my feet by your culinary talent."

Matthew laughed out loud with relief.

"You had better prepare, because it is going to be *fantabulous*!" his voice bubbly with happiness. "I will see you tonight. Oh, and Sarah… dress formally. We will have a celebration."

"Just go easy on the blue cheese, will ya, Sjjjmeet!" Sarah called after him.

"Yes, Ma'am," he literally jumped on his bike, "will do!"

Sarah biked over to Matthew's place early that evening, dressed as nicely as the bike ride would allow. She was feeling nervous and embarrassed, because she really did not know what to say to him. She shouldn't have worried. As soon as she walked in Matthew gave her such a warm hug, she couldn't be in doubt of his true friendship and she was happy for it.

"Okay, Mr. Sjjjmeet, you need to…" Sarah took a step back.

Matthew instantly understood.

They had a great evening and caught up on all that they hadn't discussed in the weeks before. Matthew cooked a fantastic meal and had bought a bottle of wine to propose a toast.

"Have you won the lottery?" Sarah asked him, teasingly pointing at her glass of wine. "Anything else I have missed?"

"Well, only that I have struck gold since I have started my part-time job as a waiter!" Matthew smiled broadly at her.

"Gold, huh?" she chuckled.

"It just so happens that my experience at Kemptville Community Hall was highly valued during my job interview," Matthew winked.

"My darling Sarah," Matthew raised his glass, "please know that you will always be *'my darling Sarah'*. I hope that in our very own way we will grow old together as the greatest of friends."

He looked Sarah straight in the eyes. "I know we will always be looking out for each other and taking care of each other. That is the true love I can offer you."

Sarah was completely thrown by the intensity of his words and a deep feeling of gratitude came over her.

"Matt, that is the sweetest thing anyone has ever said to me," Sarah said softly. "I'll gladly drink to that!"

As they were having a last cup of coffee that evening, Sarah couldn't help but notice the sad smile on Matthew's face and asked him what he was thinking of.

"Oh, nothing special," he answered too quickly.

Sarah turned to face him and looked at him questioningly, trying to catch his eye. Matthew tried to ignore her, but couldn't.

"What?" he asked with slight irritation.

"Come on, Matt, what is that sadness on your face? I thought you would be happy that we are talking again! That's not what I'm seeing, though."

Matthew suppressed a sigh but didn't want to be too harsh on her by saying that this was not about her.

But Sarah would not let go. "What's bothering you?"

Matthew shrugged his shoulders and started telling her some more about his family.

"It occurred to me as I mentioned Kemptville Community Hall, that my family really doesn't know anything about me anymore. I mean, they know I am at Dalhousie, but they don't know anything other than that. They don't know I have stopped going to church. It's not like I can go back home and tell them about my big secret, now or in future."

Sarah stared into her cup lost for a response.

"Matt, surely there will come a time when you can tell them," Sarah said encouragingly. "They're your family; your parents have raised you with every kind of love they have in their hearts. That is what I always get when you talk about home." Sarah paused for a moment. "Maybe they will need some time to adjust to the idea that you might not bring home a girl and make them grandparents, but I'm convinced they will not love you any less for it." Sarah looked at him questioningly.

"Sarah, our house is ruled by God and his rules are sacred," Matthew sighed and got up to clear the table.

"I mean, what is the concept of God anyway?" Matthew vented, coming back from the kitchen. "Sometimes I get the feeling that through God people express what they miss in those who have passed away."

"What do you mean, Matt?" Sarah tried to keep up with his reasoning.

"Somehow God has different characteristics, depending on who you talk to," Matthew said emotionally. "When I listen to my Grandma, God takes on the form of my late Granddad."

"That is surely to do with the fact that they are devout in their belief," Sarah said, trying to reason with him. "I think it can be a great comfort to people – think about it, if you could truly believe?"

"You don't honestly think that, do you?" Matthew sneered at her. "What if G.O.D. is just an abbreviation; 'gathering of dead' or 'greatness of deceased'." Once he got started there was no stopping him. "I mean, if God really is a creature, will he know how often his name is abused!"

"And what would 'Allah' be the abbreviation of?" Sarah challenged him, clearly disagreeing. "Come on, Matt, you don't mean any of that! You're just taking out your frustration at being 'different' from others," Sarah air-quoted, "at being misunderstood."

"You don't understand, Sarah, how things are back home," he almost whispered, sitting down.

"My family is so different from yours," he said quietly. "My aunts, uncles, cousins, they all live very close by in a very tight community. They all attend the same church, play in the same cards club."

Matthew shifted on his chair, obviously struggling with this. Sarah did not respond.

"My parents never have friends over; they don't socialize outside this small circle. No one in my family has ever come home with the message of being gay. Imagine the shame I would bring on them!" Matthew choked.

"You should hear the way my father talks about homosexuals. He thinks it is an outrage, a disgrace, a disease. And all this is said in the name of God; he says it's written in the bible that two men are not meant to be together."

"It is? I did not know that." Sarah tried to look at it from a different angle. "Now, *that* is an interesting piece of information!"

"Sarah, that is **not the point**!" Matthew yelled at her.

"Don't you see? It is!! That is exactly the point!!" Sarah said, clearly not impressed.

"It means that at the time the bible was being written, men were obviously already involved, you know – showing signs of homosexuality – otherwise there would have been no reason to write it up as unacceptable behavior!" Sarah said.

Matthew thought about this for a moment.

"You know, you do have a point," he said and sighed. "But it's not going to change anything in the situation."

"I know," Sarah said.

"What will happen to my parents if I tell them, or the rest of the family finds out? I'd be putting my parents in total isolation from all the people they know and love," Matthew said, sitting there paralyzed. "My family has done nothing to deserve being shunned from their community. I cannot and will not be the cause of that!"

Matthew's eyes had filled with tears and he put his face in his hands. Sarah was at a loss. He'd lived with this for a number of years now and she saw that this was extremely hard on him. She wished there was something she could do. For now the only thing she could do was to listen to him.

As Sarah biked home she once again realized how different things were for Matthew. The internal struggle for him was immense. As she was dealing with her own confusing feelings, one thing she knew for sure: being gay was not Matthew's choice.

Chapter 10

The next years at University seemed to fly by, since they were usually working so hard. Apart from seeing each other every day at Dal-U and their Wednesday dinner evenings, Matthew and Sarah had their own schedules. Sarah was coaching a team of young girls at basketball at her old club and Matthew had decided to take up playing an instrument. He had found a new passion in listening to classical music. He took up violin lessons, much to the dissatisfaction of his housemates; as with everything he did, Matthew practiced very diligently.

And every time Matthew went home to Kemptville, he would be asked the same questions. Was he studying seriously? Was he taking good care of himself? How was church? Every time it got harder to answer particularly that last question. Matthew had kept his promise and met with father Johnston from St. Patrick's, but he'd had that same, cornered feeling. How often he had wished he wasn't different in the way he was. Life would have been so much simpler. He knew as none other that this was something that could not and would not be changed.
It was fortunate that Kemptville and Halifax were two worlds apart and that his family hardly ever left Kemptville. Halifax was Matthew's safe haven.

Although Matthew only went to St. Patrick's church a few times over the years, something good had come out of it one day; another well-kept secret of Matthew's.
At some point in their graduation year, Matthew had seen there was a Gay Community Centre close by. He hadn't seen it before and although there was a modest sign above the door, Matthew had spotted it instantly. He decided that one day he would walk in the door, as soon as he felt brave enough.

Matthew was now almost 21 years old, but the issues that had haunted him all those years were still deeply bothering him. He decided he would focus on graduating first, try to find a job in the Halifax area and then see if he could truly face the most important issue he was struggling with. He felt comforted by the thought that apparently there were more people dealing with what he was going through. This did not reduce his anxiousness about the questions that he would have to answer for himself. Since he had put this issue on the back burner so often, another few months would not matter. Although a few other people, like Beatrice and Thierry, now knew about Matthew's secret, Sarah was the only one who knew how sad and frustrated he could be. In some ways it was comparable to a mourning process people go through when they lose a loved one; from shock to denial, guilt, then to anger, depression, resignation and acceptance. Apart from the shock and denial – which Matthew had probably gone through even before they met - she saw the same stages in Matthew. The only difference was that Matthew from time to time was thrown back to the guilt phase and it would start all over again. Some form of guilt was always present in Matthew.

It was quite a surprise and shock to Sarah when she fell in love again 6 months before graduation. His name was Noel, also a student at Dalhousie at the Mathematics faculty and a year younger than Sarah. Noel was kind, modest and very much in love with Sarah, too. It was some weeks before she told Matthew about this. Sarah did not quite know how to broach the subject. She knew how much Matthew would wish for her to fall in love, but she also knew it would make him feel even lonelier than usual.

One Wednesday afternoon at Dal-U she went over and sat on Matthew's lunch table.

"Excuse me, Miss, food is being served on this table," he protested. "Would you mind removing your…"

Sarah shushed him and gave him her brightest smile.

"Speaking of food, can I bring a friend this evening?" she asked abruptly.

Matthew looked at her suspiciously because in all those years she had never invited 'a friend' to join them.

"Mais oui, mademoiselle," he teased, "of course you can bring 'a friend'. Anything I need to know about this *'friend'* before this evening?"

"No, nothing much…" Sarah said nonchalantly.

"Does this *'friend'* have any special dietary wishes, or does he or she just want to eat you?" Matthew was still staring at Sarah to gage her expression.

Sarah blushed and got off the table.

"His name is Noel, and he himself is a dish, but to eat him would be a crime and a shame. You'll see!" Sarah sounded naughty. "See you this evening!"

Matthew did not have a quick reply, but was happy to see Sarah in such high spirits.

"Matthew, can I introduce you to Noel?" Sarah said, walking into Matthew's room. "Noel, this is *the* Matthew I have been telling you about."

Matthew felt shy in his own room; three was a crowd to begin with in this little space. He still found it somewhat difficult to meet new people. He wondered what Sarah would have told Noel.

"So, Matthew, you play the violin I see," said Noel, pointing, "nice instrument, that."

Matthew nodded as he walked in with the salad bowl.

"I have started playing a few years ago, but I haven't gotten very good," he said modestly. "I do enjoy playing – more than my housemates enjoy me playing, that is." He shrugged with a smile.

"Not true!" Sarah interjected. "Matt plays very well and has already been asked by two orchestras and a string quartet that plays chamber music."

"Do you play an instrument, Noel?" Matthew asked, trying to keep the conversation going.

"No, I spend most of my time improving my chess game, I'm afraid," Noel replied. "I find it fascinating to see mathematical constructions in how people build up their game. I can watch it for hours on end. Do you play at all?"

Matthew laughed and said: "I can hear that I will be a most uninteresting opponent to you. Have you played with Sarah at all?" Matthew blushed uncomfortably and added: "I mean, have you played chess against Sarah? I would be quite interested to hear how she did."

Sarah looked at Noel with an infatuated smile and said they should play chess sometime soon.

Matthew winked meaningfully at Sarah. The subject of chess apparently had not yet come up. She hit him softly and looked away to hide her embarrassment.

The evening was pleasant and uneventful, though Matthew was surprised to see the change in Sarah. She was all girlish and giddy. He had never really seen her like that and it was amusing to watch.

The next day at Dal-U, Sarah spotted Matthew at the entrance. "So, Sjjjmeet, what did you think of my date, yesterday?" she asked. Matthew looked around to see if anyone could overhear them. "He really is a dish, but so much better to look at than to talk to," Matthew said. "Sarah, he is nowhere *near* adventurous enough for you. Where did you come up with this chess-player, anyway?" Matthew gave a fake yawn for effect.

"At a basketball game, coaching my girls - my team," Sarah said dreamily.

"You know *'your girls'* sound so more interesting than Noel does, even to a gay guy," he teased.

Sarah did not listen anymore and started walking over to the library. Over her shoulder she said haughtily: "Jealousy, kind Sir, is no virtue."

In the months following Sarah and Matthew only saw each other at Dal-U. The Wednesday dinners were often swapped for the chess evenings with Noel.

"Hey, Matt! Yo, Sjjjmeet, can we convince you to join a chess practice tonight?" Sarah called out one afternoon at the bike racks. Matthew walked up to her and whispered: "Is that what you call it these days? Chess practice?" Matthew grinned knowingly.

"In my time we called it hormonal hide and seek!"
As soon as Matthew said it, he sensed that Sarah wasn't comfortable to be teased in this way; not by him, anyway. Sarah looked away and got on her bike and leaned on his shoulder for support.
"Really, in your time, huh?" Sarah nudged him. "That makes you, what, seventy-eight?"
"And I still look this good at my age!" Matthew pushed her bike off, laughing.

At their graduation party, Matthew proposed a private toast to Sarah.
"Here's to you and your bright future, Toots!" Matthew smiled warmly at her.
"Right back at you, Matt, I'm sure that you will conquer the world in your own way!" Sarah laughed.
"Where's Noel, by the way?" Matthew asked, looking around.
"You said he might be late – this is beyond being fashionably late, though!"
"Yes, about that… I'd been meaning to tell you," Sarah sighed, "I made an interesting discovery about my *darling chess-player*." The irony in her voice was unmistakable.
"Pray, do tell!" Matthew exclaimed. "It's going to be juicy, am I right?"
"No, not exactly juicy… wait," Sarah grabbed one of the bottles. "I think we need more bubbles," she said, re-filling their glasses.
"So what is this discovery you made?" Matthew prodded curiously.
"Are you ready for some shocking news?" Sarah paused.
"Give it to me straight!" Matthew winked at her.
"He knits!" Sarah shrieked.
"What does that mean, '*he knits*'?" Matthew looked puzzled. "What kind of jargon is that?"
"Just that!! He knits his own sweaters," Sarah said incredulously, "together with his mother."
"Oh, so *that* is where he gets those dramatic patterns that he covers that gorgeous body with!" Matthew snorted.

"Yep! He's a knitter and proud of it," Sarah said. "And if that isn't enough, he mentioned he dreams of one day living on a small farm with me and having sheep and goats for our own wool and milk, cheese. Go all self-supportive, have our own generator..." Sarah rolled her eyes at the thought.

"And *sooo*???" Matthew asked, egging her on impatiently to tell the rest.

"And so I told him that although I love his green way of thinking, maybe our future dreams are a little too far apart," Sarah stated, matter-of-fact.

"What a shame!" Matthew said, "I think you would look adorable; a real farm girl with rosy cheeks." He paused a moment. "I am sure I could arrange an internship for you with my brother Paul. He'd love to have you!" Matthew gave her his most encouraging smile.

"Yeah, right, you know me so well!" Sarah sighed. "Mind you," she winked naughtily, "with your gorgeous blond hunk of a brother, I wouldn't mind trying that internship."

"I think this calls for a new toast," Matthew said with a wicked smile.

"Let me guess," Sarah said, "something like 'here's to Sarah, cheese-maker and goatherd.'"

Matthew started singing loudly: "High on the hills was a lonely... Come on, Sarah! Yodelayhee… Yodelayheehoo..." Matthew gulped down his champagne and walked off to find a bottle, still singing: "Edelweiss, Edelweiss, every morning…"

Sarah called after him: "Could you be more *gay*?" The moment she said it, Sarah looked around in shock at the party guests. No need to worry, though. They all laughed at Matthew's silly singing. Besides, most of them knew.

"Oh, Sarah," Matthew sighed happily, walking back holding up a trophy bottle, "sometimes, you have me in stitches!"

"So glad I could be of service," she stated drily. "At least I have entertainment value for you."

Matthew stopped teasing her and raised his full glass.

"Now, I propose a toast: If we are both still single when we turn 50," Matthew looked at Sarah expectantly, "we will get married so that at least we will have someone to push our wheelchair."

"Matthew, I thought you'd never ask!" Sarah beamed ironically at him. "I gladly accept your kind proposal."

The sound of their champagne glasses clinking closed the deal.

"The question remains: Who will be pushing who?" Sarah teased.

"You will be pushing me of course!" Matthew said, without a shred of a doubt. "*And* you will look fabulous in gray hair and wrinkles. Life is just not fair," he sighed theatrically.

Chapter 11

Sarah had set the alarm for 7am so she could go into the office early. She had missed much the past weeks so her team had had to cover for her. Now it was necessary to go back. At the first ring of her alarm, she hit the snooze button. As she slowly woke up, she felt she would be getting up with a monstrous headache. The realization that life would have to get back to normal, as if nothing had happened, hit her like a ton of bricks. She reminded herself that she had to be thankful that Matthew was now at peace; he was no longer in pain or fearful of what would happen. But this feeling was soon washed over with a deep sense of loneliness. By the third snooze, she folded her legs out of bed and got up as best she could. The bathroom mirror told her that she looked the way she felt; a mess both outside and in.

Upon arrival at the office Sarah was greeted by the new receptionist. No sooner than she put down her laptop, did her colleague and friend Janet walk in. Janet just looked at Sarah and stood on her toes to give Sarah a warm hug. Sarah softly cried on Janet's shoulder.

They had been working together for such a long no words were needed. They had shared many worries and happy moments in the past.

"Sorry to get you all wet," Sarah apologized to Janet.

Janet shrugged carelessly. "Don't worry about it."

She took Sarah's arm and walked her to the coffee corner. They were early, there was no one there yet.

"I think it is time for a cup of *Nova Scotia brew*," Janet said kindly to Sarah.

Sarah nodded without speaking.

"Janet, I don't know where to begin," Sarah said a few moments later, "it all seems so unimportant to me. It is unbelievable that life goes on."

"I know how you feel, Sarah," Janet said, studying her friend's sad face. "it's exactly what I struggled with after my brother died so suddenly."

"Yes," Sarah said softly.

"I was almost aggressive towards people asking me – what I thought were – stupid questions," Janet's voice still filled with emotion. "I could not grasp they didn't see that none of it mattered!"

"I can't imagine getting back into the running projects," Sarah sighed deeply.

"You know, Sarah, each day gets a fraction better," Janet said, trying to comfort her.

"Does it?" Sarah did not sound convinced.

"Soon I found it comforting to concentrate on other things than just the grief of missing him," Janet explained.

"Really," Sarah said weakly.

Getting into her usual routine did not come easy to Sarah. Every morning she had to overcome the longing of just staying in bed so she wouldn't have to face the endless stream of tasks and meetings. She could not understand that prior to Matthew's illness, her job at the CAPF – the Canadian Acadia Preservation Foundation – had been her life, her mission.

After graduation she had applied for a job as Junior Project Manager and was hired to start after the summer vacation.

"*You Infidel!!*" Matthew had exclaimed when he heard about this. "You are quitting the dream of becoming an architect!"

"Your dream, Mr. Sjjjmeet, not mine exactly."

Sarah had always known that she did not possess the same talent that Matthew did. She also did not have the patience for all the necessary final details of a design. She had been thrilled with the opportunity at the foundation; she could use her knowledge for the projects related to Nova Scotia's typical design style. On top of that she would be able to use her people skills; it would be great!

By now her aspirations of living abroad had vanished. She had seen both her sisters Nicola and Madeline go off to work in the Canadian diplomatic service. They had been stationed around the world for different periods of time. Apart from the fact that Sarah had missed them so dearly, she had also seen how hard they'd struggled having to adjust to a new environment and to leave their friends behind when they were transferred to a new location.

All of a sudden Sarah had seen that that would not be for her. She would be heartbroken to constantly be so far away from everybody that she held dear. She had also come to realize how much she loved Nova Scotia; its coast lines, the ruggedness of Cape Breton, the harsh winters and the bright summers.

Working at the CAPF she would be able to contribute to doing justice to the heritage of Nova Scotia. She would plan to travel around the world for work and leisure, but she knew she would always want to come home.

She had steadily built her career climbing the project management ladder. A while back she had been appointed Program Director and as such was responsible for a large part of the decisions on future projects.

These responsibilities now weighed heavily on her and it was hard for her to cope. She tried to set up new projects, but her heart was not in it and the team around her picked up on it. Her creativity was gone – she was no longer able to surprise people with her different perspectives and solutions; now *she* waited for her team to come up with new ideas.

After a few weeks back at work Sarah saw that she was invited for a meeting with the CEO of the foundation, John Faraday. John had entered the foundation some years ago and was a great boss to work for, although sometimes very tiring when it came to discussing project funding. John seemed to be very good at steering the funding towards his pet projects, mostly involving the preservation of the lighthouses of Nova Scotia. Most of the team – including Sarah – had a special place in their heart for the typical style lighthouses, but there was so much more that needed their attention. The maintenance of the numerous smaller museums, the docks, the housing; they, too, deserved support.

In her calendar the topic for the meeting was indicated as

'Catching Up' and she wondered what that would mean. They talked to each other frequently and so she felt they were pretty much up to speed. She crossed the hall to John's office.

"I see you wanted to catch up with me," Sarah said, briefly knocking on John's door. "Good luck with that, I am so way ahead of you."

John smiled at Sarah's attempt to be witty.

"Walk with me to the fridge," John said. "I need a water," his voice clearly in business-mode.

"So John, how are the boys?" Sarah asked, searching for something to say.

"Oh, being a proud father of two boys, both in the midst of puberty," John sighed, "is sometimes not all it is cracked up to be."

Sarah laughed. "I am so glad that I was able to escape that route!"

"But you seem to be doing so well mothering over all of us; you don't need a family of your own," John said drily. "You have a real talent and it is a shame to let it go to waste," he added with the brightest of smiles.

Back in John's office, the atmosphere turned more serious. John had wanted to start by asking Sarah how she was, but dreaded the question. Instead he started discussing a project he had been looking into with the Scottish Highland Coastal Foundation.

"Let me guess," Sarah interrupted, "they have a lighthouse that needs rescuing." She heard she'd sounded sharper than she'd meant to.

Undisturbed, John continued: "In this case, Sarah, they want to learn from us how we handled the project for the preservation of the coastline of Prince Edward Island. Because of the irregular shape of the PEI coastline and the many *lighthouses*," he emphasized, "they see many similarities with the Scottish isles.

I told them we would surely be interested in sharing what we have come across."

John walked over to the window before he turned around. "Sarah, how would you like a change of scenery and go to

Scotland," he asked. "I mean, after all, PEI was your project."
Sarah wondered why John suggested she might like a 'change of scenery' but understood he meant well.

"John, I don't know that I am ready to consider a big new project," Sarah said hesitantly. "We're behind on the Widow's Walk project and there are so many other ongoing projects that need attention."

John looked at Sarah and saw her stress and discomfort.

"Sarah, I am worried about you," John said sympathetically. "You have not been yourself lately and I am trying to give you a new perspective."

"I don't know…" she said again.

"The running projects can be handled by your team," John continued.

"They are experienced enough, but you don't give them the chance to step up."

"What?" Sarah stared at him. She hadn't been prepared for the change of tone.

"I think it is time for you to take on a new challenge," John stated.

"Oh, you do, do you?" Sarah said.

Sarah was infuriated by John's words. Who in the *hell* did he think he was to judge her getting back to work and her interaction with her team? She had given them every chance of bringing in their own input. The fact of the matter was they simply had not seized the opportunity.

"Well frankly, John," Sarah started, but tears were running down her cheeks and she did not want John to see. She turned away from him and took a deep breath.

"I am sorry to hear that you are not satisfied with my work," Sarah said, swallowing hard. "I hope you will never have to go through what I have gone through recently."

John did not respond. He saw she was crying and he never had been good with crying women.

"Sarah…"

She did not turn towards him and the room went very quiet.

"Don't you understand that I am trying to help you?" John asked.

She fiercely turned around with mascara blotches underneath her eyes.

"No, I don't understand how this would help!" Sarah's eyes showing nothing short of contempt.

"Putting more pressure on me with a big new project is certainly not going to help and I resent your remark that I am not doing well by my team!" Sarah glared at her boss. "They haven't complained to me and I know they would!"

John had started the discussion and now had to follow through on it.

"Your team is worried about you, too, Sarah," John said quietly. "They don't know how to approach you. You seem vulnerable and they don't want to hurt you, but they also feel that things are not going well."

To Sarah this was a slap in the face and now she really started to sob. John had never seen her like this before.

"They went behind my back," she choked, "and came to you to complain?"

"They only… they had to…" John raised his hands in despair, not knowing how to explain the situation to her.

The silence in the room was oppressive.

"John, I think I've had enough for the day," Sarah tried to regain composure. "If you don't mind, will go home and talk to you tomorrow."

With that Sarah left the office, leaving John at a loss for words.

Chapter 12

Sarah was sad and angry over her conversation with John. Going home did not help, however. When she stepped into her apartment she saw the papers with Matthew's instructions. There was no escaping it; the grief was always there. For the first time since Matthew's death, she resented him for loading this all on her.

Why couldn't he have appointed his mother or brother? Sarah knew the answer far too well; they had gone over this a hundred times. His mother and brother did not know Matthew for who he really was and he sure as hell did not want them to find out after he passed away. There had not been enough time to clean up and sort through all his papers and photographs and he point blank refused to let them go through his house.

The phone rang and Sarah walked over, leafing through her stack of mail as she answered it.

"Hello!"

"Hey Aunt Sarah…" said her nephew Walter on the other side.

"Hey Walt, what a pleasant surprise!" Sarah said warmly. "How's my big nephew doing these days?"

"Well, I was calling to thank you for the present…" Walter said excitedly.

Present, which present?? Sarah's brain racing, but she did not remember.

"… the kite is really great, Aunt Sarah!" Sarah heard Walter saying.

Shit-sugar-dandy! Was today the 23rd? Walter's birthday! How could she have forgotten?

"Well," Sarah cleared her throat, "I'm so glad you like it, Walt…" Sarah swallowed, "Sorry I couldn't be there for your birthday today buddy!"

"I know, Mom explained it to me," his voice sounded so grown-up for a moment.

"Next time I come over, we'll go fly the kite together, okay?" Sarah said, hitting herself on the forehead.

"Sure, that'd be fun!" His enthusiasm gave him away: all kid again. "Bet you can't beat me!" he teased.

"Betcha I can!" she smiled in spite of herself. "Say, is your Mom in? Can I talk to her?"

"Sure, she's in the kitchen, probably eating the leftover birthday cake," he whispered and chuckled.

"MOM!" Sarah heard him yelling, "Mom, it's Aunt Sarah!"

"Hi Sarah, how are you?" Nicky said coolly.

"Hello big sis, why didn't you call me to remind me of my nephew's birthday?" Sarah asked in an accusatory tone.

"Well... *little* sis," Nicky said painstakingly slowly, "I did... I left two messages on your phone and did not hear from you." Nicky paused. "Besides," she added, "it *has* been his birthday for twelve years to this day."

"You DID?" Sarah was overcome, had she not checked her messages? "God, Nicky, I am *so* sorry!" Sarah was dumbfounded. "How can I thank you for getting Walter a gift on my behalf?"

"Well, let me see. You can thank me by joining *the land of the living* at some point!" Nicky said, without a trace of a smile in her voice.

"Sorry, what?" Sarah swallowed hard.

"You know, Mouse, I am really sorry for what happened with Matt, but you need to get a grip!" Nicky said in a harsh tone. "Other people are dealing with difficult situations too. It's been months now. You *have* to move on at some point!"

"And who will decide for me when to move on, *you*?" Sarah yelled.

"No, Sarah," Nicky said matter-of-fact, "nobody decides for you – but people will decide for themselves how long they will wait for you."

"Geez, thanks Nicky," Sarah now stammered into the phone, "for that reality check!"

Sarah swore she heard the word 'welcome' coming out of the receiver, just before she hung up.

Well that was the last straw. Two slaps in the face in one day. Still Sarah did not feel this to be fair on her. She tried to calm herself down. The signals she was getting were pretty strong; she had completely focused on one thing, totally neglecting others that also deserved her attention.

Trying to turn her emotions into something more constructive she called the public notary to make an appointment. After that she called Matthew's mother to inform her.
"Sarah, I am so grateful that you are taking care of all this," Mary Schmidt said in a croaky voice.
Sarah tried to imagine the loneliness at the farm, especially after Paul had moved out when he'd gotten married.
Sarah knew Paul had lunch at the farmhouse every day while he was at work there. Paul's wife Helen was there frequently, trying to balance her time between the care for her own girls and their grandmother.

"All right, Mrs. Schmidt, I will see you soon."
Before Sarah hung up the phone, Mrs. Schmidt said softly: "In future, would you mind calling me Mary?"
Slightly thrown by this, Sarah said: "Yes, I'd like that, Mary. I will see you in Halifax soon."
Over the past years Mrs. Schmidt, Mary, had frequently expressed she felt that Matthew and Sarah would make a lovely couple.
It was at times like this Sarah needed to be on guard not to make a witty remark. By now, most of their friends in Halifax knew about Matthew. So Sarah always smiled and said that was not in the cards for them, trying not to feel guilty towards Matthew's family for not being honest.

Sarah had often wondered if Matthew's family hadn't really had any idea of his secret. He never did bring home a girl – besides Sarah, that is. Matthew defied all the rules of the stereotype homosexual. Matthew dressed conservatively and did not actively involve himself in the gay community, apart from his guiding young people at the Gay Community Centre in Halifax. He did not date at all. He had only ever truly been in love that Sarah knew of, with a cellist from the quartet, called Tim.

Although Matthew and Tim had had a short fling, Tim was already in a steady relationship and had made it clear from the start that he would not consider giving that up for Matthew. That was the only time Sarah had known Matthew to be deeply depressed. He had been impossible to communicate with at the time.

Chapter 13

"I don't understand you, sometimes, Matt," Sarah said one Wednesday evening over dinner. Ever since he had arrived, Matthew had been very quiet.

"What do you mean?" Matthew asked cautiously.

"You are setting yourself up for a major disappointment," Sarah stated bluntly.

"Oh, boy, here we go!" Matthew sighed, knowing full well what Sarah was getting at.

"Matt, ever since you have hooked up with Tim, you have lived in hope that he will choose you!" Sarah looked directly at Matthew. "You seem to be always waiting when he can talk to you or be with you."

Matthew only glared at her.

"I don't recall asking for your opinion, Sarah," he said.

"Well, I'm sorry, you're gonna get it anyway!" Sarah started to talk louder.

"I don't have to listen to this!" Matthew got up from the table.

"You have chosen to be the mistress, the 'floozy on the side' for Tim," Sarah said defiantly.

"Any more labels you would like to add?" Matthew was livid by now.

"You want me to be your best friend and your best friend is worried!" She yelled at him.

"You await Tim's instructions on when and where you can meet. *It's pathetic!*" Sarah was only just getting started to vent her frustration.

"Sometimes you can be so tactless, it's shocking!" he tried to stay calm.

He walked into the hallway to get his coat.

"Thanks for a *lovely* evening," Matthew said with cold cynicism, as he slammed the door behind him.

The situation between Sarah and Matthew became volatile from that point on. Sarah could not and would not understand why Matthew chose to be in a situation like that. Matthew concluded that Sarah's resistance was driven by jealousy. She did not wish the best for him and she failed to see he was really and truly in love.

What hurt Sarah the most was the fact that Matthew did not turn up for her father's funeral. Bill McFadden had passed away very suddenly of heart failure, an immense blow to Sarah and her family. Bill had been the steady engine keeping all of them connected with their busy lives.

This came at a moment in Matthew's life where he was struggling with his unresolved issues and selfishly felt he deserved an afternoon to himself. He had expensive tickets to some Mahler concert, right there in Halifax.

The Wednesday after the funeral, over dinner at Matthew's house, they had a monumental row.

"Do you have any idea of how much I needed *you*, of all people, to be there?" Sarah confronted Matthew.

"How **dare** you?" Matthew immediately responded. "I would have expected you, *of all people*, to understand that I have been going through a tough time."

"Well, I haven't exactly had a picnic myself, you know!" Sarah tried to remain calm, but failed in the attempt.

"If something happened to your family, I wouldn't dream of not being there!" she screamed at him. "I would have gone through a brick wall to be there for you!"

"Oh, please... Let's not pretend that would mean anything to you." Matthew knew this wasn't true, but he couldn't deal with her *knight in shining armor* behavior for the moment.

"You really have no idea, do you, Matt? You selfish, egotistical bastard!" Sarah started crying and walked out.

It was the only time they had not been on speaking terms for a number of months. Both were locked in their own feelings of bitter disappointment in the other. For the first time Sarah had seen that the level of her commitment to Matthew and their friendship was totally different than his. Sarah mourned the loss of her father and the break-up with the friend, the love, she realized she never really had. They had made it too complex. Were they both substitutes for a promise of someone better suiting in future? Meanwhile, they shared all of it; travel, theatre, parties, nursing the other through flues. They were always there for each other, though apparently not always. Sarah often wondered how it was possible she had not corrected herself in her expectations. What would have happened if Tim had been single? What would it have meant? For the first time it occurred to her that she could also have found someone. Never in the 11 years before had this dawned on her, which in itself indicated the depth of her commitment. How realistic were the expectations she had of him? How much of a promise had Matthew really broken to her? Her final conclusion was always: good friends would also be there for each other at sad times.

Beatrice eventually settled the dispute. They were both just too stubborn. After many months, she called Sarah.
"Hi Sassie, how are you?" Beatrice asked.
"I'm good thanks, how are you?"
"I just talked to Matt," Beatrice introduced airily.
"So?" Sarah inhaled sharply.
"So, he really misses you," Beatrice said softly. Beatrice left out that Matthew had not exactly said it, but she felt it was implied enough.
"And, you're telling me this because…" Sarah exhaled slowly.
"He said to say 'hi'," Beatrice said simply. That part was true. She'd had the exact same phone conversation with Matthew first. Beatrice knew, like none other, that they were both too pig-headed to admit it. They missed each other like crazy, but would never come out and say it.
"Next time you speak to him, will you say 'hi' back?" Sarah said, her heart racing. "I miss him too," she admitted.

About fifteen minutes later, Sarah's doorbell rang. Matthew leaned in the door, looking at her with a shy smile. They fell into each other's arms and hugged for what seemed like minutes.

They agreed never to fight like this again, though neither apologized to the other.

"You know, Sarah, you were right about Tim," Matthew said honestly. "I am sorry to have to come to that conclusion, but you were totally right."

"I am sorry about that too," Sarah clearly meant it. "I have sincerely hoped for it to work out," Sarah said.

"It's my silly, romantic notion – if you want something badly enough, it will happen." Matthew shrugged briefly. "That's just for fairy tales," Matthew smiled in spite of himself, "no pun intended."

"That's why you like Walt Disney so much, I bet!" Sarah laughed.

"I always look for a happy ending!" he sighed. "Not with Tim, though, he quit the quartet. It was just too hard to see each other so frequently."

"You know what? I think we should get profiles on one of these Internet dating sites. Check out the possibilities!" Sarah jokingly suggested. Matthew winked at her. He knew she would never seriously consider this.

"Well, Sarah, you know you have forever spoiled me for other women, don't you?" he pushed her teasingly.

"Yes, well, truth be told: you have spoiled me for other *women*, too!" Sarah pushed back.

"Naughty, naughty! As long as I haven't spoiled you for other men, then I can live with it," Matthew said meaningfully.

"Don't worry, I'm sooo over you!" Sarah hurried to say.

"I bet if we went online, we would come up with the same men, so let's not go there!" Matthew chuckled. "We would have to compare notes and whatnot."

So many years later, it caught Sarah by complete surprise, right after Matthew had been diagnosed with terminal lung cancer, Tim re-entered the scene. As soon as he had heard about Matthew's illness he immediately contacted Matthew in an emotional state. They had agreed to meet and soon the situation started all over again.

Matthew was happy that Tim was back in his life and felt blessed he would have Tim's love and affection until he would pass away. He fluttered like a teenager in love. He called it the silver lining on his cloud. Matthew said to have no expectations from Tim, who was still together with the same life partner. "Sarah, it is so wonderful to have Tim around any moment he can spare to be with me," Matthew said. "Somehow it's easier now. We don't have to make any promises for the future; we know I don't have one."

"Don't say that, Matt," Sarah pleaded with him.

"I am just so happy to know he has not forgotten me," Matthew's eyes gleamed. "We have really missed each other in all those years."

Sarah did not respond. She sincerely tried to feel happy for Matthew but she did not trust Tim.

"Matt, how is Tim going to explain being with you when your situation worsens?" Sarah asked him, point-blank.

Matthew looked at her as if she had slapped him in the face.

"What do you mean?" Matthew challenged her. "We have made plans to go to New York together and booked tickets for Carnegie Hall. I do not *plan* to have the situation worsen!"

"I don't understand you," Sarah said, retreating slightly.

"And I don't *believe* you!" Matthew hissed at her. "Tim has indicated from the start that he does not intend to leave Joe, but that does not mean that this isn't very special to me. Can't you at least be happy for me, or are you still jealous of me and him?"

Sarah felt the wind being knocked out of her and tried to catch her breath.

"What I meant to say," she said softly, "is I am worried that you are going to get hurt again."

"Yeah, sure... whatever!"

"Have you noticed, Matt," Sarah asked him, "that the only fights we ever have, are about Tim?"

Sarah had so hoped to have the wrong end of the stick. However, as soon as Matthew's situation worsened, Tim visited less and less frequently. By the time Matthew's last experimental chemotherapy sessions had started, he was suffering both physically from the pain and mentally from being left by Tim once more.

Tim slowly stopped all forms of interaction, much to Matthew's grief. No longer did Matthew's phone buzz with text messages and Tim could hardly face visiting anymore. Sarah could only conclude that in the end Tim realized he could not offer the support that was needed and was too big of a coward to tell Matthew.

Sarah could not help but wonder how a person can do something like that to another human being they claim to love, but for once wisely decided to keep still.

Tim's betrayal to Matthew had been a blow he was unable to overcome. He withdrew from everybody and everything. He no longer read the papers or watched the news. He couldn't listen to music anymore because it was too tiring for him. He couldn't face talking to Beatrice, or Thierry, or any of his friends.

He completely shut them out. They simply no longer existed to him. His world slowly shrunk to the size of his house and only few people were allowed in. Sarah felt Matthew slip away more and more, unable to doing anything to help him. There were no issues she could address; no questions she could ask without a silent glare in return.

He would tune out since the outside world no longer involved or concerned him. It was too confrontational that everybody seemed to be moving on. In the end it became virtually impossible to reach him.

Chapter 14

"Hi Mom, how sweet you are to cook extra for me!" Sarah entered the house that had always been her home and breathed in the familiar, comfortable smells.

"I could not face having dinner by myself; I had a hell of a day at the office!" Sarah said emotionally.

Tracy McFadden embraced her daughter and told her to take off her coat.

"We're only having lasagna, sweetheart," she apologized.

"Hmmm, sounds marvelous, Mom."

As Tracy was finishing up in the kitchen after dinner, Sarah walked in to the living room where her father's chair still stood. All his books were still there, giving the place such a special atmosphere.

"You want coffee, Sarah?" her mother called from the kitchen.

"I would love some of that cappuccino you always make, if it's not too much trouble," Sarah said.

Sarah ran her hand along the Encyclopedia Britannica, one of the treasured pieces her father had been so proud of. How she missed him and what she wouldn't give to be held by him so he could tell her everything would be all right. Her mother entered with two steaming mugs of cappuccino and sat down with her.

"So, tell me about this rough day at the office?" Tracy asked patiently.

Sarah took a sip from her cappuccino. "Hmm, that is God's gift to coffee," Sarah paused for a moment. "Anyway, my day at the office," she continued. "can you believe that *a-hole* – 'scuse my expression – John Faraday? He says my work is not what it used to be and he wants to send me off for a project in Scotland, so I can have a *change of scenery*," Sarah air-quoted, pulling a long face. Tracy wisely kept quiet, letting the verbal storm whizz by before she said anything.

"Who does he think he is anyway – I mean really?" Sarah vented. "I am perfectly capable to decide whether I need a change of scenery or not. Telling me that my team is complaining about me? I don't even think it is true. Right now, there are just too many loose ends to Matthew's estate and I have to do it all myself." Tracy studied Sarah's pale face, the bright red blushes and her bewildered green eyes.

"Sarah, sweetheart, could it be that John is worried about you?" Tracy asked openly. "You have been working with him for such a long time, and have always gotten along so well. To be honest," she added, "I am sort of worried about you myself." Sarah looked up from her mug.

"What do you mean? I have just lost my very best friend," Sarah said defiantly. "I can't just leapfrog over this and pretend nothing happened, can I?"

Sarah sighed deeply. "I know you mean well, Mom," she said softly, "but it is hard enough as it is right now."

Tracy ran her hand along Sarah's cheek. "Wouldn't it be wonderful to go to Scotland and make the trip you were planning to make with Dad?" she asked. "Maybe you could combine this. You had your plans all lined up."

Sarah looked at her mother in mock-suspicion.

"Have you been talking to John Faraday, or what?" she winked. Tracy smiled and teased: "Yes indeed, we have a conspiracy going on – in fact I am having a wild affair with John, but that's not supposed to come out." Tracy winked back at her daughter. "He secretly likes older women, but I'm sure he doesn't want you to know about us!"

Sarah laughed out loud as she pictured this in her mind. "Mom, stop it!! You're grossing me out, I'm having a visual!" Suddenly she stopped laughing and stared out of the window. "I can't believe I forgot Walt's birthday."

As Sarah drove home that evening, she thought about what her mother had said about going to Scotland. This was actually not a bad idea. They'd always wanted to find out more about their ancestors and her father had done quite some research on that. She was sad, though, that they couldn't make that trip together. Her father would have been able to explain so much more about what he'd found out. As she pulled up at a traffic light, she broke away from her reverie. She wondered how long the project would be that John was thinking about. She also knew she owed John a big apology.

The next morning Sarah walked straight into John's office. He was talking to his assistant, Lisa. As they saw Sarah come in, Lisa said she would get John and Sarah their 'Nova Scotia brew' to get them started. Lisa was aware of the situation and wanted to give them a chance to talk, bless her.
Sarah gratefully accepted her cup of coffee and smiled at Lisa as she walked out before facing John.
"John, I want to apologize to you," Sarah started, "I was out of line and should not have talked to you the way I did. I am so very sorry – I am not handling things as carefully as I wish I could."
John nodded briefly.
"Sarah, I understand that you are going through a tough period," John said. "We're trying to help. If a change of project is not going to help you, then please be aware that your team is searching for a way to work with you."
Sarah had also given her team some more thought and knew John was right. She had been impossible the past weeks; irritated, short-fused and not very inspiring for sure.
"John, you're right – my team can do much more than I give them space to do," Sarah shrugged apologetically. "My control-freakish nature does not help, I'm afraid," Sarah paused for a moment – John, however, did not protest.
"John, please tell me some more about the project you mentioned in Scotland?" she asked. "What are you working on and how can I help?"
Sarah added honestly: "Maybe you are right and I do need a change. Besides, I definitely qualify, being of Scottish descent, and all," she winked at him.
"Yes, you and the rest of us, for that matter!" John replied teasingly and felt relieved that he saw a faint glimmer of the old Sarah.
John got up and said: "Let me get the project description from

Lisa and walk you through it."

Sarah's excitement grew the more she heard about the project. It matched her knowledge and her experience. She loved the challenge that it would be the first real international project she would run.

She almost felt a buzz considering going out to Scotland, despite all the things she still had to do.

"When would I have to leave, you think, and how long would I be gone?" Sarah asked, her eyes gleaming by now.

John explained that the first step was to go over to Scotland to explain what they had done in Nova Scotia and PEI. Then the scope could be determined and aligned.

"So that means I could fly over there, meet with the team for a few days and then take a few days off to travel around Scotland?" Sarah asked.

"Sure, as long as you send me the information we need to determine the next steps, you can dink off as long as you like," John smiled at her.

Sarah nodded in agreement and smiled at him quietly.

"I had long planned a trip to Scotland with my father," Sarah explained, "which we unfortunately were never able to make together. Maybe now would be a good time to investigate where we McFaddens came from and where my roots lie."

"Sure Sarah, that sounds like a good plan to me. I would come for the business part if my wife would not kill me first when I introduce the subject," he sniggered. "She can't imagine being alone with the boys for too long, for she might go berserk. She needs a strong man by her side to cope with things," he took on a flying hero stance, his belly slightly wobbling over his belt.

"Where would we be without strong men in our lives?" Sarah flashed her eyelashes. "Say, is your Superman cape still at the drycleaners?"

"Yeah, yeah, go on and start scheduling your trip and get out of my sight," John laughed. "I will inform 'your tribe' that you will be coming, so they can get Scotland Yard informed."

For the first time in a long time Sarah felt she had a spring in her step.

A few days later, Sarah met up with Mary, Paul and Helen at the notary's office. They had postponed this meeting several times, because none of them had been ready to deal with the practical side of Matthew's passing. The notary informed them of what Matthew had defined in his will.

Matthew had taken excellent care of his family. The house in Dartmouth would be sold, because none of the family wanted move there. Sarah would be in charge of dealing with the house, as was expressly Matthew's wish.

The architecture business would be sold and Sarah would look into this with Matthew's right hand at the office, Frank. Matthew had invested heavily into new design tools and a new office. They would have to see what the financial status was. There had been talk of a merger with another firm, so that might be a route to explore.

Sarah explained to Matthew's family her plans for Scotland. She promised that as soon as she was back she would start on the house. The money from the sale of the house would be put into an education fund for Paul and Helen's girls.

The money Matthew had saved would go to his mother, increasing her monthly budget.

His car and all the travel books in his library were left to Sarah. Matthew had discussed with her that it was time she got a decent car and his fancy model sure would be a treat after her banged up little 4x4, with its duct-tape features.

But Sarah was much happier with the travel books. Especially his precious book on English palaces and castles he had so treasured as a child.

Matthew's violin, sheet music, CD's and books on classical music he left to the Halifax School of Music where he had started his violin lessons.

Matt's DVD collection of period drama was left to Sarah, because Matthew's family never really watched TV or movies, except for the Disney DVD collection, which would go to his young nieces.

Matthew had documented his wish for his ashes to be spread among the big trees in the orchard on the farm in Kemptville. That way he would always be home. Matthew's family hadn't known that that was his wish and felt very moved.

Finally, the notary informed them that Matthew had also left all of them a personal letter. They looked at him with a mixture of shock and surprise.

Not even Sarah had known that he had written them all something personal. They choked as an envelope in Matthew's meticulous handwriting was handed to each of them. None of them opened the letter then and there. They would wait for a good moment to read this.

To my darling Sarah,

I know I will surprise you with this letter. You thought you knew everything, but fortunately that is not the case. I am happy to report that you do know the most of it, which is exactly the reason I wanted to write you this letter. There's something I should have told you long ago.

First of all I would like to apologize to you for sometimes being such an insensitive bastard of a guy who did not always deserve your friendship. In my incompetence of expressing myself, and dealing with situations in my life that I did not know how to handle, I have sometimes mistreated you. I have admired you for <u>always</u> knowing what to say and how to discuss things, but we both know that I was never blessed with the same talent. I sometimes hoped that at some point you would also be at a loss, but you never were — and that was confrontational too, from time to time. I know that I have been selfish at times you really needed me, and I feel horrible about that now. Just wanted you to know that I did register this and wish I could set it straight. This is the only way I know how. Sorry, sweetheart, for not being able to tell you this in person.

Second of all I wish to tell you how much your friendship, your undivided love and attention, have enriched my life. Thank you for that. You were the only real love I have ever experienced and I can't tell you how grateful I am. Even as I feel my health is fading, I know that I have your love to guide me through. I see how much it pains you, and still you never give up. I now see that that is what true love means. I am sorry I was never able to fully return this feeling. I'm also sorry I could not express how important this has been, to not feel lonely at this time.

We promised to push each other's wheel chair and I hate that my time came so much sooner than we both envisioned. I would have done all of that for you, too, had I been given the chance... We would have made a great team walking down the aisle when both 50 and single. That would have been a scream, wouldn't it?

Sarah, please be well and remember all the things we have been through together. Remember them with a smile, rather than tears. We were blessed to meet each other so young and to have had so much time to spend together. No one can take that away from us, for it is engraved in both our souls.

I can only wish for you to meet someone who will return all that love. You have so much to give, you're so smart, funny and so loving. I hope you will find someone worthy of this, so you know what it's like to be at the receiving end of it. I can honestly tell you: It's wonderful!!

It's hard to imagine I will no longer be able to hug you and be with you. I have booked a lifetime place in your heart, so I know I am covered.

I love you Sarah, forever,
Yours, Matt   Xxx

Sarah had to stop reading a few times, because the tears in her eyes blurred her vision and she simply could not read on. It had taken her a few days to find the courage to read the letter, but decided she wanted to know what he had written to her before she left for Scotland. She read it on the side of the bed, the day before her flight.

Her suitcase was packed and ready. She craved a good night's sleep. Getting to sleep proved impossible after reading Matthew's letter. She would cherish it forever, although she knew she couldn't read it again anytime soon. It was just too painful. With a strong sense of ceremony she placed the letter in Matthew's favorite castle book. She crawled into bed and stared at the ceiling. She wondered if she had taken the right decision to go to Scotland. In some undefined way she felt she was deserting Matthew and was overwhelmed by sadness.

Marc arrived at Sarah's apartment early to pick her up and found her wiping her red eyes in the living room.

"Sarah... oh, don't worry; you're going to be okay," Marc said and hugged her.

"If not, give me a call and I will come get you the same day," he said warmly. "All right?"

Sarah nodded.

"I must look a mess. How am I ever going to attract attention from the handsome pilot this way?" she said, trying to smile. Marc laughed and replied that the handsome pilot first had to get her to Edinburgh safely, which would give her enough time to redo her make-up on the way.

They said goodbye at the airport. Marc said he hoped she would start to feel better during her trip. What he didn't add is that he was worried that she was going to do the things she had planned with their dad; another stroll down another memory lane. Sarah was very sweet, but could do with a little less theatrics sometimes.

Her sensitive nature was her talent in many ways, but it was her pitfall too. In no way did he mean to do injustice to her sorrow over losing Matthew, but he felt it was also necessary to keep a focus on real life. As much as he had liked Matthew, he also felt that his little sister had been at the receiving end of a number of surprisingly egotistical actions on Matthew's side. He admired Sarah for always staying loyal and forgiving, but sometimes wondered with exasperation why Sarah's otherwise strong character faded in the background when dealing with Matthew.

As Sarah got on the plane, she remembered Matthew's letter. She wondered if his family had read theirs yet. She felt she should have called Mary yesterday, but couldn't bring herself to having the same conversation with Mary they seemed to have every time. She also dreaded having a tearful Mary on the phone without being able to offer her any comfort. What a coward she was turning into.

Soon after departure, Sarah dozed off. After a few hours of sleep she was woken by the sound of the stewardesses serving breakfast. Sarah didn't feel like eating. She looked at the screen that was displayed and saw they made good progress. Taking out the in-flight magazine she leafed through the destinations the airline serviced. Her eye fell on Bristol and her heart missed a beat.

One of the best trips with Matthew had been their first trip to England. Just after graduation, Matthew had saved enough with his student jobs and for Sarah it was her graduation present. Ever since the second year of university Matthew and she had planned to make the trip, because one of their Professors had extensively talked about the rich architecture in England, especially in and around Sarah's beloved Bath.

Of course, Matthew would not consider going across to England and not making it to Castle Howard, too. Although much more to the north, it was still too close by to fly home without having seen it.

Chapter 15

"Matt, have you seen all those perpendicular accents on the Abbey?" Sarah nudged him.

Sitting next to Sarah on a bench in Abbey Square, Matthew felt like he had never felt before.

"I am still trying to get over that mindboggling experience just now," Matthew said earnestly.

"What mindboggling experience?" Sarah asked in surprise.

"This invasion of the body snatchers I witnessed," Matthew studied Sarah closely.

"What?" Sarah

"Have they left, you think?" Matthew kept staring at her and tapped Sarah's head.

"Stop it!" Sarah pushed Matthew. "What is the matter with you?"

"Someone took possession of your body a moment ago!" Matthew exclaimed. "Someone sounding very British!"

"You are silly!" Sarah laughed.

"I didn't know you did such a good British accent!" Matthew smiled at her. "In future can you warn me in advance, otherwise I might burst out laughing."

"God, I'm knackered, I's been on me bacon 'n' eggs all day! I could do with a cup of rosie," Sarah said in broad Cockney.

"Well, don't do it again; you sound like a stand up comedian without a good joke!" Matthew laughed.

"Why, Gov, a girl can't 'elp it, now can I?" Sarah shrugged.

"You know, Sarah, I have decided not to return to Nova Scotia with you," Matthew stated seriously. "This is all so amazing, this is so very *me*, I now know for a fact I was born in the wrong place at the wrong time."

Matthew looked like the cat that found the mouse on a serving platter.

"Look at it; have you ever seen anything so gorgeous?" Matthew sounded so excited. "By the way, it is perpendicular gothic, just so you know."

"I knew you would like it, Mr. Know-it-All," Sarah enjoyed him looking so happy. "I mean, have you seen those ladders on the turrets with the angels ascending? A real Stairway to Heaven. How cool is that?"

"You probably mean the depiction of Jacob's Ladder," Matthew said in his lecturing voice.

"If you say so, my talented tour guide," Sarah yawned.

"Do you see those two angels who want to go back down, like against the current?" Sarah pointed up. "Listen," she held her hand behind her ear, "you can almost hear them screaming: *no, no, let me go – I'm too young to go to heaven*! *Pick someone else!*" Sarah's high pitch voice attracting some attention around them.

"Sarah, please!" Matthew looked around apologetically, pointing at her head indicating clear lunacy and madness on his friend's part.

Sarah closed her eyes to the sunshine and decided Matthew was right about one thing: "I could sit here for hours, especially now that the sun is out," she sighed happily.

"Hmmm," was Matthew's only reply as he looked around him.

"It's so good to be back here," Sarah's voice sincere. "I was happy to see the house on Alpine Gardens was still there and Hedgemead Park where Marc used to take me to the swings. I can't believe how small the Park felt now; I used to think it was huge when I was smaller." Sarah sighed happily. "I guess now you and I will have to make this an annual event."

Matthew considered this for a few moments.

"Nah, not good enough," Matthew nodded 'no'. "It's final, I'm definitely staying here."

"I know, it's lovely here, isn't it?" Sarah said with a sense of pride.

"I could have done without the smells of these Roman Baths, though," Matthew complained.

"Oh, bah-humbug!" Sarah snorted and looked at her watch. "I am getting hungry, how about you?"

"I shall live on the food for the soul that I am harvesting," Matthew said earnestly, pressing his hands on his heart.

"No can do, mister, you need to get real food in you, too." Sarah poked him until he looked at her. "Can I tempt you with another scrumptious Sally Lunn's bun with Welsh rarebit?

As we will be leaving Bath tomorrow morning, this will be our last chance!"

Matthew still did not move from the bench.

"*Must* you remind me of leaving?" he asked pleadingly. "Sarah, I implore you…"

Sarah cut in. "Don't think I will enjoy leaving; but life goes on! Come on!" Sarah got up and pulled his arm, but he would not budge. Sarah let go and started walking along the Pump Room and looked at the menu near the door.

Too fancy, too expensive for poor students – but one day… once they made their fame and fortune, she daydreamed.

"After Sally Lunn's I would like to go and admire the Pulteney Bridge by Adams, inspired by the Ponte Vecchio and the Ponte di Rialto," Matthew said behind her. "And then sit in the Parade Gardens!"

Sarah looked over her shoulder; she knew he would come.

"I have many memories of Sunday afternoon concerts in the sun," Sarah remembered, on the colored beach chairs. "But this time, Matt, would you mind if I walk over to the Assembly Rooms? I would love to see the Museum of Costume again with all the old-fashioned dress styles. I used to love that as a child."

"Sure," Matthew shrugged, "but I feel it only fair to warn you: don't expect to see Colin Firth there in his wet Mr. Darcy outfit."

Sarah smiled. They both loved the BBC Pride & Prejudice series so much they almost knew it by heart.

"Well, a girl can always dream, can't she? Besides, who knows? Bath is considered to be Jane Austen country," Sarah's smile full of promise.

"Funny though, that nobody here mentions she absolutely *hated* the place. Not good for business, of course…" Matthew set her straight.

"Oh Jane, Jane," Sarah sighed, "you and I agree on so many things. You poor misguided child – hating Bath… what were you thinking?" Sarah looked at the sunny skies.

"Right?" Matthew waited in expectation, wondering what Sarah would come up with next.

"It must be walking around Bath in silly, silky heels, through the mucky streets," Sarah said forgivingly. "I mean," she continued, on a roll now, "in her day and age there was so much to admire in Bath already! Even if you hadn't studied architecture, you would still see the beauty of it. I mean, think of it: she danced at the Assembly Rooms, had lunch at Sally's, went to church in the Abbey, strolled along the Circus, the Crescent; seriously, what was not to like?"

"You silly woman!" Matthew snorted. "Some of those buildings and structures were extremely modern buildings in her time."

"No, I'm convinced. It must be the shoes thing!" Sarah said with a sigh. "If only Jane had known that we women have liberated ourselves in the modern western world. We don't wear heels if we don't want to!" Sarah said, deep in thought.

"McFadden and Austen to the rescue of Women's Lib!" Matthew raised his fist in protest.

"At least in our day and age we would have sent Mr. Collins packing, wouldn't we? ... All-girl families can now inherit, yesss!! … Poor Charlotte, having to put up with this horrible, presumptuous man!" Sarah said indignantly.

"Have you quite finished?" Matthew laughed at her as he held the door open for Sarah and bowed deeply. "Sally awaits!"

The next day they took the bus to Stourhead House and Gardens. Matthew had not exaggerated that he would be sad to leave Bath. He was very quiet as they got on the bus.

"Don't be sad, Matt," Sarah squeezed his arm softly. "I know what's coming next and you're gonna go all googly-eyed at Stourhead and you will soon have forgotten about Bath."

"Impossible!" he said disgruntledly.

After about 45 minutes they got to the Stourhead car park. Matthew got out and schlepped his suitcase off the bus.

"Why did you have to bring a suitcase, Matt? I told you it would be a hassle to drag around," Sarah sounded irritated. Matthew stopped to stare at her.

"Haven't we had this conversation about twenty times now? I like my clothes to look as if they haven't been crumpled up all the time. I was never a blue jeans kind of guy, and never will be," Matthew said in exasperation.

"You know, for someone who's been here many times you forget the English are classy people and expect that kind of class," he added with his nose in the air.

They walked up the lane to the main house and instantly fell silent. The house itself was amazing, the gardens surrounding the house were simply stunning!

"Wow, Sarah, this Henry Hoare knew his stuff, didn't he?" Matthew exclaimed.

"Who?" Sarah asked him, teasingly.

"Good God, woman, did I not teach you *anything*?" he looked at her in frustration.

"Henry Hoare is considered to be the inventor of the landscaped garden. Often the name of Capability Brown is mentioned, but Henry Hoare created these Stourhead landscape gardens when old Capability was still in 'nappies'." Matthew looked around admiringly and added: "I am so glad you convinced me to leave Bath and come here. I have dreamt of seeing this house and these gardens forever."

"See, told you!" Sarah said triumphantly, her face radiant.

"Okay, Miss Know-it-All, lead the way…" he lugged his suitcase behind him.

They visited the house first and admired its green and white Regency library. Matthew chuckled and pointed at the huge marble statue of Queen Victoria.

"I expect the sculptor will probably have been beheaded for making the statue to actual life size," he whispered in Sarah's ear.

"Why?" Sarah whispered back.

"Queen Vic was never very realistic about her own respectable size, but this sculptor has spent enough marble on doing it justice!"

They suppressed their laughter in the serene atmosphere of the house.

For both Matthew and Sarah the 18th century Palladian style of the house was a treat. Matthew explained the many details of the picture gallery and Chippendale furniture. Sarah was, as ever, deeply impressed by how much he knew about all this; he was a fantastic guide.

The Stourhead gardens lying there in a bright summer sun were truly a sight. They decided to take the long walk through the gardens, around the fabulous lake to see all of the buildings; the Temple of Apollo and the Pantheon.

Years and years later, how thrilled they had been to see the new Pride & Prejudice movie was filmed partly at Stourhead gardens. They instantly recognized it; Elizabeth running across the Palladian bridge – standing in the pouring rain underneath the Temple of Apollo, spitting at Darcy: *"And those are the words of a gentleman?"*
They had liked the movie, but still preferred the BBC series. Though Matthew used to say that the movie portrayed a more realistic version of the rougher life style of the gentry in those days - the BBC series was a little too polished.

A message from Frome to Home

Dear Mom and Dad,

I am sending you this special card from Stourhead. Frome; one of the many special places for us as a family. I have been showing Matthew around Bath and now Stourhead. I have been reliving all the happy moments we have had here together. I have revisited it all: Alpine Gardens, the swings in Hedgemead Park, the Abbey, the little second hand book store, the seconds dishware place, and I have bought some lovely soap – just like we used to every year. That wonderful smelling box in the attic, hmmm.

I remember it all, the visits to the castles, the fantastic stories Dad used to tell us about how life would be in these drafty, cold places. Taking the train through England. Cuddling ponies and pussycats at the old stables.

I also realized that I have not taken the chance to thank you properly. Not just for the present for my graduation, so I got to go back here, but more importantly for all the good advice you have given me. I know that I gave you a hard time, but going to Dal-U turned out to be a great decision (on your part, of course!). Although I may not have portrayed this always, I am very grateful for all you have done for me to get me prepared for my adult life, which I think and hope I am now entering. I am looking forward to starting my new job at the Foundation after the summer and hope to have your guidance for a long time still.

I'm sending you all my love from this beautiful, historic and happy place. Yours with all my heart,

Sarah,
xxxx

From Stourhead they journeyed through the Cotswolds to Oxford. At a small Bed and Breakfast in Cirencester – a town name that they never agreed on how to pronounce - they met a German couple the next morning.

The German man was telling the other guests at the breakfast table: "We haf driven zru ze Cotswoldz, we haf wokked zru ze Cotswoldz, it alwayz rainz in ze Cotswoldz."

Sarah did not dare look at Matthew and nearly choked on her English bangers. The full English breakfast was another reason for Matthew to be in love with England. He could eat 'the full English' every morning; he could and he did.

"It's just not fair that you can stay slim eating the way you do," Sarah complained.

"It is equally unfair that you have a head full of gorgeous hair, whilst mine started thinning at birth – but you don't hear me complain, do you?" Matthew retorted sulkily.

They enjoyed the little villages in the Cotswolds; the picturesque and quaint places they saw were numerous; Upper and Lower Slaughter – baptized "The Slaughters"; the honey-colored cottages and rose gardens all too chocolate box perfect to not take pictures of. All those many medieval churches, some still completely intact, others rebuilt in different styles at a later stage. They were going to spend a fortune on having their photographs developed.

"On to Castle Howard, my dear Sarah, finally I will get to see it for myself!!"

Sarah laughed at Matthew's excitement.

"It is the epitome, the embodiment, no – the quintessence of everything baroque," Matthew sighed with longing. "It is also where 'Brideshead Revisited' was filmed, another one of my favorites," he added.

Sarah gave him a teasing look. "Anymore synonyms? I think you may have left out: exemplification!" she laughed.

"Well, I can't help it that I was born in the wrong country, can I?" and with that Matthew stared at his book for the rest of the bus trip.

Castle Howard would always remain Matthew's absolute favorite house. Sarah never forgot the expression on his face as he laid eyes on this grand house for the first time. He looked like he was ready to hug every wall and every pillar in the Great Hall he had come to know so well. He probably made a better tour guide than any of the employees there and never needed the descriptions offered per room. He also told her about the characters Charles and Sebastian from Brideshead Revisited, and how Castle Howard played an important role in the series as the Brideshead House.

Matthew was right: Castle Howard was a dream to baroque-fans.

Sarah didn't want to spoil Matthew's experience by saying she thought it was just a tad too much baroque for her taste. She just quietly witnessed Matthew jumping around the place in pure joy.

"Can you believe this house was designed by John Vanbrugh – who had no experience as an architect whatsoever, but was a playwright and a friend of the 3rd Earle of Carlisle? I mean, imagine that!" Matthew shrieked in disbelief, beside himself with happiness.

The grounds of Castle Howard were spectacular, with big peacocks striding around the south side of the house. Matthew pointed towards the mausoleum. Too bad it was closed to visitors. They lingered around the fountain and the Temple of the Four Winds, where Matthew reminisced about the scenes filmed there.

"You know, Matt," Sarah patted him on the arm, "when we get back, I will have to watch the series more closely. It didn't quite grab me the first time, but I would like to see it again."

Chapter 16

As the plane made a rather sudden drop, Sarah was distur-
bed from her deep thoughts. Too bad, she was enjoying her
reverie of their first trip. The gentleman sitting next to her
looked up from his book and gave a faint smile.

The pilot finally broke the spell of her daydream announ-
cing their arrival at Edinburgh airport. It was less welcoming
than Sarah had hoped. She walked out of the terminal to
face an icy wind. She picked up her rental car and looked
for the address of the B&B in Perth she had booked for the
night. It was only about a two-hour drive so that wasn't too
bad. Tomorrow she would drive up to Inverness to make her
acquaintance with the team. As she got to the car, she reminded
herself she would be driving on the 'wrong' side of the road
again. She instantly made the mistake of wanting to get in on
the passenger side. This would be interesting; it had been a
while since she had driven in Britain. Fortunately, this time she
had asked for an automatic gear, one less thing to focus on. It
was strange enough to have the mirror on her left hand side,
let alone that she would have to change gears manually on the
left. She would be too busy with all that to keep her eyes on the
road, especially now that she was driving alone. She got out of
the parking lot and had to think hard to take the roundabout
the right – or better, left – way around. By the time she got to
the B&B, she was exhausted. The concentration on the drive
had been tiring; she had completely missed the view from the
bridge over the Firth of Forth, which was supposed to be quite
something.

She was welcomed by a smiling woman in her fifties, with a
soft Scottish accent – Jill – who showed her to her room. It was
an old house with wooden floors and it smelled of apple pie;
very homely. Before leaving Sarah in her room Jill had some

instructions on the do's and don'ts during her stay.

"I don't allow smoking in the house; please don't eat or drink in your room," Jill said sternly, "breakfast is between 7 and 8 am and check-out is before 10. Oh, and you can't use the pay phone downstairs because it is broken."

Sarah wondered if Jill had ever heard of cell phones but decided not to ask.

Meanwhile Jill rattled on: "I don't give out keys to the house, so you can come in until 10 this evening. After that I lock the door," Jill's smile had now vanished completely. "Unless we agree on another time, that is, but never later than 11 pm. I need my sleep, you see, and I have to get up very early to start preparations for breakfast. Extra blankets are in the cupboard. Used towels go in the bathtub. Any more questions?" Jill finished her military drill.

Sarah made the mistake of asking for a suggestion for dinner. The list of suggestions was endless and Sarah wished she hadn't asked.

Sarah decided to walk into town later on and find somewhere cozy. From the few impressions she had caught from the car, Perth looked very nice. She found a lovely pub advertising good 'pub grub' on the sign near the door, 'The Scottish Arms'. She did not expect a culinary experience and she certainly did not get one, but the traditional pub atmosphere was priceless and she thoroughly enjoyed herself. The locals had their pints and got merrier with every refill. The landlady was very good at selling them more, since the 'liquids evaporated so quickly'.

As Sarah walked back to the B&B she noticed the distinct smell of smoke in her clothes and in her hair. Jill would probably think she had been smoking in the house and have a fit, Sarah thought with a wicked smile.

The next morning Sarah realized she had not been alone in the B&B. There was a young man at the breakfast table tucking into eggs and baked beans. Jill pointed out to Sarah to choose any table she liked and would she like tea or coffee. Still slightly sleepy and jetlagged Sarah opted for coffee. With the first sip

she was instantly reminded that the British have a different idea
of coffee than the Americans and Canadians. Still, breakfast
was lovely and got her jumpstarted for the day ahead. She felt
quite excited about driving north to Inverness and meeting the
team in the afternoon. The other guest had meanwhile finished
his breakfast and was checking out with Jill. Sarah finished her
orange juice.

"I have to get ready too, Jill," Sarah said, "I have quite a drive up
to Inverness today."

Jill waved this away. "Och, as long as you get on the A9 and
stay on, you'll be there in a jiffy. Too bad you don't have time
to visit Scone Palace; it is quite the pride of Perth. It used to be
the crowning place for our Kings, you know. It has wonderful
grounds with Highland cattle." Jill looked at Sarah with that
studied hostess-smile. "Still, maybe on your way back, eh?"
Sarah nodded and decided not to start a new discussion. She
really needed to get on her way.

"Inverness, here I come!" she said to herself as she again made the
mistake of walking to the wrong side of the car. "Or, maybe not…"
It was another freezing day, which explained the signs for the '
Indoor Highland Games' – it was even too cold for the sturdy
Scotsmen, Sarah thought with a chuckle.

The drive to Inverness was pure joy. Sarah now saw why
they were called the Scottish Highlands. The views on the
rugged terrain were amazing. The bright sunlight, blue skies
and white chasing clouds completed the picture. No wonder
the early settlers in Nova Scotia had seen the similarities and
name it the 'New Scotland'. It looked like driving up to the north
of Cape Breton.

The difference in bright colors was breathtaking. Sarah had to
restrain herself not to get out of the car every few minutes to
take pictures. She would do that as soon as her vacation
started.

Now she had to get to Inverness for her meetings. Besides, it
was far too cold to get out of the car for every scenic view.
'Get on the A9 and stay on' she reminded herself and 'be there
in a jiffy'.

As Sarah arrived at the visitor desk of the Highland Coastal Foundation she had trouble tuning her ears to the strong Scottish accent of the receptionist. This might prove to be a bit more of a challenge than she had expected. Being of Scottish descent apparently did not mean that she had a talent for grasping this language quickly. She looked admiringly around the old building and the main hall with the huge fireplace. Too bad the fire wasn't burning; she could have done with some warmth.

Sarah was introduced to Jaime Stewart, the Director of the Foundation, and to the project team, Allan and Maggie. They instantly offered to get her some lunch and coffee or tea.
"Would you like some haggis, or have you already had some?" Allan asked.
Sarah had been warned about haggis, a traditional Scottish dish of stuffed sheep stomach.
"No thank you, I'm fine," Sarah smiled coyly. "A tea would be lovely."
Jaime and his team started to laugh.
"Neu wurries, lass, eunly jeukin' wi'ya," Jaime's laugh thundering as he briefly slapped her shoulder.
After a moment's consideration she decided it meant they were only joking. She laughed more out of relief than anything else, but understood they meant well. She was served tea, flaky white with milk. *Oops, should have said 'black tea',* Sarah thought to herself.

Sarah's presentation of how they had run their PEI coastal project was received well. Jaime and his team were impressed with the results they had achieved and asked about their time line and budgeting procedure. After the meeting Sarah was invited to join Jaime and his wife for dinner, which she gratefully accepted. Jaime said that then at least they could get some 'prupper fodder in ya'.

Sarah went to her hotel where Jaime and his wife would pick her up at 7 pm. The hotel was a gem; an 18th century merchant's house in early Georgian style. For a moment she admired the tall terraced town house before walking up to the gracious panel-wood door. The Reception desk was located in the central hall, with a magnificent marble fireplace. This must have been some well-to-do merchant!

As soon as she got to her room, she saw that every piece of fabric in the hotel had a check pattern; the carpeting, the curtains, the bed spreads – everything was tartan and it looked amazingly good. Had anyone explained it to her beforehand, she would probably have screamed at the idea, but here it totally worked. She decided to take a hot bath before dinner. The huge sash windows in her room and bathroom were fantastic. She loved this simpler style of building and decorating, although she knew it originated from the less romantic influence of industrialization; the mass production of brick and sheet glass was what had enabled this building style. With every new detail she saw, she could not help thinking that Matthew would have thought this wasn't nearly extravagant enough in its ornamentation, being the baroque-fan that he was. She wondered if these reflexes would ever go away. She felt guilty thinking this and pushed it from her mind. *Live in the moment Sarah, **in** the moment.*

She dressed up for dinner and wandered around the hotel a bit. The big wooden stairways, the many fireplaces, the family crests – it all breathed history. Sarah curiously studied the family crests and wondered if the McFadden's one was represented there. That was homework for later on.

Jaime and his wife Andrea were wonderfully bubbly company. They took Sarah to a really nice French restaurant and shared all their stories about how they had met and how Jaime had joined the Highland Coastal Foundation. They also wanted to know everything about Sarah, managing somehow to not sound nosy. It was an enjoyable evening. The seafood was delicious and the wine divine. As they drove her back to the hotel Sarah felt slightly tipsy. She hadn't had this much wine in a long time. She hoped Jaime and Andrea hadn't noticed because she didn't want to make a bad impression. *'Goodytwoshoes'* she heard Matthew's voice in her head. Although she was spontaneous enough, Matthew had often teased her she was too dependent on other people's opinion of her. She could be way too hard on herself sometimes.

The next morning with Jaime and his team Sarah discussed ways of applying for government funding. She explained how this was organized for them at the CAPF and how they also got sponsoring from larger companies. The team had never dealt with company sponsoring before. In a one-on-one meeting, Jaime told Sarah his team had been very pleased and impressed with getting to know her and the work at CAPF.

"We would like to move forward and start a collaboration as soon as possible," he added with a smile.

Sarah was immensely happy about this and couldn't wait to tell John. With a shock she remembered that she hadn't sent him the promised message yesterday. She asked Jaime if she could give John a call from their offices and Jaime showed her to a meeting room.

"John, hi, it's me," Sarah said as she got through.

"Oh, hi Sarah, good to hear from you," John's curiosity sounded in his voice.

"I'm sorry I did not mail you yesterday," Sarah hurried to say. "The good news is, I have just heard the Scots would like to move forward and get started with the collaboration."

"Sarah, that's great news! I knew you would do a good job, well done!" John happily congratulated her.

"I will call you tomorrow from the hotel, okay, but I didn't want to keep you waiting any longer," Sarah said.

"Thanks, that's great – wow, our first international partnership. I am very happy 'bout this, Sarah!!"

"Yes, me too. I think I deserve a glass of bubbles this evening," she said with a chuckle, remembering she hadn't exactly run dry the evening before.

"You sure do, you deserve a bottle. I will have one chilled and ready for when you get back," John promised.

"Thanks! I will look forward to that. And John…" Sarah said meaningfully, "thanks for the opportunity. I'm having a great time."

"You're welcome, Sarah, glad to hear it."

"Talk to you tomorrow, John. Bye."

Chapter 17

Having gotten all of her work meetings out of the way Sarah could now start planning the rest of her trip. Since she had left for Scotland in rather a hurry, she'd focused on preparing the work meetings with Jaime and his team first. She had brought the preparation notes she had jotted down with her father, so she could plan the rest from there. In tracing back their ancestors Sarah's father had gotten as far as 1848, when the Renfrewshire McFaddens had left from Glasgow port for the long crossing to the land of the free; destined for Philadelphia. One of the family members had died on the crossing.

From Philadelphia on the McFaddens had moved around the Northeast of the US, until their great-grandfather had moved to Nova Scotia in 1896 as a young man for a job with the Halifax rail company. Sarah looked at the clipping of an old brochure, moved that her father had put it in the logbook.

> 1897
>
> **Glimpses Along the South Coast**
> Compliments of the
> Coast Railway Company Ltd.
> Nova Scotia

Finding out more of their family lineage fascinated Sarah. She knew from her father's information that he had planned to start in Glasgow, at the McFadden Society. She studied the map of Scotland to see how far the drive was to get there. From Inverness she would take the road that led south directly along Loch Ness. She would spot 'Nessy', take a quick picture and drive on to Fort William. She had considered driving west first to see Eilean Donan Castle. It would have been nice to go but it was such a monstrous detour, she decided against it. Sarah understood by now that the roads in Scotland were comparable to the roads on Cape Breton; always taking up more time than originally planned.

She would find a B&B near Fort William and Ben Nevis whilst she was there. Both Jill and Jaime had told her it was *the* mountain of Scotland to see, so she felt this to be a must.

Sarah stopped at the first parking on the banks of Loch Ness and was almost disappointed that 'Nessy' did not show himself. She did see people with binoculars staring out over the lake and suppressed a smile; what were they trying to see, seriously? Sarah took a few pictures of the Loch. She would have to paste a smiling 'Nessy' in for the team back home; they would love that. With a pang she remembered again how hard she had been on the team in the past months. She would use this time off to relax and get back to her old self. She fervently hoped she would get to that point. Stressing about it, she decided, was not going to help her. She walked along the loch some more and was surprised about how many people were there in March, which must surely be off-off-season.

For her next stop she had planned some time at Urquhart Castle, situated right on Loch Ness. Once she got there, though, she saw it was merely a castle ruins. Somehow, she had completely missed that on her map. She pulled into the parking lot and got out. She decided not to walk around too far. It wasn't very nice to be outside; it was sunny but very cold and windy. Getting a coffee at the café would be very welcome, though. She hadn't had enough coffee for the time of day.

She walked back to the car and headed onward to Fort William. Farther to the south of Loch Ness on the turn to a little town called Invergarry, she spotted a hitchhiker with a backpack. A tall man in his early forties stood beside the road hoping to catch a ride. He did not have a direction sign with him, but he looked like he had been standing there for quite some time. There were not many cars coming this way. Sarah considered taking him with her, but drove on, looking straight ahead.

You could never know whom you were taking, could you? She passed him and felt somewhat sorry. Although he was hardly her responsibility, was he?

She drove on to Fort William and looked at her B&B guide. She had dog-eared the pages of the places she had pre-selected and looked up the first address she would try. As she entered Fort William, she recognized the signs stating: 'Ceud Mìle Fàilte' – 'a hundred thousand welcomes' in Gaelic.
She reached the street and found the small B&B easily enough; it was just off the main road. The street overlooked the town of Fort William, over which the sun was now setting. The B&B looked nice and Sarah was in luck. They did indeed have vacancies and Sarah checked in. She walked up to her room, turned the key and couldn't help laughing. Where at the hotel in Inverness everything had been decorated in a check pattern, here everything had a floral theme and not necessarily matching in colors. *They should hand out sunglasses with the room key*, Sarah thought to herself. It was a good thing she would spend most of her time here with her eyes closed.
She took a long soaking bath and slipped on a pair of jeans and a warm turtleneck. She would take the car into town and find a restaurant. She walked downstairs and got somewhat of a surprise. At the small wooden reception table she saw the hitchhiker she had passed on the road, making enquiries about a room. She noted a hint of an accent, Danish perhaps, or German? She wondered if he had ever 'wokked in ze Cotswoldz' and sniggered. He looked at her curiously, but did not say anything.

She got to her car and saw that it was blocked by another car. The driver was still in the car on the phone, gestured an apology and started the engine.
In the meantime the Danish/German had come outside to pick up his backpack.
"I see you have met my chauffeur, James," he said, "I will ask him next time not to be so rude and block other people's cars."
"So, is 'James' taking you into town too?" Sarah asked.

The Danish/German nodded 'no'.

"If you're planning to go into town, I can take you if you want," Sarah offered airily.

"You'd better be careful, young lady, offering rides to strangers," the Danish/German smiled widely at her, "you never know what trouble you get yourself in to."

Young lady?? What the…

Sarah turned towards him to look at him more closely, but he had started walking down the street and did not look back.

Sarah felt like a schoolgirl, caught at cheating; he had obviously recognized her from along the route.

Still, she couldn't care less – or could she?

'Goodytwoshoes' it rang in her head again. She passed him on the road, honked loudly and waved – *that* would take care of him!

Sarah had another interesting pub meal. As she ordered at the bar she gave her name. They would call her as soon as her food was ready. Sarah chose a table near a big fireplace and looked around the pub, enjoying the atmosphere.

Her choice of deep fried mushrooms in a beer batter was very good and she sprinkled her fries richly with salt and vinegar. Yummy!

Sarah tried to catch some of the conversation around her. This Scottish tongue was hard to grasp, especially if the locals started talking to each other. Some time later, Sarah spotted the Danish/German across the room; the DeeGee, as she had now baptized him. He waved briefly at her and gave her another one of those wide smiles. She couldn't help but laugh back, knowing full well he was teasing her.

In the meantime at the bar they kept calling out the food orders; "Order for the two pretties" and two less-than-lookers of men got up to pick up their food. Sarah chuckled; she loved this sense of humor, that the British and the Scottish seemed to have in common. They had a great way of not taking themselves too seriously.

Something I could learn from, Sarah thought to herself.

She wondered what name the DeeGee would have given at

the bar, something like: "Order for the honky burger from the Continent".
In the end she missed it in the hustle and bustle of the pub, as she peeked over and saw he was already eating.

After the meal Sarah got back to the B&B to her floral pattern room and picked up the e-reader Matthew had given her. She hadn't been reading for months and was looking forward to it. She had uploaded some books before she left. She decided to open the latest book by one of her favorite authors who had given her many a laugh-out-loud moment, sometimes to the embarrassment of people around her. But Sarah had problems concentrating. She didn't know whether it was the quality of the book or the fact that she felt too uneasy to read. She turned off her reading lamp and pulled the blankets up to her nose, shivering. She should have picked a warmer season to come than the end of winter.

Chapter 18

Sarah woke up in the middle of the night. Her t-shirt was soaked and her heart was racing. She tried to find the switch for the lamp but knocked over her water glass. Good grief, she'd been having a horrible nightmare about the time that she and Matthew had learned of his lung cancer and the possibilities for treatment.

In first instance Matthew had been very brave, but over time he became more and more withdrawn. Sarah had tried to get Matthew to go on daytrips, to have new experiences.

One day as she drove him back from the hospital she said: "You know, Matt, now that this string of chemo treatments is behind you, I think it is time we start planning this trip to England we said we would make. We still have to book this chocolate box cottage to stay in and 'do like the English do.'" Matthew smiled at her vaguely, understanding her good intentions.

"Of course it will have to be close to Bath," Sarah continued purposefully, "or even *in* Bath. What do you think? We could rent an apartment right on the Royal Crescent!"

Matthew turned toward her in his car seat and thought about this. "You know, my dearest Sarah, that is actually not a bad idea," he said. "I mean, it's not like I have to leave my money behind for anyone. I say, we might as well enjoy it," Matthew raised his hands, adding: "Who knows, we could walk under a bus tomorrow and never have lived like the English live."

Sarah was happy he was warming to the idea of making the trip they had been talking about for ages. The long silence that followed indicated they both realized it could be their last, though neither expressed it.

Eventually, she broke the silence.

"All right, I will start Googling for chocolate box cottages with a rose garden, teapot in the kitchen, located in a quaint village.

When do you wish to go?"

Matthew took out his cell phone and studied his calendar. "Why don't we try to go around the end of April?" he suggested. "That will give us a few weeks to plan the trip; the weather might be a bit better then. It also matches with my schedule for the next scan."

The next morning Sarah sent the first links to Matthew by e-mail:

Subject: House 1

How about this cutie, and in a picture perfect village too – only 40 km from Bath!!!!
I can just see us walking along the high street with a wicker basket to go to the bakery. Hmmm.
Will send some more options later.
XXX

Subject: House 2

This one is unbelievable, look at the garden around it – small but perfect for us!!
What do you think?
I wonder if the cat comes with the house?
Ciao bello, later!

Subject: House 3

We could also go bigger – this manor house in Babington – we could be lord and lady of the manor. Doesn't sound half bad either. We will have to fight over who gets the lush master bedroom, though… ;-))
Sorry, I've got to get back to work, Mister!
Kissies, Sarah

Within an hour she had a reply from Matthew:

> **Subject: You ARE Crazy!! And I LOVE you for it!!**
>
> House 1: adorable, let's consider it – very chocky boxy indeed!
> House 2: too small and too far away from Bath; you'd get attached to the cat and never want to leave …
> House 3: unaffordable – meant for 12 people – but lovely library and an AGA in the kitchen; close enough to Bath. Castle Howard is quite a long way but nothing we can't handle. I'd say – let's go for it.
> Double kissies back, Matt, xx
> NOW GET BACK TO WORK!

They mailed back and forth about another number of stately homes for rent and had great fun considering all the options. At the end of the afternoon Matthew grabbed his cell phone.

"You missed Dyrham Park and Buckingham Palace, my darling Sarah!" Matthew said sniggering.

Sarah was glad that he sounded so happy.

"Well, Dyrham Park is way too small for us, as you well know," Sarah stated matter-of-fact, "and I did try Buck Hall, but it seems to have been rented out to something-something Windsor in the period we want to go. Bugger all!"

"Did you actually say 'bugger all'?" Matthew's laugh thundered through the line. "My dear Ms. McFadden, that is so highly uncalled for!"

Sarah snorted loudly at the other end.

"You know, this manor house in Babington sort of stuck in my mind," Matthew sounded more serious now.

"Wouldn't it be a hoot if we could rent this for a week? I'm game if you are," he said hastily, "I mean, it's not like *you* have to leave all your savings to your children and grandchildren!"

"How *rude* you are!!" Sarah tried to sound offended, but her voice gave her away, "at my age there is still a glimmer of hope of finding Mr. Right and starting a family."

"So how's about it?" Matthew asked eagerly, "fancy going on a trip to Babington with your own Mr. Wrong?"

Sarah heard the excitement in his voice and asked: "Do you have *any* idea how much 3,000 British Pounds is in Canadian Dollars?"

"Nope, don't know and don't care!" Matthew said soberly. "Come on, Miss Program Director, now is not a time to be stingy! I mean," he sighed theatrically, "it will be a very medicinal trip for me… and I do not have a manipulative nature, as you well know!" He snorted into the phone.

"You horrible, horrible man, you!!" Sarah teased him, "not even shying away from emotional blackmail… Well, maybe we could knock something off the price since there will be only the two of us," she said in hesitation.

Sarah heard Matthew's happy laughter at the other end; something she hadn't heard in such a long time.

"If anyone can negotiate, it would be you!" Matthew said with tooth-aching sweetness.

"Okay, Mr. Smooth Talker, why don't I give these people a call and see if we can arrange something?" Sarah gave in. "I mean: to be 'Lady Babington' for a week, I do like the sound of that!"

"You're serious? No, really? I'm game if you are!" Matthew shrieked. "So my little negotiator, see what super deal you can get us and let's go! It is out of season and we will treat the house so well, no children, they should be happy we're coming!"

The intermediaries of the house did indeed contact the owner and they got a 35% discount. Sarah could be very convincing if she wanted to be. *Still a small fortune, but for a very, very good cause.*

She immediately called Matthew and told him she had closed the deal and they were definitely going.

"My darling Lady Babington," Matthew said softly, "I can't believe this is actually happening. I can't wait to go. We will have to rent a car so we can tour the area and drive up north."

"Yes, shall I look into tickets and a car tomorrow?" Sarah offered.

"Would you?" Matthew sounded so happy. "I think it's good that this time we will be staying in one location, instead of touring around from place to place," Matthew added softly, "I think that would be too tiring for me."

It was one of the first times Matthew himself indicated he knew he had lost a lot of his physical condition as a result of the chemotherapy.

Sarah arranged everything: the house, car, plane tickets – everything was prepared. She had called ahead to the contact person, Anne, who would meet them at the manor house. They had a few phone conversations in which Sarah explained to Anne the situation of Matthew's health and asked her how she could call for a doctor if necessary. Anne couldn't have been more helpful in getting all the information to Sarah before they left.

"You will love the house, it is ever so nice," Anne explained enthusiastically. "And the new owner, Mr. Lambert, has decorated it in a very posh style. You will have bags of space, of course, it being just the two of you."

"One last thing, Anne," Sarah said, "can you advise us where to go for dinner on the evening we arrive?"

"Well, you could always go to the local pub restaurant," Anne said. "It is quite fancy and they do a lovely menu, mind, you do want to get a reservation. People from all around the area pop over for a meal, it being a Saturday 'n' all. Which rooms would you like me to prepare for you?"

Sarah even considered lending a dog to stay at the house; Matthew loved dogs as long as they were not in his own pristine home. She also enquired about having their portrait painted to complete the M'Lord & Lady feel, but it would mean that they would be tied down in their schedule. She knew she had a tendency to go overboard with her ideas and these might qualify, so she restrained herself.

There were times when Sarah wondered if making this trip was too much of a risk, or might be too hard for her to handle.

But when she saw Matthew's text messages in the days leading up to their departure for England, she was convinced it had been a good decision.

Bleep!

> Hullo, M'Lady BABS, have you packed already? Should we bring our own port decanter, or will they have one? What do you think, old girl? Love, Lord BABS, xxx

Bleep!

> My darling lady BABS, have Chef, the butler, gardener and maid been informed of our arrival? Hate to have them stay at the wrong house and come home in the cold, wouldn't you? BABS himself, xxx

They had agreed beforehand that Sarah was going to do all the driving in England, since Matthew was often too tired. Matthew had offered to deejay along the way, so he could play her new classical pieces he had discovered.
"We're starting with an oldie," Matthew said with a wink.
Sarah instantly recognized it. 'I vow to Thee My Country', from 'The Planets' by Holst.
Sarah looked to her side and saw Matthew choke when he heard the phenomenal choir and wondered if it was a smart idea to play this kind of music. She did not say it, though. The drive along the M4 went so fast they decided to take a touristy route for the final part into Babington.

Babington was a lovely village, with a quaint 18th century church. They would walk over to the church later after they had accepted the key to the house.
Driving up the lane to the manor was amazing. Anne had opened the front gate and waved them on to drive up to the house. The photographs they had seen online of the garden leading up to the house did not do justice to how exquisite it

was in reality. The joy they experienced upon seeing the house was indescribable.

"Can you believe our luck?" Sarah asked, deeply in awe, "being able to stay here for a week??"

Matthew took Sarah's hand from the wheel for a moment, kissed it softly and whispered: "Thank you…"

Sarah looked at him as she stopped the car.

"Lord Babington, allow me to welcome you home," Sarah said with happy, watery eyes.

Nothing could have prepared Sarah for the change she saw in Matthew as they stepped in the door. Anne led them around the house and in her enthusiasm explained about the Grand Hall, the library and the different building stages. Sarah thoroughly enjoyed the tour but noticed Matthew did not give much response. She looked around a few times to see if he was still with them as he followed them in silence. In the main wing of the house they went up the stairs to the bedrooms Anne had prepared for them. All of it more impressive and grand than the pictures on the Internet had shown.

To stay in a manor like this… it was just overwhelming.

Sarah had brought a few cookbooks so they could prepare their dinners together and try out the AGA.

Anne walked into the master suite, decorated in off-white with black accessories, with an enormous four-poster bed. The view of the garden, the trees in blossom, was better than an English postcard. They followed Anne into the en-suite bathroom with a traditional bathtub and taps.

"Yes, I will take this room for the week," Matthew said and Sarah looked at him in surprise, realizing he was serious.

Anne then led them to a room next to the master suite, a little smaller but also stunningly decorated in powder blue and off white, the smaller leaded glass windows offering a view of the rolling fields on the other side of the house.

Anne showed them that this room also had an en-suite bathroom with a shower, done in an old-fashioned style.

Sarah looked at Matthew, but he ignored her completely.

"I will take this room, Anne, it's beautiful – thank you," Sarah said,

"I prefer a shower."
This was indeed true, but Sarah would have appreciated to discuss it first.

"Now, that has you sorted for the bedrooms," said Anne and walked downstairs again to explain about the Internet access, alarm system and of course, the kitchen.
"I have lit up the AGA, since the Lamberts hadn't been here for quite some time. The AGA stays on all the time during your stay, so you needn't worry about that. We have chilled a bottle of champagne in the fridge for you and there is a welcome basket of assorted teas, coffees and shortbread. We do hope you will have a wonderful time," Anne added kindly.
Sarah had brought Anne a gift from Canada; hand-carved wooden lighthouse tea coasters. Anne accepted the gift in grateful surprise. She hugged Sarah and said to call if they needed anything else. Matthew said a brief 'goodbye' and walked back to the Grand Hall.
Sarah walked Anne to her car.
Anne opened her car window and called out: "Enjoy your dinner this evening!" as she waved and drove off.
Sarah waved back. "We will, thanks again, Anne!"

After she got out of the shower Sarah heard thundering classical music coming from the Grand Hall. She put on her black dress with the lacquer boots and looked in the mirror; not quite Lady Babington, but close enough. Walking downstairs and opening the enormous carved wooden door to the Grand Hall she was overpowered by the loud music. Matthew sat on the stone floor in front of the fireplace, trying to light it.
"Lord Babington, can I invite you to go out and dine with me?" she had to raise her voice to be heard.
She kept staring at Matthew's back as he slowly turned around.
"Sure," he said.
"Did you want to get changed before we go? We have a reservation in 10 minutes, but I'm sure it is just a short walk – small village," she smiled.
Matthew got up and said he would quickly wash his hands.

"Are you okay?" Sarah asked.

"Yes, I'm fine. Just a bit tired from the trip," Matthew said.

Over dinner Sarah almost felt like she was invading Matthew's privacy by addressing him. Sarah had never seen him like this and wondered what had brought this on.

The next morning Sarah suggested they would go for some grocery shopping, so they could fill the fridge.

"I have to take my medication first, so we have to plan around this in the mornings," Matthew said.

"Of course, Matt, how can we do this?" Sarah asked.

"After I take these," Matthew said, picking up his pills, "I cannot eat for an hour."

"Then let's go to the grocery store in Radstock and stock up on some things for breakfast and dinner this evening," Sarah said, with her usual practical tone. "I can't wait to try out this traditional AGA," she said as she held out the cookbook.

Matthew gave no response whatsoever.

"I can go alone if you want to stay in," Sarah offered, studying Matthew. "Grocery shopping wasn't high on our list."

"I have to say I resent your tone," Matthew glared at her as he walked toward the front door, "I am not that sick yet."

Exasperated by this remark, Sarah stopped in her tracks.

"Matt, I didn't mean…" but he did not look at her, leaving her baffled for a few moments.

They bought all the ingredients to cook a full English breakfast on the AGA for at least half the week. They divided the work to prepare breakfast and Matthew went over to the Grand Hall to put on some music. She could hear the music through the dining room all the way to the kitchen.

The cozy kitchen was a joy. Matthew was happily preparing his favorites: bangers and black pudding. They had their grand breakfast in the huge dining room, served on beautiful plates.

"Shall we both sit at the far ends of the table?" Sarah laughed. "You know, like in The Duchess?"

Matthew pictured it and snorted. "Let's both sit near the window and look at this amazing garden," he suggested.

"Our first homemade full English," Sarah said proudly, "enjoy, Matt."

Matthew instantly tucked into the enormous portion of food and beamed at her.

"Hmmm, delicious M'Lady!" his eyes sparkled. "Too bad we gave the staff the day off. Now we will have to do our own dishes."

After they finished having breakfast, Sarah started clearing the table and Matthew disappeared to the Grand Hall again.

"What do you want to do for the rest of the day, Matt?" Sarah asked as she walked in.

He looked up from his book with slight irritation. "I thought I would just read today – bad weather, nothing open on Sunday," he said.

Sarah noticed again how Matthew made his own decision and tried to remind herself how different his situation was from hers.

The entire Sunday Matthew played loud classical music in the Grand Hall. He tried to light the fire and read a book without so much as speaking a word to her.

The silence weighed heavily on Sarah's shoulders; she didn't know what to do. She said she would start preparing the meal and stayed in the kitchen for most of the time.

The next days Matthew really didn't want to be at the house anymore.

"How about," he suggested the next morning, "I take my medication, we drive to Wells. We can have breakfast there."

"But… we have a fridge full of breakfast ingredients," Sarah said, not understanding.

"Are we going to go poor over a few groceries?" Matthew ridiculed her.

"It's a shame to let it go to waste," Sarah said. "I also thought we rented the house so we could spend some time in it."

His only answer was a noncommittal stare.

Something in Matthew froze and Sarah was unable to get through to him. She had become his chauffeur and his guardian; the facilitator of the trip. Never in her entire life had she felt this lonely. There were moments he seemed unaware of her presence, even. He was lost in his emotions, in his fear. He ran from his computer to the library. He ordered books online every hour like there literally was no tomorrow. He played music in the Grand Hall, loud enough, Sarah thought, not to hear his own thoughts. He would pick up a book and put it down again after a few minutes. The restlessness in him was omni-present. It took every last bit of Sarah's strength not to shout at him that she was there also; this was her trip too. Sarah intuitively understood that confronting Matthew with this could potentially mean a final break between them. So instead of letting the situation explode, Sarah literally imploded – letting her strong will eat away at her for not standing up for herself.

It was after the way he treated her on their visit to Bath Sarah realized this trip was a big mistake. They were sitting on a bench near the Abbey, the sounds of the Roman Baths coming from behind them.
"I would really like to climb the spire and walk around the roof," Matthew said, pointing up to where he saw some tourists walking. "Good idea," Sarah said, not voicing her concern that the climb might be too tiring for him. "You know what? I will wait here and take a picture of you; soon as you appear up there!" Sarah offered with a smile.
"That would be nice," Matthew nodded in agreement.
Every time Sarah would look up and see a new group of visitors appear, but there was no sign of Matthew. She waited in the pale sunlight for almost 45 minutes, camera in hand, until she decided to check at the Abbey entrance around the corner to see if there was a queue. At the entry of the spire tours there was no one there.
Sarah wondered where Matthew could have gone. She was worried that he had not been able to finish the climb. She tried calling him on his cell phone, which was switched off.
Sarah decided to walk into Bath on her own, see the old familiar places. Sarah's mind was racing, though, and she failed to enjoy being in the place she held so dear. She spent an hour in

Bath, constantly checking her phone, before she walked back. She instantly saw Matthew sitting on one of the benches in front of the Abbey, where they had sat so many years before. She slowly walked over. As soon as Matthew spotted her, he said with a radiant smile: "Sarah, you have really missed something great!"

She looked at him, completely taken aback. "What do you mean?"

"Well, there was a waiting line for the spire tour and I saw a poster for a choir concert in the Abbey at noon for the bank holiday. I decided to catch that instead!" Matthew said delightedly. "It was amazing!"

Sarah couldn't believe what she was hearing.

"But… I was waiting for you to take your picture!" she stammered. Matthew did not reply.

"Why didn't you come and get me?"

"You don't even like choir music!" he retorted defensively.

Sarah pointed to the other side of the Abbey. "I was only 50 meters away on that bench over there."

"You don't mean to tell me you actually waited for me," Matthew said, "don't be ridiculous!"

"Of course, I promised! I waited there for almost 45 minutes," Sarah swallowed the rest of the sentence '*I will not be able to take that picture of you after today*'.

"Don't be stupid!" Matthew said. "I would have left after 10 minutes."

Sarah sat down next to him with watery eyes. "Well, that's apparently where you and I are different," she said.

They sat there without saying a word. The wind was picking up, bringing in dark cloudy skies. More and more people left. Finally, after what seemed like an eternity, Matthew said in a strangled voice: "We're sitting on the Abbey Churchyard and I feel like those two angels… rushing against the current." He nodded up toward the Jacob's ladder on the Abbey. Then he dropped his head, stared at his hands and whispered: "You and I both know I don't stand a chance."

The long silence that followed was only interrupted by Sarah's sobs.

The day before leaving for Halifax, they drove up north to Castle Howard. Seeing Matthew walk around the Castle that last time literally broke Sarah's heart.

Upon her arrival home, Marc was just filling her fridge.
"Hey, sis, welcome back!" he hugged her. "How was your trip?"
"Don't ask..." Sarah sighed and started to cry uncontrollably, all her pent-up frustration now surfacing.
"That difficult, huh?" Marc said. "I think you are very brave; not many friends would have dared to undertake such a trip with someone so ill."
"No, Marc, that's just it," Sarah said, "it didn't feel like friends, most of the time he didn't even notice I was there."
"What do you mean, did not notice?" Marc looked at her in surprise.
"He never really talked to me during this whole trip," Sarah sobbed as she told Marc the rest.
"What an asshole!" Marc exclaimed. "The fact that he is ill, doesn't give him the right to treat you like that, now does it?"
"I have never felt this lonely before, Marc, in my entire life," Sarah's shoulders shook with her deep sobs.
"My goodness, Sarah…" Marc sounded sad for her.
"You know, this trip just was a huge mistake. By making it so special and so big, we emphasized that this was a last," Sarah said, wiping her eyes.
"And you did not *scream* at him for the way he acted?" Marc said incredulously.
"No, I couldn't," Sarah stared out the window, "I really did not know what response to expect. I mean, I couldn't risk breaking off this friendship at a time like this, could I?"
"Sarah, when will you ever stop making excuses for the guy?" Marc sounded clearly frustrated. "You did not deserve this!"
"Every day I would have given a fortune to crawl back home," she said.
"Well, Sarah, you must have superpowers in you. I know I wouldn't have been able to cope," Marc sighed deeply.

Subject: News

Hi Sarah,

I am sorry to send you this message via e-mail. This is something I cannot bring myself to tell you in person.

I did not want to spoil our trip, so I did not tell you that just before we left for England I had another scan done of my head. I have been feeling dizzy often and suffer from excruciating headaches.

This morning I received a phone call from my doctor to come in a.s.a.p.

The short of it is: they have discovered a large brain tumor. There is nothing they can do about it. They have warned me to tell my close relations that this is a major setback in my treatment. It may lead to mood swings, blindness and paralysis.

Sorry, Sarah, for e-mailing you with this news.
I am at a loss for words...

Matthew

Chapter 19

Sarah got up the next morning feeling groggy and grumpy. Reliving that last trip with Matthew had been devastating. It had brought a mixture of feelings back to life that she could well do without.

She got down to the breakfast room knowing she looked like death warmed over. However, no amount of make-up would do just that: make up for it – too much to expect from a jar. Fortunately, there was no one there. She hadn't looked at her watch properly because breakfast hadn't started yet. The kind landlord immediately offered her a coffee and said breakfast would only be a few minutes. She took her coffee to the big living room and picked up a magazine. She stared at the pictures but the information did not sink in.

After a while the 'DeeGee' walked in and mumbled a 'good morning'. She nodded and went back to staring at the pages.

"Are you considering taking the Ben Nevis tour?" the DeeGee asked as he sat down opposite her.

"Excuse me?" Sarah looked up.

"I said," he repeated politely, "I see you are looking at the Ben Nevis tour."

She re-examined the cover of her magazine and saw what he was getting at.

"Not really, no," she shook her head. "I was just waiting for breakfast… Are you taking the tour?" Sarah asked.

"Nuh-uh, me neither, I am trying to get south to Glasgow, hitchhiking," the DeeGee said with emphasis, "I am on my way back from the Island of Skye and am preparing to get back home." Sarah waited if he was going to say something about the previous day and was relieved he didn't.

"Have you been hitchhiking all this way?" Sarah asked, clearly impressed. "Seems like the wrong season to do that."

"Yes indeed, not the best of choices, but some things come unplanned," he shrugged lightly.

The landlord came in and stated that the breakfast room was ready for them.

"Enjoy your breakfast," he said.

She looked at him with a moment's hesitation. "Would you care to join me?" she offered.

He looked somewhat taken aback but joined her at her table. Sarah couldn't help thinking '*don't feel like you have to on my account*'.

"So, 'James' is not driving you all the way to Glasgow, then?" she asked with a smile.

"No, no such luck, I'm afraid," he smiled back shyly.

Breakfast was served in floral dishes, of course it was, and Sarah couldn't suppress a chuckle.

"Is it my imagination, or are you finding it hard to hide your joy at the fact that I will have to face the cold again?" he winked at Sarah.

She looked directly at him. "Well, time to toughen up," she teased him, "I'm sure in a few days someone will probably come along to pick you up."

If anyone didn't look like they needed toughening up, it would be him, Sarah thought, peeking at his tall build, his unshaven face and weather-beaten, tanned skin.

"Where are you from, the US?" he asked. "Is that where they tell strangers to toughen up?"

She quite enjoyed this cat'n'mouse conversation.

"No, I'm Canadian – Nova Scotia – the new, *improved* Scotland," she whispered the last bit not to offend their host.

"And where are you from that you can't stand a little cold, South Africa?"

"Not a bad guess considering my accent," he looked at her in surprise, "but I'm from The Netherlands – Friesland to be exact."

Oh, so *that* was what she had been hearing; he was Dutch. He had very good vocabulary, though.

The DeeGee stretched out his hand to introduce himself, but

all Sarah could make of it was: 'Abbah Maggagga'.

She shook his hand and said: "Sarah, Sarah McFadden. How do you spell your name because I don't recognize any of those guttural sounds."

He took out a pen and wrote on his paper napkin 'Abe Makkinga'.

"That is not at *all* what that sounded like!" Sarah laughed. "Anyway, Abe, if I may call you Abe, I am driving in the direction of Glasgow and now that I know you are a trust-worthy non-flying Dutchman I am offering you a ride."

She would quite enjoy having some company on the road.

"That sounds great, thanks," he looked at her gratefully, "and please, yes, do call me Abe."

They enjoyed their breakfast. Abe also ordered the continental and added with a wink that he should not eat too much since he would not be hiking but hitchhiking. Sarah did not comment but wondered what he had to worry about. There was no indication of handles anywhere. Not that she was the expert. God knows how long ago it was… She broke her train of thought; *'now would be a good snappy-outy moment'*.

"Shall we say I meet you at the car in fifteen minutes?" Sarah suggested instead.

"If you haven't changed your mind about taking a hitchhiker," Abe said hesitantly, "then yes – see you in fifteen."

She assured him it was okay, but appreciated him giving her an out for her spontaneous offer.

Seeing Sarah come downstairs with her luggage was quite an unexpected sight.

"Did you pack your whole household or do you have more stuff back home?" Abe asked her with a wide grin.

"Hey, listen," Sarah swallowed the word 'buster' right in time, "just because you make the mistake of hiking doesn't mean we all fall for the romance of packing light."

He helped her put her luggage in the car.

"Now I just have to rush back in to get my coffee," Sarah said frantically.

"Your what?" Abe sounded surprised.

"My coffee-to-go… my travel cup," Sarah studied Abe for a moment, deep in thought. "Maybe that kind of innovation hasn't quite reached Europe yet?"

Abe laughed as he got in the car.

A few moments later Sarah came walking back with a huge thermal cup.

"For a moment there I thought you were joking," he said drily.

"Coffee is no joking matter," she retorted earnestly as she got in. "You are much safer on board when I have my cup of coffee, trust me."

"I will take your word for it, ma'am," Abe smiled at her.

"Oh, I almost forgot – we also need good travel music," Sarah jumped back out of the car.

"Don't tell me you brought along your CD rack!" Abe was laughing out loud by now.

"Yes, and my stereo system with huge speakers, woofers, sub-woofers…" Sarah's muffled voice came through the back hatch. "I'm sure they must be here somewhere…"

Sarah re-appeared at her door. "Don't tell me you're hiking without having music with you!"

"Guilty as charged," Abe raised his hand ceremonially, "I do have my MP3 player with me, yes."

"Aha!!" Sarah pointed at him getting back in. "And might I ask what you play whilst hiking? Is there anything that helps you forget the cold, the wet and the sore, blistered, feet?" she asked, going through her bag for a decent CD to play.

"Wow, no need to ask you if you are a hiker, then!" he grinned broadly. "As far as music goes, I have a wide variety. I like all kinds of music, really."

"That 's good, 'cause we're getting Neil Young for the first part of the journey," Sarah said as she slipped the CD into the front loader.

"Had to be good ol' American music of course," he stated soberly, "but I am very happy that you won't play bag pipe music in the car," Abe's expression grateful. "I have gotten quite an impression of Scottish music and have heard enough to last me a lifetime." He rolled his eyes as he said it.

"Can I just interrupt you there," Sarah said firmly, "Neil Young is Canadian. Granted, he's not from Nova Scotia – Winnipeg originally – but we still like him."

"Why pardon me, ma'am," Abe said in almost perfect southern drawl, "for being so ignorant."

She replied with a twinkle in her eye: "Well don't let it happen again!"

She wondered how come it felt like they had known each other for a very long time and were comfortable enough to joke like old friends.

They drove south for a while listening to Neil Young.

"This sounds good," Abe said, listening intently. "I mean, he doesn't come close to Neil Diamond, of course, but it's quite good."

"Really, a Neil Diamond fan, huh?" Sarah snorted. "You were right: with a hitchhiker you never know what kind of trouble you get yourself into."

"Neil Diamond is fantastic!" Abe said defensively. "And I like The Eagles, that sort of thing, Hotel California, Peaceful Easy Feeling – great music," he said trying to look cool and playing the air guitar. "Me and my brother had a traveling disco-show when we were teenagers." Abe smiled at the memory of it.

"Really?" Sarah said with a teasing smile.

"Well, the traveling was done by bike," Abe said drily, "and the records 'n' disco-ball were transported on our windsurf cart," he chuckled.

"Wow," Sarah laughed, "that sounds positively – how shall I put this…"

"Don't laugh!" Abe protested, "we were quite popular with the girls, you know!"

"I bet you were," Sarah said, her voice dripping with irony.

"You do know that more music was written since the 70's and 80's, don't you?"

"U2 new enough for you? My favorite band of all times," he said with an air of finality.

She did not want to spoil the moment by mentioning she absolutely hated U2. "Okay, close enough," she shrugged.

As they drove past Loch Linnhe, laying there in mystic pale sunlight, Sarah asked Abe to change the CD after Neil Young had started anew.

"Any preference?" Abe asked her.

"Not really," Sarah smiled, "Sorry there is no Neil Diamond on board, or any of your other 'golden oldies.'"

"Are you mocking my taste in music?" Abe asked in a wounded tone.

"Hey, you got any complaints, you can catch the next ride!" Sarah briefly touched the breaks for effect, and laughed out loud.

Sometime later, Abe turned towards Sarah to thank her for taking him along, as he saw tears running down her cheek. He stopped himself just in time. Sarah stared over the steering wheel, her knuckles white with holding on.

> *How can you accept me, tell me what you see*
> *When all I can do, is run from myself*
> *How can you believe me, tell me what I say*
> *When all that I feel, can't hide from myself*
>
> *Can I really trust you, build on your foundation*
> *Why don't you deceive me, it has been the trend*
> *When all that I can do, is to give up on me*
> *I only receive, I've got nothing to send*

He listened intently to the lyrics and wondered what was bothering Sarah and what her reason was for being here in Scotland. Abe turned away from her and stared out of the window. The Loch was on her side so he looked up towards the hills, or was it mountains? *Whatever!*

In his mind he started planning the rest of his trip after Glasgow. For the umpteenth time he wondered what he would head home for.

Chapter 20

It started to drizzle on the windshield. Sarah reached for a tissue and wiped her nose. She hoped Abe had not seen her choke. How stupid she had been to burn 'Accepting Me' on the CD. It was the only pop song that Matthew had liked and even knew the lyrics to.
Matthew had always claimed the piano parts were originally meant for harpsichord – very baroque – and since it was obviously inspired on Bach he could tolerate it. His opinion had never changed: all pop music was created by copycats who 'borrowed' from the great composers.

"Why don't we try some genuine Scottish radio?" Sarah said as she fumbled with the dials. "Ah, here we go."
The radio kicked in and they heard some kind of honky-tonk, country-sound.

> *If you think me bitter*
> *I just read on Twitter*
> *You and me broke up today*
> *The turn that my gaze took*
> *As I saw on Facebook*
> *I'm goin' my own sep'rate way*

"Very genuinely Scottish, by the sound of it," Abe snorted.
"Ahhh, much better! Bag-pipe free, Scottish country line-dance music," Sarah said and avoided Abe's look.
Abe smiled briefly, hearing Sarah struggle to pick herself up.

It would have been kind, though,
If you'd shared your mind, though,
To save me from hysteria
My friends are a-callin'
The note cards are fallin'
How social are these media?

"That's an interesting combination of old-school country with a modern day theme, sung by a Scotsman," Sarah was slowly relaxing, her hands getting back to a pale pink on the wheel. "How would you like to stop somewhere on the Bonnie, Bonnie Banks of Loch Lomond?" Sarah proposed.

"As long as it's bagpipe-free, count me in!" he replied.

"Boy, you weren't joking when you said you'd had enough of those, were you?" Sarah laughed.

"Nope, noisy bastards," Abe said with feeling, "I mean the pipes of course, not the pipers!"

"Too bad they won't have a Jay Jones in Scotland. I could kill for a sweet snack," Sarah said longingly.

"Who's Jay Jones and why would you kill for him?" Abe asked.

"Jay runs a great deli in Halifax; they have the greatest pastries, you know *Danish* 'n stuff," Sarah smiled inwardly.

"Well, let's see if we can find you an Angus Jones for the local specialty," Abe offered.

"My turn to say: as long as it's haggis-free," Sarah said.

"You don't like haggis?" Abe looked surprised. "I thought it was exquisite, never had anything better in my life."

"To be perfectly honest, I haven't tried it yet," Sarah confessed, "but I don't care for the idea of haggis."

"To be perfectly honest, I *did* try it and let's say it was not an experience I would care to repeat," Abe beamed at her. "Makes you wonder why we came to Scotland, we don't seem to have grasped a taste for the local specialties, do we?" He laughed good-naturedly.

"Bit like going to Holland and disliking windmills and wooden shoes?" Sarah asked him.

"Impossible!" Abe exclaimed.

"Well, I came to Scotland on an important mission to find my ancestors," Sarah said looking directly at Abe. "What brings you here?"

"Och, Lassie, plenty o' rrreasons," Abe tried to sound Scottish and did not volunteer any more information.

"That's a terrible Scottish accent!" Sarah said.

"Aye, Lassie, Ah knoo," Abe said, unfazed, and got out.

They had a simple lunch of soup and a roll at a nice little place on Loch Lomond just north of Dumbarton.

"Is this what they call going Dutch?" Sarah asked as they both chipped in to pay.

"Yes, we are quite famous for being frugal – or better yet: cheap!" Abe laughed. "We are a tormented people, we are. Consider it; Double Dutch, going Dutch, the Dutch treat."

"Yes, a big burden indeed..." Sarah said with feeling.

"It gets worse," he sighed, "in recent years we Dutch have acquired quite a name for ourselves. The world thinks we are all drug dealers because of our cannabis laws, or hookers in view of our prostitution regulations. The fact that we have a much lower rape statistic as a result, is usually overlooked. Then there is the fact that we are seen as murderers because of our abortion and euthanasia laws. To top it all up pretty much every American sitcom calls us crazy because we allow homosexuals to marry," Abe added more seriously.

Sarah remembered Matthew always referred to Holland as an exemplary country for how they treated 'people like him'.

Abe continued: "Sometimes having progressive ideas is not widely understood. Mind you, it is just as true as the stereotype that all Americans carry a gun and you can get shot anytime, anyplace. Or all Scottish men wear kilts without underwear."

"Yes, that was a bitter disappointment!" Sarah mock-sighed.

"But sometimes it is interesting to see that people flinch if you say you're from Holland – The Netherlands – to be exact," Abe explained.

"I thought the term The Netherlands was only used by the Dutch to refer to Holland," Sarah challenged him.

"No, no," Abe replied seriously, "Holland was just one of the counties of the 'Low Lands' many centuries ago and so many Dutch people do not feel they are addressed by the term Holland." Abe winked at Sarah. "And this concludes our lesson for today. Sorry to bore you."

"Not at all," Sarah laughed, "my father was a history teacher. I guess we never did cover Holland all that much. I mean, The Netherlands," she corrected herself.

"So, Abe, anywhere I can drop you off as we head in the direction of Glasgow?" Sarah asked after they'd been on the road for some time.

"I think I will stay in Glasgow for the night and tomorrow look up possibilities to get to Newcastle upon Tyne," Abe replied. "That is where I will be taking the ferry back. Catching the ride with you has speeded up my progress immensely. Thanks for that."

Sarah smiled at him. "You're most welcome, it's been fun having you on board."

"Where are you going next?" Abe asked.

"I will look up the McFadden Society in Glasgow tomorrow," Sarah explained how far back her father had traced their genealogy and about the trip that they were planning to make to Scotland when her father had suddenly passed away.

So *that* was the reason she had been so sad, Abe thought immediately.

"I am sorry to hear that, Sarah. I can imagine you have mixed feelings about this," Abe said with a kind smile.

She looked at him in surprise and saw the kind look on his face. The little lines around his nose and mouth were curved in the cutest way.

"Yes, thanks," Sarah said softly, tearing her eyes away from him. "I am happy to be here, but it would have been so much better to be here with my dad. I do miss him."

"I know," Abe said, staring out his window, "I lost my father a while ago and it's hard to not be able to talk to him anymore. I feel like grabbing the phone every day still."

It was the most personal information he had voluntarily rendered so far.

Sarah briefly touched his forearm and said: "It does get better with time and grief makes place for gratitude for all you have shared." Abe looked at her gratefully.

After a while Abe concluded: "So, we both need a place to stay in or around Glasgow, then?"
"Yep, sounds like it." Sarah wasn't quite sure where he was headed with this.
"How about we look for a B&B or a small hotel and I buy you dinner this evening to thank you for giving this lone Dutchman a ride?" Abe suggested, beaming at her.
Sarah's brain told her to think about this, but her heart made a leap.
"So, no Dutch treat then?" she teased him.
He laughed out loud. "No, sorry ma'am, definitely no Dutch treat."
She smiled warmly at him. "I'd really like that, Abe, thanks."
Abe felt he did not often meet people he could have such easy banter with and concluded she was fun to be with.

They found a small B&B in Sarah's guide, right on the edge of the city and agreed to meet at 7 pm to go to dinner. Sarah said she'd look up some restaurant options.
"Don't tell me: you also brought your entire office with you!" Abe teased.
She stuck out her tongue to him. "Consider yourself lucky I am so well organized!"

As Sarah walked down the stairs to meet Abe she heard a soft whistle and Abe's voice: "I am glad I shaved for the occasion. You look very pretty this evening."
"I am sorry, I am meeting someone for dinner," she deliberately looked past him, "someone in hiking boots."
She had hardly recognized Abe for the hitchhiker who had walked up the stairs in front of her less than an hour before. He had lost his beard and was dressed in dark jeans, slim black t-shirt and brogues.
She looked at him again. For the first time she noticed his

blue-gray eyes underneath his thick graying hair. He actually looked quite distinguished, businessy.

"What would you like to eat?" Sarah said, somewhat confused. "I have found a nice Italian restaurant not too far away, so we could walk and both have a glass of wine. Another option could be to go Asian and take the car."

"Italian sounds wonderful and a glass of wine even better," Abe answered. "Remember, it is my treat this evening." Abe said, courteously opening the door for her.

"You really don't have to do that; it was a pleasure to have you on board," Sarah curtsied and she walked on.

"No, no, I insist – dinner is on me!" Abe clearly did not expect any more discussion about the matter.

Sarah looked up at him. *Gosh, he was tall.*

"So, about that glass of wine; do you have a preference, red, white?" Abe asked her as soon as they were settled at a lovely window table.

"I am more of a white wine drinker, to be honest," Sarah said. "You?"

"In summer, yes, but in winter I prefer a deep red," Abe said as he gestured to the waiter. "Let's order by the glass; what kind of white would you like? Chardonnay?"

"Yes, or a Sauvignon Blanc, maybe?" Sarah said doubtfully. "Chardonnay can be a bit too oaky for my taste."

He looked at the wine list and smiled approvingly.

"Could we have a bottle of the Marlboro New Zealand Sauvignon Blanc?" he asked the waiter. Sarah almost jumped in, a bottle was way too much – she wouldn't finish a whole bottle. "And two glasses please," Abe added.

"Didn't you want a red wine?" Sarah was puzzled.

"As soon as I saw the Marlboro I decided to join you," Abe said. "It is my favorite white wine," he smiled with relish.

Sarah wondered how the rugged non-descript backpacker had vanished. He looked so different, very… attractive.

"Funny that you now look less like a Marlboro man than you did before!" Sarah said, openly studying him.

Abe roared with laughter; he loved her sense of humor.

They enjoyed a relaxed evening. Abe was surprised by Sarah's open responses and felt happy to spend the evening with her. Sarah felt comfortable in his company. She tasted the wine, which they had with their seafood appetizers.

"I have ordered a light red so that you can enjoy the combination of the veal with the wine," Abe briefly put his hand on her arm. "Trust me, I think you will like it."

Sarah tasted the wine and took a bite.

"So glad I trusted you," she winked at him, clearly savoring the combination, "the tastes go together perfectly."

"You don't know this yet," he stated seriously, "but I am a very trustworthy Friesian guy."

"Well, for a trustworthy Friesian guy you are getting me awfully drunk!" Sarah complained unconvincingly.

"There is no such thing as getting drunk if you are of Scottish descent," Abe protested. "I think I am in more danger than you."

"Speaking of which," Sarah said, "I am excited to go to the McFadden Society tomorrow and find out more about my Scottish ancestry."

"Weren't you the one saying we need to live in modern times – teasing me about old music? Yet, here you are ready to bury yourself in heaps and tons of old stuff," Abe winked. "Seriously, what do you think you will find?"

"I don't know, that I am the heiress to a grand castle maybe?" She looked at him with a twinkle in her eyes.

"And then what, move to a draughty old castle in Scotland?" Abe asked, trying to picture this.

"Nah, I suppose you're right – that wouldn't be me," Sarah said sipping her wine. "I am more of a new improved Scotland kind of girl.

"I agree, I don't think I could live here either," Abe said.

"You are probably only built for living in your Netherly Lands?" she asked more than stated.

"Well, actually, my brother moved to Colorado many years ago and seems to be doing well," Abe told Sarah. "So we Makkinga's do have a talent for making it elsewhere."

"Really, what brought him to Colorado?" Sarah was enjoying hearing some more about Abe and his roots.

"The usual," Abe shrugged briefly, "you know, true love."

"Wow, is that really 'the usual'?" Sarah sat up straight. "I seem to have missed that turn!"

"Well, I just got divorced, so I guess you're right," Abe's voice sounded more serious, "calling it 'the usual' is maybe the wrong way to put it. It's more 'the uniqueness'. Anyway, my brother and his wife are the living proof it exists. After all those years they're still very much in love. She was living in Alaska when they met, he was in New Jersey and they decided to meet in the middle."

"Wow," Sarah said again, "that sounds like a big step for the both of them. How wonderful that it worked out!"

"Is your divorce the reason for you to backpack Scotland so out of season?" Sarah asked Abe with an open expression on her face.

"Well, the short version is: my father passed away, I got divorced and I just sold my company," Abe said.

"Geez, Abe, sound like you've had your share recently," Sarah tried to gage his expression.

"I guess so," Abe continued, "the moment I sold my shares in the company and was considering what to do next, my wife came home to confess she had been having an affair for quite some time and asked me for a divorce."

"My goodness Abe…" Sarah didn't know what else to say.

"It's true what they say: life is a female dog!" Abe smiled briefly. Sarah couldn't help chuckling. "Whoever says that?"

"Well, people who are just too polite to use the 'b'-word," Abe said haughtily.

"You are somethin' else, Abe, you are so funny," Sarah said, still laughing. "Even when you talk about very serious stuff."

"Anyway," Abe said, "you would think that no amount of backpacking would get that squared away, would you? But it was exactly what I needed." He added with a smile: "I don't know if it was the backpacking or the frickin' cold that worked for me. Excuse my French."

"You know, your English is sometimes just a bit too good – a little on the American side, but very impressive," Sarah said truthfully. She did not experience any problem conversing with him.

"Thanks, lots of practice I guess," Abe's face clearly portraying pride at receiving the compliment.

"So, now you've heard my situation in a nutshell, or should I say *nuts-hell*," Abe sat up straight, looking expectantly at her. "Your turn! Is your father the only reason for you to come to Scotland?"

Sarah's heart sank a moment and her face glazed over.

"I'm sorry," Abe instantly picked up on the change in Sarah, "none of my business, of course."

"I came to Inverness for work and decided to combine it with the McFadden search," Sarah exhaled slowly. She felt she was not being fair on Abe. Why should she not share the real reason to come here? After a pause she added: "And I have just lost the most important person in my life to cancer and I needed a change of place."

Abe nodded in understanding. "I am so sorry to hear that, Sarah, so sorry for your loss."

"Thanks, Abe," Sarah stared into her wineglass for a few seconds.

"Is it helping you to be away from home?" Abe looked at her with genuine interest.

Sarah looked at him thankfully for responding so warmly. "I have found that I can relax a bit. I had a lot of my shoulders – maybe more than I could carry."

Abe saw her expression and suppressed the idea of taking her hand. To hide his confusion he divided the last bit of red wine into their glasses.

Sarah noticed that his eyes had gone watery and felt comforted by his presence. He had obviously gone through a lot and somehow, that helped her. She felt less lonely for a while.

As they got back to the B&B Sarah thanked Abe for the wonderful evening and the delicious meal.

"It was way too much for just a ride to a place I already needed to go to," Sarah said warmly, "but appreciated all the more."

"Sarah, thank you for a wonderful evening, I had a great time," Abe said, looking shyly at her. "Will I be seeing you for breakfast tomorrow?"

"Sure, shall we sleep in and meet at 9?" Sarah blushed slightly at the suggestion of 'them' sleeping in. She stammered on: "I mean, we got up really early this morning…"

Abe nodded in agreement and briefly caressed her cheek. "Sweet dreams, Sarah, see you in the morning."

Sarah felt she hardly touched the stairs as she went up; she reprimanded herself for having too much wine again – or was there another reason she was floating? She touched her cheek and smiled. He was very gentlemanly in a European way and it was lovely.

Chapter 21

The next morning Sarah woke up; she had slept like a log all through the night. She couldn't remember when that had happened recently. Instantly she looked at her watch – she had to get dressed to meet Abe for breakfast. With a pang she realized that this would be the last time she would see him and wondered how come she felt she would miss him or at least wanted him to tag along some more. *Get real, Sarah, you just met the guy!*

Abe had woken early and dressed restlessly. He decided to take a walk before breakfast. There were so many thoughts going through his mind; traveling on, catching the ferry that would take him back, going home, not seeing Sarah after this morning…

Abe wondered what bothered him most; that he was going back home or saying goodbye to Sarah. She was ravishing, had a great sense of humor, smart, sensitive, sweet – *all right, enough with the advertising!*

He had the idea that she had also felt the connection, but she had just lost her significant other and he knew she was in deep mourning and would be for a long time.

"Good morning, Sarah, did you sleep well?" Abe took a seat next to her at the long breakfast table.

"I did, indeed, I can't recall when I slept so well," Sarah said, looking at him. "I'm sure that wonderful red wine had something to do with it," she sniggered. In a broad Scottish accent she added: "Quite medicinal."

"Have you found out where the Society is located yet?" Abe asked to make conversation.

"Yes, I will take a cab from here and leave the car. I have decided to stay another night so I can go to the library after that. And you? I see your hitchhiker outfit is back!" Sarah said with a sinking

heart, knowing this meant it was time for him to move on.
"I don't know just yet, but I will go to the railway station and check it out. I will get there somehow," Abe said calmly.
"Sure you will... More coffee?" Sarah held up the pot.
"Darn, I forgot my thermal cup to-go!" Abe said teasingly.

After breakfast they reluctantly said their goodbyes and both felt powerless. Abe gave Sarah a white envelope and said: "My contact details in case you are ever in Friesland."
Sarah heard him swallow. She looked up at him and again noticed the warm expression in his blue-gray eyes. She took a business card out of her purse and handed it to him.
"Just in case you're ever traveling to Nova Scotia; look me up!"
Abe clumsily wrapped his long arms around her and gave her a kiss on the top of her head. Sarah lingered in his embrace for a moment. Why couldn't great guys like Abe be found in Nova Scotia?
"All right, Mr. Maggagga," she said stepping back, "have a safe journey home and take good care of yourself."
"You too, Sarah, you too… good luck with the…" Abe almost whispered.
Sarah nodded.
With that he picked up his backpack and walked out the door. Sarah stared at his back and wanted to run after him, shout at him to not go, but her legs did not move and her voice did not make a sound.

Later in the cab she tried to convince herself she should be happy she did not make a fool of herself. He had more than enough going on in his life without Sarah and all her issues. Her head told her that, but her heart said that now he was still close to her in Scotland and the distance would be growing soon. '*Tell the driver to go to the station*', a voice rang in her head.
"And then what?" she muttered.
"Come again?" said the cab driver.
She smiled at him in the mirror. "Nothing, sorry, just talking to myself," Sarah said, feeling stupid.

The cab driver smiled briefly and focused on the road again. She wished she had taken the envelope with her. She had put it on her bed before she left. Anyway, she now had to focus on the McFaddens and her family history.

The elderly lady she talked to at the Society was most helpful, but Sarah had trouble concentrating on the abundance of information that was handed to her. She tried to take notes on all of the sources she should continue to look at.
Apparently the McFaddens, or MacFadyens and MacFadzeans at the time, had their own family crest in blue and gold with a white swallow flying at the top and they had been dependents of the MacLaines' clan of Lochbuie. Sarah had no idea what that meant. She was shown the tartan of the MacLaines and couldn't help thinking that at least they were not cheated with awful colors. *Not really the point, Sarah! FOCUS!*
From time to time Abe's face would pop up in the pictures she saw. She giggled softly; he looked quite good in a kilt, actually. She was told she would probably find a lot more information at Lochbuie. With shaking hands the lady took out a map to show her how to get there.
"It is to the west from Oban on the Isle of Mull," she pointed out.
Sarah thanked her for all the helpful information and said she would come back if she had more questions. She decided she would first try to continue with the information she had received.
In the cab back she looked at the map. With a start she remembered why the town name Oban rang a bell; she had seen signs for Oban as she drove down from Fort William yesterday. She hadn't passed it, but it was quite a way back to the North – and the Isle of Mull was even further to the west.

Sarah got back to her room and without taking off her coat took the white envelope from the bed.

Hi Sarah,

I found this card at the local newspaper stand this morning.
I thought it was appropriate for giving you my address details
in The Netherlands.
I cannot tell you how much I enjoyed meeting you. To me it
felt like we have known each other forever. I don't know how
it's possible that you turned this shy guy into someone who
can talk about what's been going on in his life, but consider it
a gift, Sarah.
Thank you for the fun time. I hope you will find a way to deal
with your great loss. Should you ever have plans to come to
'Holland' let me know. I would love to see you again.
Yours, with fond memories, Abe, xxx

P.t.o. for my address details!

Sarah sat down on the bed and slowly turned over the card
and looked at an impressive sailing ship. In the sail Abe had
written the address, phone number and e-mail. In the sky
around the main sail he had scribbled in different corners:

"Great sailing in Friesland, too!"
"The weather is <u>always</u> beautiful!"

In the water at the bottom of the card he had written in
capital letters:

"CAN'T WAIT TO SEE YOU AGAIN!!!"

How stupid she felt for letting Abe walk away. Didn't his card indicate that he really liked her too? Well, it couldn't be helped now. Sarah couldn't remember when she had felt like this. She felt like a sixteen year old, all giddy, giggly and excited.

She stared at the card over and gazed out of the window. Would he still be in Scotland or would he be on the evening ferry? How far was this Friesland anyway?

She took her camera out of her luggage. At least she had a few pictures of him, taken during their lunch. She stared at them and was surprised again at how different he had looked all shaven, an entirely different man.

That evening she decided to go for the Asian dinner. The food was terrific but the restaurant was almost empty and her feeling of loneliness returned with a vengeance. In her mind she pictured Abe sitting across the table. His kind eyes looking at her…

Sarah paid up at the restaurant and as she drove back to the B&B she heard her cell phone deep in her tote bag.

As she walked up to her bedroom she looked at the missed call; her sister Nicola. Nicola had also texted Sarah to give her a call.

"Hi Nicky, it's me live from Scotland," Sarah said.

"Hi Mouse, how are you?" Nicky sounded happy to hear her youngest sister on the phone.

Sarah smiled hearing her nickname 'mouse'. She knew it meant she was forgiven for her stupidity.

"I am most wonderful," Sarah said. "How are you?"

"We're fine and you sure *sound* wonderful. Have you fallen for a red-haired Scotsman or have you finally found the McFadden fortune?" Nicky asked, chuckling.

"No, I have not fallen for a *Scotsman* and as far as the McFadden fortune goes, I am having a slight setback there. I need to travel quite a way for the next step, they say."

Nicky was always very perceptive and had picked up on the emphasis on Scotsman. "So if you haven't fallen for a Scotsman, who is it *this time*?" she asked with irony. Nicky was always the one complaining that Sarah did not take action to find a nice boyfriend.

"Oh, only a Flying Dutchman this time," Sarah sighed with a swoony voice.

"So, you had a nice pilot; hardly impressive, Mouse! Surely, you can do better than that!" Nicky laughed.

"Well, you never know, do you?" Sarah said mysteriously. "Anyway, I am going to have to take a small detour before I get to the family fortune."

They chatted some more and Nicky was relieved to hear Sarah so happy and bubbly. It seemed like it had been a good idea to get away from Nova Scotia for some time. She sent a text message to Tracy, Marc and Madeline:

> Just spoke to Mouse – sounds like she is getting her energy back. She will send us an e-mail with her progress, but needs a slight detour before claiming the family fortune. Don't quit your daytime jobs yet. ☺ xxx

In the meantime Sarah decided to send a text message of her own. She wanted to thank Abe for his card. She hoped that the telephone number he had given her was a cell phone that she could text to. She thought about how best to write the message without sounding too mushy.

> Hi Abe, tnx for the card! Tried the Asian tonight – food great; missed your company, though! Where are you now? Love, Sarah. Xxx

She pressed 'send' and hoped it would reach him soon. She got in the shower to get ready for bed. Warmed by the shower, she decided for her jogging pants and t-shirt. It was just too cold at night. She checked her phone but she hadn't received any new messages. Oh well…

Chapter 22

Abe's train connections had worked out better than expected and he got to Newcastle much faster than he had imagined. The ferry had already docked and disembarkation was in full swing. He honestly couldn't say he was looking forward to going home. He checked in and walked over to the ship. He was sorry he didn't have a reason to stay in Scotland longer; trains on time, no storm to cancel the crossing… sounded like a dream schedule, not to Abe though. Whatever happened to good old-fashioned train delays and the hardship of being stranded?

The emptiness in his life hit him. At home he had so many things to decide, to arrange – and what for? What would he do after all the arrangements were made? His relationship ruined, the house up for sale, his shares sold and his job handed over to the new co-owner. Not a very attractive prospect. Still, it had to be done.

He looked up his cabin and left his backpack behind. At the check-in he had booked a private hut at a small extra charge, since the ship was not fully booked. He decided to have mercy on his fellow-passengers. No use getting into trouble over his snoring if he could avoid it, he thought with a smile. He locked the cabin and walked up to the bar for a glass of wine. The bartender offered him a choice of chardonnay or merlot. Abe smiled a private smile and chose the merlot.

"It is a good evening for a red wine, besides I've recently learned that chardonnay can be too oaky," Abe said knowingly, as he smiled inside.

The bartender smiled briefly as Abe turned around to find a table.

Around midnight, as the ferry had long departed New-castle, Abe decided to go back to the cabin. He picked up his backpack and got out his phone. He saw the light blink

indicating he had a new message. He was very happy to see it was from Sarah. He read and re-read the message. He felt sorry he hadn't responded straight away, especially now he saw that the connection was weak. She had missed him and he realized he missed her too. This was ridiculous, how could you miss someone that you had just met? He wasn't that kind of man. He also wasn't the kind of man to leave behind cards. Had he really done that? With all those scribblings?
He looked at the end of the message: *'love, Sarah. Xxx'*
He would send her a message in the morning as soon as they docked.

Bleep!

> Dear Sarah, sorry for the late response. Was on the ferry already. Am back in Holland now. Friends picked me up to drive me home. Glad you liked the card. I meant it!! How's the search going? Cheerio, Abe.

Since it had taken a while for him to answer she had wondered if she had imagined their connection. She saw the *'cheerio, Abe'*. Not a very promising way to end. She longed to talk to him, hear his voice.

A few hours later as Sarah was studying the map of Scotland for the route to Lochbuie her cell phone bleeped again.

> Hey, Sarah, I'm back home; but it doesn't feel like home. Do you sometimes wonder where we are and where we are going? Philosopher Abe, Xxx

This time Sarah's heart literally jumped. She knew for a fact where she was and pondered where she would be going.

> Hi Abe, Sorry your homecoming wasn't really that. Wish you were here. Practical Sarah, Xxx

Bleep!

Sweet Sarah, I think 'home' will be a moving target for me, somehow. Wish you were here too! Abe, Xxx

Sarah stared at her phone for a while and closed the map in front of her. She was wondering what the next stop on her trip would bring her.

Chapter 23

Discussing the sale of the house with his ex-wife Anne-marie and her new partner, Erik, was easier than Abe had imagined. They met up at the now half empty house. Annemarie had removed the furniture they had agreed she'd take. Erik and she seemed very happy together and the discussions about the house were mutually respectful. Abe was to stay there until he made a decision on his future steps or until the house was sold. As Erik and Annemarie were getting ready to leave the doorbell rang. Abe got up and stopped in his tracks as he saw who peeked through the glass in the front door.

Surely, he was imagining things, surely.
Abe opened the door to see Sarah standing there with a big smile, dripping with rain and waving Abe's card in front of him.
"I have a *written* guarantee that the weather is **always** beautiful in Friesland and I want my money back!" she exclaimed, beaming at him brightly.
Abe was too overcome to respond. Meanwhile Annemarie and Erik looked at him expecting an introduction, but none was offered.
After an awkward pause, Abe said: "I'm sorry, Sarah, this is Annemarie and Erik… Guys, this is Sarah."
He gestured onward into the living room. "Sarah, please do come in. Shall I make a new pot of coffee?"
In perfect English, Annemarie responded: "No, no, don't mind us, we were just leaving. Erik? Shall we go?"
"Yes, darling. Nice to meet you Sarah – welcome to rainy Fries-land," Erik said, walking out the door. He unfolded an umbrella and stepped into the rain. "I'll get the car, Annemarie, you wait here."
As she walked out the door, Annemarie couldn't help

whispering to Abe: "No wonder you look so different."
Abe was at a loss for a response.

"I'm so sorry, Abe, I shouldn't have barged in like that.
I didn't know you had company," Sarah said, absolutely
mortified. "To say I'm completely embarrassed is an under-
statement, if it's any consolation to you."
Sarah turned away from Abe. This wasn't at all the welcome
she had expected and Abe sure wasn't looking relaxed. He still
did not say anything.
"Maybe it is better if I leave," Sarah said, getting up. "I'm sorry
Abe. Me and my foolish impulses. I shouldn't have come
unexpectedly."
"No, no, Sarah, I'm just surprised – that's all…" Abe's voice
sounded unconvincing. "Please take off your coat and let me
get you something warm to drink."
Sarah sensed, however, that Abe's mind was somewhere else
entirely.

As Sarah dried up and Abe recovered somewhat they had a
cup of tea. Abe looked outside and gave her a shy smile.
"You were right with your claim for a refund, the weather is
truly horrendous," Abe joked sheepishly.
"Abe, I really don't know what to say," Sarah sensed his discomfort. "I will finish my tea and think of what to do next. Is
there a B&B or small hotel I can stay at?"
"No, Sarah, you can stay here," Abe offered hastily. "I'm sorry,
I'm all in favor of spontaneous plans, but I'm terribly out of
practice. I'm really happy you're here." The expression on his
face was saying something totally different, however.

In the evening as Abe was making up the bed in the spare
bedroom, Sarah could have screamed at herself. She hadn't
thought the whole situation through at all. She had just wanted
to see him. She had played the situation in her head like a
movie scene, where he would scoop her up as soon as he saw
her. Instead, she found herself alone in a spare bedroom with
bare walls and a storm tearing at the windows. It had been

ages since she had followed her impulses, but it hadn't worked out well. She brushed away a few tears and made a decision to return to Scotland the very next day.

> Hey, Nicky, do me a favor; next time I plan something spontaneous, will you please do everything in your power to stop me? Love, Sarah

Bleep!

> Sure, Mouse, if ever you will tell me what's up and how you think I can exercise that power – gladly. Knowing you, you're hard to convince otherwise. Now go to sleep – it's the middle of the night in Bonnie Scotland! Love, Nicky

Sarah stared at her phone. Bonnie Scotland, if only that were true. *How could you be so stupid!*

Abe went to bed feeling awful. All the way back home from Scotland he had thought about Sarah and how much he wanted they'd had more time together. Now she was right here and he didn't know how to respond. He felt stupid. Poor Sarah; she must have expected something different, surely.

Chapter 24

The next morning Sarah looked all around the house. There was no sign of Abe. In the kitchen she did find a very nicely set breakfast table and the inviting smell a pot of coffee brewing. She looked outside and admired the terrace and garden from the big French doors. There was a boat landing at the back of the garden, and large open water to sail away on.

The storm had made way for a sunny day although it still looked freezing cold. The branches of the trees outside sparkled with frozen droplets against the sunlight. Sarah decided to pack her things upstairs so she would be ready to leave after breakfast. From upstairs she heard the front door open. Her heart thumped as she wondered how she would face Abe. She felt so silly. She should have crept out of the house while she had the chance. Well, too late now. She looked in the mirror, really not liking what she saw, and went downstairs. As she walked into the kitchen Abe turned around and walked over to her. He brushed her cheek briefly and simply said: "Sorry…"

Sarah looked up at Abe, stared into his lovely blue-gray eyes and nodded 'no'. "I'm the one who should be sorry. It's just that I haven't done anything spontaneous in such a long time and your text message said…" Sarah felt she was rattling. "I should have called you before I decided to jump on a plane. Well, that'll teach me to…" She couldn't finish her as Abe wrapped his arms around her and kissed her softly.

"I should have done that yesterday, but with my ex-wife there, that was a bit awkward," Abe gave her an ironic smile.

"That was your ex-wife?" Sarah was dumb-founded. "You never said... Wow, have I said sorry enough yet?"

He laughed and nodded a fervent 'yes'.

"Plenty of sorries, now let's have breakfast," Abe said pointing at the table. "I have gone out especially to get you a fresh traditional Friesian sugar loaf. Try it with only some farm butter. It is to die for."

"Is that real butter?" Sarah asked. "You mean it's to die *of*? Do you know how many calories are in that stuff?" She gave him a wink and took a bite. He was right; it was delicious.

Over breakfast they both relaxed and re-found their original ease of talking to each other.

As they were clearing the table Abe asked what she would like to do. Sarah looked over to him.

"Abe, I feel it would be better if I…" but he turned around, took her hand and pulled her closer. He looked down into her bright green eyes, now shy and insecure, not knowing how to ask her what he wanted to ask her.

"Sarah, I'm not…"

"Abe, let's not…"

They spoke at the same time.

Abe kissed her softly and only whispered: "Stay!"

Sarah felt all of her resistance fade. "Okay," she said in a croaky voice and they lingered in their embrace.

"All right, Miss McFadden, are you ready to learn some more about the history of my province?" Abe asked with the brightest of smiles.

"Why, yes, Mr. Maggagga," Sarah said complacently. "I am most interested in knowing more. Where are you taking me?"

"You strike me as a woman who enjoys combining a sporty challenge with some historic touches," Abe said trying to read her. "Am I right?"

"Indeed, but might one ask as to the nature of the sporty challenge?" Sarah tried.

"No, Miss McFadden, one might not," he chuckled. He was totally going to enjoy this.

Before Abe got his car out of the garage he changed the CD selection. Abe drove Sarah from his home, just outside of Grou, to the bigger city of Heerenveen. He deliberately took a scenic detour, which would take them quite a bit longer, but with so much more to see. Sarah quite enjoyed looking at the scenery. First they drove through wide open spaces with scattered low farms, which gave the impression of a long forgotten era – almost as if the last few centuries had passed it by.

"That is an interesting shape, that farmhouse," Sarah said, pointing over to a large farm just off the road.

"Let's see, how can I translate that," Abe thought for a moment, "literally it's a 'head-neck-body' or 'head-neck-trunk' farm. If you look at it, it resembles a cow lying down." He slowed down the car to point it out.

"Oh, yeah, I see it!" Sarah said.

"The head is the part where the farmer lives, the neck is the original storage area. In the older farms, the trunk was built on if the crops were good and more space was needed. Over the ages, this became the typical Friesian farm."

Sarah was surprised by the amount of lakes they passed. "This lake you see on the right hand side, called the Sneek Lake," Abe pronounced it 'Snake Lake', "or Snitser Mar in Friesian. It is where my dad took my brother and me sailing. Together with my uncle, we had a traditional Friesian sailboat, called a skûtsje – which was kept in pristine condition." Sarah noticed the pride and longing in Abe's voice.

"And does it have any snakes in it, this lake?" Sarah asked. Abe roared with laughter. "No, the spelling is S-N-E-E-K – so Sneak Lake, hmmm – none of this sounds about right, anyway... The skûtsje is no small boat you know, it's more of a ship. Our skûtsje was almost 50 feet long with a total sail surface of over a thousand square feet."

"And how do you pronounce that? Skoochah?" Sarah tried.

"Yep, Skoochah, very good!" Abe laughed encouragingly at Sarah.

"Say, why do you tell me stuff in feet?" Sarah asked. "We use the metric system in Canada, you know! Although, I have to admit, in Acadia not everybody has left the imperial age yet."

"All right, Miss Canada, in that case it would be 16 meters long and almost 100 square meters in sail," Abe explained patiently.

"Wow, that is indeed quite something!" Sarah sounded

impressed. "That would even qualify for the smaller traditional classes of the Nova Scotia Tall Ships!"

"Well, these ships have no keel because they were built to sail the rivers and lakes for transportation inland. They are literally *flat-bottomed*," Abe sniggered. "You cannot sail them on open sea." Abe paused for a moment and looked around.

"There is actually a really fierce competition every year in summer, the 'skûtsjesilen', with some 15 skûtsjes," he continued enthusiastically. "It is just as much a competition between the towns and the skippers. It's great fun."

Abe drove around the lake to show Sarah where some of the skûtsjes were moored in the Sneek marina. Sarah could see the romance in the old wooden ships, the thick brown and gray sails – the big wooden blades on the sides functioning as a keel. It was hard to imagine, as Abe mentioned, that this was the means of transportation through Friesland less than a century ago, the skipper living on board with his family. She loved it all the more because Abe explained it all with such passion.

"What happened to your Dad's ship, Abe?" Sarah asked.

"It was sold when my dad passed away. My uncle had died before him; my brother was already in Colorado and Annemarie didn't like sailing," Abe said with regret. "I am still sorry that I couldn't hold on to it. At the time I thought the ship deserved a better owner than me. I worked in Amsterdam and made long hours. Big mistake in retrospect, I guess," he paused, "it would have made a great new home for me. Goes to show we never know what the future has in store for us."

"Yep, I guess you could say: Life is a female dog!" Sarah pushed him playfully.

They drove on to Heerenveen and Sarah was still in the dark about the surprise Abe had planned for her.

"What is this music?" Sarah asked.

"This, my dear Sarah, is the great Frank Sinatra!" Abe said, knowing almost what kind of response to expect.

"Really, could you be more corny?" Sarah teased.

"You mean, you don't know the greatest piece of music that ol' blue eyes ever made?" Abe looked astonished.

"What is it with you and old music?" Sarah nudged him with her elbow.

"This is not old, this is *brilliant*!" Abe looked abruptly at her. Sarah sensed he really meant what he was saying. What a strange, complex man. There was a sensitivity about him that Sarah had never noticed in other men.

"What is it? It sounds different," Sarah listened intently.

"This collection is called Watertown and I think it was one of the first things that Frank Sinatra actually produced himself," Abe said calmly. "If you ever have the patience to listen to the lyrics the songs on the album make a complete story. It is just wonderful."

Sarah laughed. "What's wrong with my patience, anyway?" she quizzed him.

The sober sounds of the music completed the atmosphere with the quiet, pale sunny weather and the wide-open spaces around them. Sarah sat and listened for a while. Abe was right, the lyrics and the mellow way it was sung made for a very moving composition.

"Geez, Abe, that really is very good. Gives me goose bumps all over. This is almost fragile and understated," Sarah turned towards Abe and stared at him. "Not at all that loud, big-bandy sound…"

"I hoped you would like it," Abe said smiling. "I'm surprised at your open mind – you seem to have your opinion ready rather quickly," he teased Sarah.

"Any more *constructive feedback* for me, Mr. Maggagga?" Sarah grinned about what she knew to be true. She could be quite judgmental and quickly label. Abe was not the first person to tell her this.

Some time later they arrived in Heerenveen, one of the main cities of Friesland. Although the architecture was very different from Nova Scotia, Sarah recognized the same structure as in Halifax; hardly any high-rise buildings, typical for areas where space was not an issue.

Sarah pointed at a sign and turned towards Abe: "How do you

pronounce that word – T-H-I-A-L-F? Thai-Alf? Thigh-Alf?"

"I can see you are ahead of me," Abe said, "it is indeed where we're going. *Teeejalf.*"

As they walked over to the huge oval building, Abe's smile broadened with every step. He had taken a large bag with him. He grabbed Sarah's hand and looked at her with expectation. "Let's see how well you do on ice skates," he said, "Thialf is the home of many a world record in speed skating."

"Is that all you've got for me?" Sarah looked at Abe with a perky smile. "Did I not mention I was practically *born* on ice skates?"

"Is that so?" he challenged her.

"Yes, indeed," Sarah nodded fiercely, "when I wasn't playing basketball, I was ice skating with my brother and sisters in Halifax. It's been a while but I suspect it's like riding a bike, you never really lose the feel for it," she said confidently.

Abe could not wipe the smile off his face. "What size do you need?"

At the rental counter Abe got a pair of skates for Sarah. They sat down at the side of the oval ring and Abe gave her the skates. To Sarah's unpleasant surprise they looked quite different from the ice hockey skates she was used to. The shoe was low around the ankle and the actual skate looked almost twice as long. Sarah, however, managed to appear utterly unfazed and put them on.

Abe suppressed another smile and stepped onto the ice in front of her. He looked behind him to see Sarah get on the ice. Her ankles collapsed in every direction as the skates hit the ice and after two glides she fell mercilessly. She didn't look at Abe and got up, her lips thin with determination. She clung to the boarding for the next glides with a grim expression of concentration. This wasn't going to get the better of her. She would get the hang of this, if it killed her. Meanwhile Abe whizzed by, skating a few rounds laughing a little louder each time he passed her.

Much to his surprise, after Sarah had gingerly done a few rounds herself, she was getting the hang of it. As she got more confident she picked up more speed.

Abe came alongside and said: "It's important to place your skates horizontally on the ice. If you hit the ice with the front point of the skate, you will be sent reeling."

"Gee, thanks Abe, that is most comforting to know," Sarah called after him. "Thanks a bundle!"

"Don't mention it; you're welcome!" he called back.

She was impressed with how much speed you could build up, but was unpleasantly surprised at the turns she could make, or rather couldn't make. She smacked against the ice with chattering teeth and turned on her back.

He stopped right next to her, looking down with a worried frown.

"Are you okay?" Abe asked, as she did not move to get up.

"Don't worry 'bout me," Sarah looked up at him and gave him the brightest smile she could muster. "I'm okay! I'm just looking at this from a different perspective."

Abe helped her up and held her hand as they got off the ice.

"I am so going to get even with you if you're ever in Halifax," she whispered in his ear.

"I can't wait!" he whispered back.

"So much for the sporty challenge, what about this historic thing you promised me?" Sarah took off her skates with a sense of relief. Her ankles were killing her; they hadn't worked this hard in a long time. Her whole body felt sore.

"The historic bit is up next – but maybe better left until tomorrow," Abe said, looking worried. "Let's go home, relax a bit and then I'll buy you dinner."

Abe took Sarah's skates and returned them at the counter. He took her hand again and she couldn't help smiling. This was such a great feeling; a sense of belonging. *Get a grip, Sarah!* She decided for once to listen to her inner voice and strengthened her grip on Abe's hand.

"I have to say Sarah," Abe admitted to her, "you were so much better at this than I could have imagined. You did great!"

He looked at her with pride.

"Don't even *think* you can throw me off scent by giving me

some lame compliments, Mister Maggagga," Sarah said with a feisty voice. "I'm still going to get even with you when I have the chance. Be afraid… be *very* afraid!"

Chapter 25

In the afternoon Abe installed Sarah on the big couch. Every muscle in her body ached after her fall on the ice. Abe went out of his way to make her comfortable, making her tea, and getting her extra pillows.

"Don't think that I am not on to you…" Sarah pointed at him. After some time Sarah dozed off and Abe sat there looking at her. He softly touched her cheek. She looked so lovely in her sleep.

Sometime later Sarah woke up and looked up at Abe. He was sitting there with a book. The look he gave her made her all warm inside. He didn't have to say it. She could see he was glad she was there after all.

"Who is the lovely woman in the photograph on your side table?" Sarah studied the photograph intensely. A beautiful woman with curved long lashes, wavy hair twisted into a Grace Kelly roll; the peach skin looking silky in the black-and-white picture.

"That's my mother," Abe said proudly. "She was some piece of work in her time – very independent and good fun."

"Wow, Abe, she looks like a movie star! Too bad you didn't inherit any of that," she teased.

"She *was* beautiful, wasn't she?" Abe said, looking over at Sarah. "She died so young…"

Sarah nodded, she remembered Abe had told her at dinner in Scotland.

"You haven't seen pictures of my dad yet – he was a rock-star in his white sailor's uniform."

Abe started rummaging in a richly carved wooden chest and dug out a picture of his father in uniform. As Sarah stared at the picture, she instantly saw the resemblance with Abe. His parents must have made a stunning couple. She turned around and burst out laughing. Abe was trying to put on what looked like a white uniform jacket with tassels.

"I take it your father was slimmer than you?" she concluded, looking at his struggle.

He pulled a face as Sarah helped him peel off the jacket. "Well, Abe, you will smell of mothballs all evening, yummy!"

"That smell is actually the cedar chest," Abe set her straight. "My dad brought it back from one of his trips to Indonesia. I am going to ship the chest to Colorado, so my brother's children can have it in future. They still remember my dad very well. He was such a loving, proud, grandfather."

They looked at some more family memorabilia. Sarah again sensed the warm bond the Makkinga's must have had. She couldn't imagine being without both parents and having only one brother so far away. For a moment she wondered what her family would think of Abe; and he of them.

As Sarah looked around the living room, she called out to Abe: "I like what you've done to the place!" staring at the empty walls. "It has that very understated, feng shui, kind of feel to it and yet you managed to steer clear of anything bordering on... a construction site," she said brightly.

Abe peeked around the kitchen door. "I was going for the minimalistic look!"

"If that is the case, you have totally succeeded," she grinned widely.

"You don't mean to tell me that you haven't seen my great painting on the wall?" Abe pointed over to the far wall of the living room. "It is the only painting I really wanted to keep in the divorce settlement," he said seriously.

Sarah walked over and stared at the painting.

"Geez, Abe, it's wonderful! It is so bright and colorful. 'Fly Daddy Fly' – what do you think it means?" she asked.

"It is a painting by Wouter Stips, my favorite artist," Abe walked across the room and stood next to Sarah. "He also makes amazing sculptures."

"I just love his direct, naive style – the way he plays with dimensions," Sarah said, studying the piece.

"You see how the male and female figure have tiny little angel wings?" Abe pointed out to her. "I like to think it is my mother picking up my father's soul – 'Fly Daddy Fly' – see?"

"That's a beautiful thought, Abe," Sarah softly nudged his shoulder with her nose.

"Only, my dad did not have a cool hat like that…" he joked, before he continued, "I know it's crazy and I don't really believe in heaven or anything, but the combination of the message and the painting itself… makes me smile," Abe shrugged.

"Sarah, I have made reservations at a nice restaurant in a village nearby," Abe said, walking back into the living room. "I hope you will enjoy it. Dress code is between formal and casual."

"Sounds great, Abe," Sarah said warmly. "Can I get in the bath or shower?"

"Sure, let me show you where to find the towels," Abe led her up the stairs.

Sarah tried not to show how her sore muscles affected her. She didn't want him to triumph in any way.

The bath was wholesome. A piece of her hoped Abe would join her but she also dreaded going too fast. She was so out of practice with anything dating-related. It was all just so confusing.

Abe had ordered a cab to go to the restaurant so they could both have a glass of wine.

"You are in no state to walk to the restaurant; besides it's way too cold," he called up the stairs.

"Yeah, yeah, blame it on the girl," Sarah replied as she walked down, trying to keep a semblance of dignity with her sore muscles. Wearing a simple black outfit she looked stunning. Her eyes glowed when she saw his admiration.

"I can't walk very far in these heels," Sarah said gratefully, "so a cab is very welcome."

He retorted instantly: "Yeah, yeah, blame it on the heels." They both laughed as he took her hand.

Catching a cab in the Friesian countryside was quite different from hailing a cab in a big city. A gleaming Mercedes turned up the driveway with an elderly gentleman in a suit at the wheel. Sarah almost felt like the neighbors would be looking out the window. Hang on, that didn't just feel like it, there were actually people standing at their windows. Sarah noticed how many of the houses didn't have curtains in the windows. Strange people, these Dutch.

"You will be the talk of the town tomorrow," Sarah said over her shoulder.

"Don't worry about that, I have been for a long time," Abe grinned. "Hey, what can I say – I do lead a wildly interesting life."

"Interesting, huh?" Sarah teased him.

"Say, is it my imagination, or does your mouth get bigger when you wear heels?" Abe laughed at her.

"No, Mr. Maggagga, maybe it is because you're worried I don't look up to you enough, now that I can almost look you straight in the eye…" Sarah flashed her long lashes at him. "Don't worry, I do so look up to you…"

"Uhuh," Abe said ironically, as he gestured for Sarah to keep walking out the door.

"Or maybe," Sarah beamed at him as she turned back, "it is because then my mouth is closer to your old ears, and you can hear the smart things I say so much better!"

The Australian chef at the restaurant prepared some typical Dutch wintry dishes. Some of the combinations were surprising, but all of them delicious. As soon as he heard that Sarah was over from Canada, he made a special visit to their table. He explained about the different ingredients he used from the local area, some of which Sarah had never heard of before; things like "boerenkool", a dark-green curly cabbage in mashed potatoes. The Chef told them of his coming to Friesland and learning about the many ways the Dutch mash up '*potatoes'n'more*' as he called it. It was a delightful evening. Sarah and Abe both felt their initial feeling of connection was definitely re-established after the rocky start of the day before.

As soon as they got back to Abe's house, however, the tension returned and Sarah sensed a distance as Abe pecked her on the cheek and said 'goodnight' at the bottom of the stairs. *What on earth was she doing here?* Why did he not take her in his arms to take her to his own bedroom? She could have screamed in frustration. They were not teenagers, for crying out loud! On the other hand, she also didn't want to come across as too easy. So *she* certainly wouldn't take the initiative. What if he had the same train of thought? Or worse still, what if he did not have those kinds of feelings for her? If only she had stayed in Scotland to find her family history. Then Abe would have been a nice memory of someone who had brought a flutter to her life. You don't respond to flutters in real life – that is for books and movies, for hopeless romantics; 'hopeless' being the operative word.

She texted Nicky:

> The Flying Dutchman is really not all he's cracked up to be; it sounded better than it really is. Remind me never to be spontaneous again. Big Mistake! How you guys doin'? Miss you! Mouse x

She put her tired body to bed and hoped her muscles would be kind to her in the morning. Come to think of it, maybe it wasn't such a bad thing that they were not having a wild passionate night. Crawling into bed and resting would probably be much better for her. How uneventful! Would Abe have thought of that and was that the reason he did not come to her?

Oh hell, she didn't know anymore. Now she was starting to think for Abe, but it did not fill in the blanks. Before she fell asleep she wondered what Abe had in mind for the next day. Then again, who cares! She didn't come for Friesland! She was overcome by the feeling that she should leave as soon as possible. This wasn't turning out as she had hoped, although what it was exactly she had hoped for – she did not dare to answer to herself. *God, she had been so stupid!*

As Abe went upstairs later he passed the guest bedroom. For a moment he paused; he wanted nothing more than to crawl into bed with Sarah and… endlessly make love to her. He suppressed his feelings and walked on to his own bedroom. Before he closed his bedroom door he stared at her door once more. *Make love to her and then what?*

Chapter 26

"If you translate it, it is called the 'Eleven-cities-tour' and it is the toughest skating event in the world," Abe said at breakfast the following morning. "It is almost 125 miles skating on natural ice in the biting cold. Especially since Friesland is so flat the wind usually becomes an issue with a real risk of frostbite for the skaters. Every year all of Holland is in a frenzy when it starts freezing and we all hope it will be cold enough for a new 'Elfstedentocht'. The last one was held in 1997." Abe was rattling nervously. "It is a regular national news item to see the organizers test the thickness of the ice. It is quite something."

"I hope it hasn't been cold enough last night," Sarah suppressed a yawn, "the skating rink was enough speed skating for me for a long time."

"I was thinking of driving you around the region to follow a part of the route of the 'Elfstedentocht' and have lunch," Abe suggested. "See, the nice part about it, is that the eleven cities are mostly quaint little villages that I'm sure you would enjoy seeing," Abe looked at her expectantly.

Sarah stared into her cup of coffee. In her head she only heard 'yadayadayada'.

What did she care about quaint villages? What was this, *the Friesland Tourist Board*? She felt ungrateful but Sarah still hadn't gotten over her frustration of last night. Although this morning Abe had woken her with a butterfly kiss on the cheek and a cup of tea, it was all Sarah could do not to drag him into bed. That idea became less enticing as she felt how stiff she was.

Again she couldn't push away the feeling; Abe was struggling with having her there. He was kind in a way that friends are, with a distance she could not cross. Something was in the way and her uneasiness would not go away.

Abe noticed that Sarah had gone really quiet and did not give him any response to his suggestions.

"Would you rather do something else instead?" he asked her patiently.

Sarah realized with a start that she had phased out completely. "What?"

"I said, if you don't want to do the eleven cities tour, would you like to do something else?" Abe repeated the question.

"No, that's fine," Sarah said noncommittally.

"Sarah, your enthusiasm is underwhelming. What's wrong?" Abe pushed on.

"Nothing's wrong. I am just a little sore, that's all," Sarah said evasively. "Do we have more coffee in the pot?" Sarah held out her cup.

Abe poured her another cup of coffee. "You are so addicted to that stuff," he grinned, but still didn't get much response.

"We could also go to one of the isles up north," Abe tried. "It is cold still, but the deserted beaches will be amazing. I can check if we can take the car on the ferry, so you don't have to bike across the island," he said with a smile.

"Yes, that sounds nice, Abe," Sarah said, but her heart was not in it.

While Sarah was getting dressed Abe called up to her that he had been able to make arrangements to go to Ameland and take the car.

As she came down the stairs, Abe said: "You're going to love Ameland, Sarah," he briefly touched her hand. "Make sure to dress up warm for the beach."

Driving to the North of Friesland, where they would catch the ferry, the awkward silence grew.

"Is something wrong, Sarah?" Abe finally had the courage to ask.

"No, nothing much," Sarah was not as courageous as Abe.

"I feel torn about what to do. I mean, after I leave here, should I go back to Scotland or return to Nova Scotia?"

"Did you find what you were looking for in Scotland?"

Abe meant well but his question inadvertently raised more doubts for Sarah.

Why did she leave Scotland, a place she so badly wanted to visit after her father died? Why did she come here; apparently not even Abe could think of an answer to that one.

"At home I also still need to take care of all of Matthew's affairs," Sarah added quietly.

Abe looked over to Sarah and saw her staring out the window, with watery eyes. She was obviously still in deep mourning over this Matthew. Although, what the exact nature of the relation between Sarah and Matthew had been, was hard to figure out. Sarah spoke of him with such love and affection, but as far as Abe understood they'd never gotten married or lived together. Maybe they'd split up and it hadn't been Sarah's choice. Maybe she'd stayed in love with him all that time. It was certain this was a great loss she was dealing with, that much was clear. And so silence fell again; Sarah lost in her thoughts – Abe never good at small talk.

The ferry across to Ameland took much longer than Sarah had expected. Walking on the windy deck had cleared her mind. She hooked her arm into Abe's.

"So tell me, what is Amyland and why does it take forever to get there?" She nudged him and smiled at him, knowing he meant well by showing her around.

"Ameland is the island you see over there," Abe pointed out, sounding relieved, "with the tall lighthouse to your left. We are now crossing the Wadden Sea; the biggest wetlands on this planet. We have to make a wide bend through the shipping lane to get there; the rest of the sea is too shallow. At low tide you can even walk across."

Abe certainly hadn't promised too much; Ameland was breathtaking. He drove her to the west side of the island, through the dunes, where the beach reached as far as the eye could see. Snuggling into her cardigan and shawl Sarah followed Abe onto the endless ivory white beach.

"Before we go back, can we stop at the lighthouse we passed

on the way here?" Sarah asked Abe. "It looked so very different from the lighthouses we have in Nova Scotia. It would be nice to have some pictures to take home."

"Sure," Abe sensed Sarah's excitement was returning, "let's walk around the point to the North Sea. I'll buy you a hot chocolate back here at the beach café and we'll see if we can climb to the top."

"Well, climb it may be a stretch for my aching body!" Sarah sighed.

The sound of the thundering sea rolling onto the beach was medicinal for both of them. Sarah loved it; the light salty smells, the waving dune grass. After a while Abe took Sarah's hand and turned her around to look how small the beach café had become behind them.

"Abe, this is magical," she said, squeezing his hand to convey her happiness. Abe looked straight down into her eyes and squeezed back.

"Has anyone ever told you, you have rainbow eyes?" Abe asked her softly.

"Not to my recollection…" Sarah kept gazing into Abe's eyes, "what are rainbow eyes?"

"I have never known they existed, but your eyes are not just green, there are so many other colors present, just gorgeous…" Abe said, kissing her eyelids. Then he took her shawl and softly wrapped it tighter and pulled her into his arms.

"Just want to make sure your ageing body doesn't catch a cold," he teased.

"You know your English is not all it's cracked up to be," Sarah complained. "You don't even know the difference between aching and ageing!" She pushed him playfully.

"Is it my English or your reluctance to face the truth, I wonder," he tapped his chin deep in thought. "I think it is very important to be honest in a relationship; you are not 17 anymore!" Abe added soberly.

"If this is your way of applying for a relationship with me," Sarah warned him, "then we need to set some ground rules about this honesty-thing... Ageing body, perish the thought!"

As they continued walking hand in hand on the deserted beach at Hollum, they hardly spoke. The wind was picking up as they rounded the point towards the North Sea. Sarah wondered if it was the wind on the beach, or the whirlwind inside her. For the first time since Sarah arrived in Friesland, she felt they were truly in sync with each other – and with this amazing island.

With a sense of pride Abe looked at Sarah and her windblown rosy cheeks. If ever the timing could be right for them, they could make quite a wonderful couple! He should have made reservations for them to stay on Ameland, Abe thought with regret.

"Do you see those clouds moving in?" Sarah looked up at the racing clouds. "Should we go back and get that hot chocolate you promised me?"

Abe simply nodded and made a 180 degree turn, sticking out his other hand. Sarah tied her windblown hair back together and beamed up at him. She didn't have to voice how happy she felt to be with him right there and then. Her eyes gave all that away. Abe put his arm around her briefly and pressed her close. On the way back Sarah picked up a few shells and a wooden stump and put them in her cardigan pocket.

"You are becoming quite a 'strandjutter', Miss McFadden," Abe laughed.

"A what?" Sarah asked.

"A strandjutter," Abe said, "I really wouldn't know the English word for it – but strandjutters were people who lived off whatever washed up on the shore."

"Oh, you mean beach combers? See, there's that poor English again!" She winked broadly at him.

With a strong wind in their backs they were practically blown back, the sun now on their faces.

"How spectacular to be on an almost deserted beach like this," Sarah sighed happily. "Nobody but us and the seals, that is."

"I know, I could be here forever." Abe closed his eyes for a moment.

"Hmmm, how very true." Sarah felt silly for having been so frustrated before. She had never been known for her patience and was probably at an all-time low on that skill that very morning. Poor Abe, she thought, he deserved better.

Hot chocolate on the deck behind glass wind blockers was a double treat. The view of the sea and beach was one she would never forget. She recaptured the feeling of how much she had always loved being on the coast; the lighthouses, water, sand and no schedule to keep.

"Too bad the Hollum lighthouse was closed," Abe said to Sarah as they drove back to the ferry.
"At least I got to walk around it and admire the height of that thing!" Sarah was still impressed. "The Acadian lighthouses are mostly made out of wood, instead of steel, and are less than half as high."
"Well, you'll just have to come back to climb it and see the neighboring island of Terschelling from there," Abe said decisively.
"Is that an invitation?" Sarah felt warm inside. "I'd like that!" she said, as she slid closer to him in the car.

Chapter 27

After another morning of waking up alone, Sarah knew there was something seriously wrong with her expectations. Ameland had been fantastic; Abe on Ameland had been a dream. She'd woken up from the dream, though, as they returned to his house. And although Sarah realized that she was being very impatient, she also knew it was driven by insecurity. The feeling that their connection seemed to be strictly platonic on Abe's side scared her by now. It was almost as if her legs gave way as it dawned on her when she had been in this position before.

Oh, goodness, no! Did the fact that he had been married mean anything? Could it be that Abe had divorced Annemarie because he had found out he had homosexual feelings? Could she have been *that* wrong in what she thought he felt for her? Was this just a matter of kindred spirits and a deep sense of friendship? What did she really know about him? Oh, God, how had she gotten herself into this?

Sarah got up and went downstairs in her jogging suit; the smell of coffee pulling at her. They ate breakfast in complete silence; neither knew how to start a conversation that was anything more than the weather. Sarah felt the atmosphere pressing down on her and she didn't know how to address her fears. Planning what to do did not deliver a conclusion as they finished their breakfast.

As they went to their rooms to get dressed, Sarah tried to go on-line on her computer to see if she could book a flight back to Scotland or even back home to Halifax. With a pang in her stomach she realized she soon would be back in the reality of things; all that still needed to happen with Matthew's estate – everything she had pushed away. How she missed the easy comfort of Matthew's company. This was so messed up;

she was so messed up! She sensed there could be the same easy comfort with Abe if only she would open up. In Abe's case, though, it wasn't easy comfort she wanted.

Abe knocked on the door and walked in. He looked surprised to see her with her computer on her lap.

"Abe, I need to start planning my trip back," Sarah kept staring at her screen. "Coming here was a mistake, I'm sorry. I don't know what it was that I was hoping to find here."

"I'm sorry you feel that way," he muttered.

Sarah did not respond.

"When were you planning to leave?" he asked her bluntly.

Sarah's heart sank as she said: "As soon as I can catch a flight."

Abe practically threw the computer aside, sat next to her on the bed and took her hand.

"Sarah, don't go. I don't know how to say this, but I haven't felt what I feel for you in such a long time. So much has changed in my life and this is all happening so fast."

Sarah took Abe's face in her hands and tried to explain as best she could.

"That is all my fault, Abe," Sarah's eyes filled with tears. "I never meant to hurry you, but I have to be honest. I have fallen deeply in love with you and I don't know what to do with these feelings. My going away will give us both the space to think about what we want."

"All I know is that I don't want you to leave." It was clear he meant it.

"Abe, being here together is only putting pressure on both of us," Sarah said softly.

"I don't want you to go," he whispered again and it tore right through Sarah.

"I must…"

Abe got up and left the room. His body language indicated his deep frustration.

Sarah took up the computer again and decided then and there she was going back home. She longed to see her family, Matthew's family and go back to some sense of normality.

Getting reservations on a flight to London and on to Halifax proved easier than expected. She could leave the same afternoon and stay over in London. The next day would get her back home. Sarah felt horrible for being so shallow and expecting so much so soon. It couldn't be helped. Was it the fact that she hadn't been in love for eons? Now that she had finally found it, she wanted all of it instantly? Why? She behaved like a starving person suddenly entering a grocery store.

As Abe drove her to the airport they hardly spoke a word. His thoughts were in turmoil. On the one hand he wanted nothing more than for Sarah to stay with him. On the other he didn't know how to approach her. She had a life in Nova Scotia. He didn't really know where he was or where he was going. Her leaving so soon was an indication of how clumsy he had been towards her. She had followed her heart in coming here and he wished he could have responded by following his own heart.

They said goodbye at the airport; Sarah with a mixture of sadness and relief – Abe crushed with all the questions in his head. What Sarah didn't know was that Abe waited for the plane to depart and stared after it until it vanished in the clouds. The feeling of emptiness hit him on the drive home. Home to what, exactly?
He didn't know what to do next. He pulled over and sent Sarah a text message:

> I feel so stupid for letting you go. I never found the right words to tell you how I feel about you. I'm sorry for that. Maybe my English isn't so good after all. Or maybe we do need more time. All I know is, I miss you already. Abe

Abe pressed 'send' knowing she wouldn't read it until after she arrived in London. Why had he found it so hard to open up to her? Too much had happened in a short time and no amount of hiking in Scotland could have set that straight so quickly. He suddenly felt lost driving through the area he knew like the back of his hand.

Chapter 28

Sarah read Abe's text message after the plane landed in London. Although it made her feel good to see he had contacted her immediately, the mixed feelings remained. There was a sense of relief to be away from Friesland and the dampened atmosphere there. Since she did not know what to write back, she decided to put it off for a while. She missed the man she met in Scotland – she could do without the Friesian, though. Not exactly text material to send, she thought with a wry smile.

Weather-wise, London was no big improvement on Friesland. It was freezing and uninviting. She had a simple meal at the hotel restaurant. She contacted Marc and Nicky that she was on the way home. Tomorrow she would see them all again.

> Maddy, I hear that you're staying with Mom. I can't wait to see you again! We'll have a real family reunion! It's been way too long!! Miss you, love you, see you tomorrow! Sarah, xxxxxxxx

Maddy was Sarah's sweet sensitive sister who was still suffering greatly from the loss of their father. Since Madeline worked in the Foreign Service, she was usually far away and much of their contact was through Skype and e-mail. The time difference with Rome did not help. Sarah longed to catch up. If anyone would understand her spontaneous plans to go to Holland, it would be Madeline. They were both hopeless, romantic fools, always ready for a romantic story or movie. Hopefully, they could laugh about her mistake of actually wanting to star in one, when she got home. Maddy would die to hear that Abe was actually Kevin Costner material, a big favorite of hers.

The next day Sarah looked at the in-flight information to see which movie would be playing. Hmmm, 'Black Swan' with Natalie Portman. Sarah absolutely adored Natalie Portman, ever since she had played the mother of the Wall-Mart baby – a movie she could watch over and over again. After all the safety procedures were taken care of and the flight information vanished from the screen, the movie was getting started. She settled into the chair as comfortably as she could. The story of a gifted young ballerina in New York, making it to the top under a buck load of pressure – from her mother, her ballet company, the director of Swan Lake – was gripping.

The way that fear of failing and reality were interwoven was masterful and Sarah was completely sucked into the story. The atmosphere was oppressive, like being pushed into a pitch-black funnel. As the movie ended she was left with many question marks. Which parts of the story did actually happen and which had Nina, the main character, imagined? Wow, that was impressive! Not a feel-good movie; the sense of what pressure can do to people would stay with Sarah for quite some time.

Just then Sarah realized she had made the right decision in leaving Friesland.

Sarah took out her e-reader and stroked the leather that Matthew had touched so often. In the past few days she had been so busy with herself and this awkward situation with Abe she had hardly thought of Matthew. She had wondered a number of times if Matthew's passing away had created an opening for her to fall in love again. Had she really still been waiting for Matthew's love all this time; for this silly wedding when they'd turn 50? It was hard to imagine this could be true. And even if it were, had she fallen in love with Abe only on the rebound?

She opened the e-reader and looked at the index of all the books he had loaded. She chose to continue with Pride and Prejudice and was soon swept away to a time when ladies were staring at their needlepoint, every conversation was guarded and Mr. Darcy was being obnoxious. *Ahh, good old Mr. Darcy; you knew where you were with him.*

At Halifax airport she was greeted by Marc, Nicky and Maddy. Sarah choked at the sight of them. It was so good to be home. How she had missed them! Marc got the car and the big sisters asked every question imaginable. They so wanted to hear all about Sarah's trip. Sarah laughed, teasing them about the family fortune that never was.

"I'll tell you later over a cup of tea, or preferably a glass of wine," Sarah solemnly promised. In the back of the car, she stared at the photo she had taken of Abe with her cell phone in Scotland. What struck her, were his kind blue-gray eyes that seemed to be piercing through the little screen. She showed it to Maddy, who winked at her. Goodness, she really was deeply in love and there was nothing she could do about it.

Tracy McFadden hurried to the front door as she heard the car approaching. How happy she was that all of her children would be home again. This didn't happen nearly often enough. What an unexpected pleasure that Sarah was coming back right at the time that Maddy was there. In the back of Tracy's mind it bugged her that something might be wrong with Sarah, seeing as she came back so suddenly. As she saw them get out of the car she noticed Sarah's radiant smile. She embraced her youngest daughter and held her tight for a few moments.

"Sarah, I'm so happy to see you again," she said into her daughter's ear, "especially with you looking so well!"

"Mom, it was good to go away and even better to be back," Sarah said with a sigh. "Can I stay here tonight so I can have a glass of wine with you guys?"

"Sweetheart, you can stay as long as you like."

"Thanks, Mom, you look wonderful too. What's the latest news?"

"Oh, nothing much," Tracy said, "I'm clearing your father's library and diaries. Marc and Maddy have been looking into all your father's scribblings. I can't believe how much material he produced. He wrote a few pages every day on what was happening in daily life and the world at large. It is quite an image of the time in which he lived. You can have a look later."

Nicky interrupted them: "Ladies, I suggest we go inside and

hear Sarah's travel stories. I think there is much we have missed so far." Nicky winked at Sarah and took her hand. They went into the large kitchen where Marc was getting out a bottle of prosecco and some glasses. They sat at the big oak kitchen table that had always formed the centre of the household.

"Here's to our unexpected family reunion," said Marc with his deep voice, raising his glass. "May we have many of these in future years!"
"Here, here!" voices from all around the table joined in.
"And to the wonderful memories of Dad," added Maddy.
"And to absent friends," said Tracy, looking over at Sarah.
"Here, here!"
"I don't know about you girls, but I'm taking a sip of this heavenly liquid," Marc said.
"No argument there!" said Nickly, and winked at her brother.
"So, Sarah, tell us all about Scotland!"
"Working with the Scottish team went very well, and we landed our first real international collaboration," Sarah said with pride.
"Not exactly the information the women are waiting for," Marc said drily, "but congrats anyway!" He bowed towards her.
Sarah blushed and continued: "Well, I did not get as far as I had planned with the research into the McFaddens..."
She took a large swig of her prosecco.
"Yes, but how far did you get with the *Dutchman*?" Maddy tapped Sarah's arm impatiently. "Mom, have you seen the picture Sarah has on her cell phone? He is *sooo* good looking!"
"Well, I met Abe in Scotland and after getting to know each other I thought we both felt a real connection. After a few days Abe had to go back home to The Netherlands." Sarah raised her empty glass to her brother and said: "I'm experiencing a severe case of dryness here!"
"And..." Nicky drew circles in the air with her hand to keep the story rolling.
"He left me a wonderful card and we texted for a few days," Sarah continued. "It sounded like he wanted to be with me as much as I wanted to be with him."

Marc meanwhile refilled their glasses. He knew it couldn't have worked out if Sarah was back so sudden. He looked over at Maddy, hanging on to Sarah's every word. *Women!*

"To make a short story long…" Marc said.

"And then you went to see him," Nicky jumped ahead in the story, gesturing to keep going.

"I made the mistake of getting on pretty much the next plane to Amsterdam. I thought to myself: why not see if there really is something between us."

"And?" they said almost simultaneously.

"So, Maddy, how's the new ambassador?" Sarah decided to tease them now they were practically all sitting *on* the table to hear her story.

"Oh, no, you don't!" Maddy almost shouted. "Tell us about the Dutchman first! The ambassador can wait."

"So I get to Friesland, bump into Abe's ex-wife and her new lover, skate on speed skates and come back home," Sarah shrugged. "That's it, really."

"Come on, what happened?" They were all talking at the same time now, typical McFadden family style. Sarah smiled and told them a bit more.

"Anyway, I think I overwhelmed Abe by suddenly showing up on his doorstep," Sarah said, giggling as she remembered it. Her voice turned more serious immediately. "I think he has a lot of unresolved issues…"

"Oh, sweetheart, what a shame!" Tracy rubbed Sarah's arm with sympathy.

"But I have to be honest," Sarah said swooning, "the time we spent together in Scotland was wonderful. The time we spent on this little island, Amyland, was magical."

"Not all bad then," Marc was about ready with this nonsense.

"It just wasn't meant to be anything more than a crush, I guess," Sarah concluded. "Now I feel stupid for not going on the quest into our family history."

They had all seen the change in Sarah's expression; she was hurting that it had not worked out as she'd hoped. Too bad too, it would have been wonderful for her to find someone.

"Well, you went on a quest of your own, didn't you?" Nicky winked. "Nothing wrong with that!"

"Yeah, I guess…" Sarah sighed. "Anyway, Holland is flat and damp – not my kind of country, so it's just as well."

She held up her glass and asked her brother for a filler-upper. "I'm staying here tonight, so an extra glass of wine won't hurt."

"You took up speed-drinking, did you?" Marc teased. "Well, trust your big brother to be there in your hour of need," he grinned broadly.

Sarah got out the gifts she had brought them, showing the McFadden family crest in blue and gold with the white swallow.

"Marc, I considered bringing you a real kilt," Sarah turned around to him, "but you would need to work on those legs of yours – so next time!"

They talked for a long time in their easy familiar way, jumping from one subject to the other and back.

Chapter 29

Soon after her return Sarah got back into the rhythm of daily life. She found pleasure in being back at work and interacting with the Scots about their progress. They would be coming over to Nova Scotia where Sarah would show them around Cape Breton and PEI and explain the effects of the work they had done so far.

The following weekend Sarah decided to drive down to Kemptville, to visit Matthew's family.
"Sarah, how lovely to see you again, it has been such a long time," Mary walked over to the front gate to hug Sarah. "Did you have a good trip?"
Sarah studied Mary. Every time Sarah saw Mary, she seemed thinner and paler than the time before.
"How have you been, Mary?" Sarah didn't want to voice her concern directly.
"It's been quiet, you know," Mary looked away from Sarah. "Especially the mornings are hard – getting the day started." Mary wrapped her scarf tightly around her.
"So how was Scotland?" Mary clearly wanted the focus off of herself.
"Scotland was very nice and the meetings were successful," Sarah left out that she had taken a detour. "Where's the rest of the family, Mary?"
They walked over to the farmhouse as Mary explained that Paul and his family were at the local school for a school play. They would be joining them later.
Sarah put her arm around Mary's shoulder, who leaned against Sarah for support.
"Oh, Sarah, I am so happy you're here," Mary said. "You have become such a dear part of our small family, Paul was just saying that the other day."

"Thank you, Mary, what a sweet thing to say," Sarah said, deeply touched.

"I know that Matthew had a life of his own in Halifax," Mary said, clearing her throat, "but he called me almost every day – I miss him so much."

Sarah only nodded and followed Mary into the large country kitchen. There was nothing she could say to comfort Mary. All around the kitchen there were pictures of Matthew; in his tuxedo at a concert, at his drawing table, sitting in the window overlooking the Dartmouth harbor. She tried to avoid Matthew's dark-brown eyes.

"And to think that his ashes are scattered right here around the orchard is something that is not really sinking in yet," Mary was saying. "I walk over every day and talk to him. Yet, I still don't understand that it is my son lying there."

Sarah exhaled with relief; they had already taken care of the ashes. Her second thought was: *Why wasn't I there?*

The rawness of the emotions on Mary's face said it all and Sarah kept quiet.

"Do you want to walk over to the orchard, Sarah?" Mary asked.

Sarah nodded bravely, sensing how much Mary wanted to go there with her. It was a moment she dreaded – to face Matthew's last resting place.

"First I have to get back to the car," Sarah said, knowing she was stalling. "I brought some flowers for you that could use some water. Then let's have a coffee or tea, I could really do with a hot drink after the long drive."

Mary walked out with Sarah and looked at Matthew's gleaming car – none of this felt right. Mary could have howled at the confrontation that everything was gone. Instead she just said: "Of course, dear, how thoughtless of me not to offer you something first."

"Here you go," Sarah handed the flowers to Mary, "red roses, Matthew's favorite flowers."

"Why don't you bring them to Matthew later?" Mary suggested. "You haven't seen it yet."

Sarah tried to swallow and nodded 'yes'. There would be no escape.

Over a strong cup of coffee Sarah heard Mary chattering away – who had been visiting; Aunty this and Uncle that, neighbor left and vicar such. Matthew had often explained to Sarah how small their circle in Kemptville was. Mary was grateful for each kind visitor; she felt blessed she could share her thoughts. It was hard for Sarah to listen to Mary's explanation of why God had needed Matthew by his side. Since Sarah did not believe she nodded respectfully and did not respond.

Sarah managed to postpone walking over to the orchard till after lunch. Standing there, this wintry day, the icy wind in her hair, on the barren soil among the leafless trees, facing her first love and best friend's last burial place was an earth-shattering experience for Sarah.

Paul and Mary had had a headstone placed:

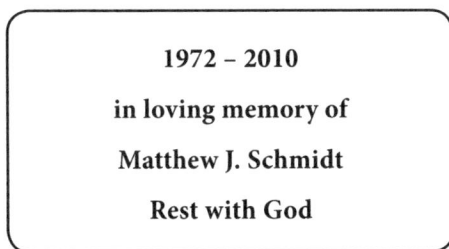

1972 – 2010

in loving memory of

Matthew J. Schmidt

Rest with God

Sarah could barely look at it. *Sod the loving memories!* Why did this have to happen to him? What had he done wrong? Lung cancer without ever having smoked a cigarette! If there really was a God, why in the *HELL* did he have to pick Matt? It just wasn't fair. Once again the finality of it all struck her. Sarah felt overpowered by her anger. Whoever had a headstone placed like this? Matthew didn't *want* a headstone; he didn't want to be buried and he *certainly* didn't want a place with God – whose representatives had always denied him to be who he really was!!

Sarah wept and wept, spreading the red roses she brought among the trees. Mary respectfully retreated slightly. It was a great comfort to her that other people mourned Matthew's death with her and she mumbled the same prayer she said every day:

> *and by Your command we return to dust.*
> *Lord, those who die still live in Your presence,*
> *their lives change but do not end.*

Sarah couldn't listen to it and abruptly turned away from Mary. How awful she felt that Mary didn't know Matthew didn't share their beliefs. How lonely he had felt their religion portrayed him as a freak. How angry he had been that it was the Catholic Church who offered a course for youngsters to brainwash them out of being gay; to convince them they were only imagining this. Poor Mary. Poor Matt. Two people who loved each other so dearly, yet were so unconnected in so many ways. Sarah leaned against a big cherry tree, willing her sobs to stop.

Slowly, Sarah calmed down and turned around to face Mary. She took Mary's arm and shivered.

"All right, dearest," Mary broke the silence, "let's get you back inside and warm you up. I have made chicken soup."

By the time they got back Paul and his family had arrived. The change in atmosphere in the big kitchen with the bubbly young girls was very welcome. The girls were excited about the school play and still wore their costumes. Paul winked at Sarah and sighed how hard it was to live with only women in the house.

"You should talk to my brother Marc," Sarah smiled at Paul, "he deals with our all-women population quite well."

Paul and Sarah walked over to the living room and made some arrangements about Matthew's house. Sarah sensed Paul had been unpleasantly surprised about his brother's decision to have Sarah take care of everything. He didn't push, however, and Sarah did not volunteer any more information.

They agreed Sarah would start working on the house the next weekend and would call him if she needed help.

Paul expressed his gratitude for all Sarah had done for Matthew and they hugged warmly as Sarah was getting ready to leave.

Chapter 30

"I'm sooo happy to see you again! It's been too long!" Sarah exclaimed as she got out of the car.

"Hello, M'Lady!" Thierry said walking over with his arms wide open to give Sarah a bear hug. "Welcome to the 'Bee&Tree Inn'."

"Oh, Thierry, your hugs are wholesome, I tell you!" Sarah said gratefully and looked at her old friend.

"I have been trained by the master," Thierry chuckled and said: "and here she is just now!"

Beatrice ran out to embrace Sarah.

"Hi Sassie, how've you been?" Beatrice hugged Sarah close.

"Oh, goodness, I am so ready for some lively conversation!" Sarah sighed.

"How was Kemptville?" Beatrice asked.

"It was hard to be out there, but somehow rewarding, too." Sarah dropped her shoulders, indicating her exhaustion. "Mary is so brave."

"Tell us all about it over our special seafood chowder," Thierry said, "recipe of my mother." Thierry took Sarah's bag and walked in.

"So, Shelburne, huh?" Sarah studied the sign on the front door and looked around. "I can see why you would leave metropolitan Halifax for this. This looks great; and I just *love* the name!"

Sarah walked into the reception area of the small inn that Beatrice and Thierry had bought just a few months back.

"Not technically Shelburne, that would be too big a city for us!" Thierry grinned.

"You mean, after Halifax?" Sarah teased.

"Yes, way too big a city," Beatrice joined in. "We have made up our nicest room for you; we have spent quite some time on decorating." Beatrice led the way up a wide wooden staircase.

"Thanks, you guys – WOW, this really is a treat to walk into!" Sarah exclaimed as she entered the room. She liked the authentic Nova Scotia style, the big quilt on the wooden bed and the view from the window overlooking the sea.

"The only disadvantage is that you will see the light from the Sandy Point lighthouse flashing by until you fall asleep," Thierry said in mock apology – knowing how much Sarah loved 'her' lighthouses.

"Well, you gotta roll with the punches, my dear Thierry," Sarah tried to sound defeated and winked at him. "You take the good with the bad… No, seriously, I love it!"

Thierry poured a glass of wine for the girls and excused himself.

"Kitchen duty is mine this evening, so you can catch up." He smiled warmly at them. "Now don't you go expecting any culinary miracles!"

"Thierry, even raw potatoes would taste good. The company totally makes up for it." Sarah patted his shoulder before she sat down next to Beatrice.

"This is a welcome glass of wine!" Beatrice said with feeling. "We've been working so hard and I feel it hardly shows."

"Not true!" Sarah said matter-of-fact, "it looks marvelous already. I'm sure you will be a major hit come summer time! I will advise everybody I know to come here!"

"How have you been Sarah?" Beatrice studied Sarah as a silence fell between them. "Are you coping?"

"You know, Bee, so much has been going on; Matt, the trip to Scotland..."

Beatrice immediately sensed there was something Sarah was not telling her. "And?"

"Well, then there was this Dutch intermezzo." Sarah gestured briefly, brushing it aside.

"Dutch intermezzo – what Dutch intermezzo?" Beatrice saw Sarah rolling her eyes and sat up straight. "So tell me; how gorgeous was he?"

"Oh, Bee, he was to die for!" Sarah shrieked.

"So what happened?" Beatrice poked Sarah fervently. "Come on; spill!"

"I honestly don't know what happened," Sarah sighed loudly. "I met him in Scotland – his name is Abe, by the way – and I followed him to Holland," Sarah stated the facts in a dry tone. "By the time I got there, he was a changed man."

"What do you mean, 'a changed man'?" Beatrice asked. "Was he married? Did he lie to you or something?"

"No, just like his spirit had sort of vanished by the time I got to Holland," Sarah still hadn't figured it out for herself. "Like he was hiding something."

"Oh Sarah, that's a bummer," Beatrice knew how badly Sarah was hurting over losing Matthew, but added light-heartedly: "Plenty more fish in the sea; as they say."

"Easy enough for you to say," Sarah said cynically, "you hooked your fish more than twenty years ago."

Sarah had always admired how good Beatrice and Thierry fit together, even after all that time. They made her feel there was hope still.

"Yes, he's an old fish by now; but still wonderful!" Beatrice said in a swoony voice, flashing her eyelashes.

Sarah laughed. "Mine are probably swimming the Pacific, I'm looking in the wrong places, darn!" Sarah slapped her leg for effect.

Beatrice laughed at her friend's silliness. "The good news is, Sarah, that you were open for something new. That's something I can't remember seeing in you for so long."

Beatrice was right, Sarah realized. Somehow her life had revolved around Matthew, her work, her friends and her family. For a long time she'd thought it would be enough. Meeting Abe had opened possibilities she hadn't considered, well, forever really.

"Do you think, Bee, that Matt kept me from being open to meeting other people; you know, new relationships?" Sarah asked her friend.

"No, I don't, Sass," Beatrice replied honestly. "I think you did all of that yourself. Matt wanted nothing more than for you to be happy."

Over dinner they reminisced about their university time and about Matthew. Sarah told Thierry and Beatrice how hard it had been for him and for those around him to deal with his disease.

"Did Matthew ever tell his family about being gay?" Thierry asked.

"No, Thierry," Beatrice said in an unusually sharp tone, "that's why he didn't want anyone there at the cremation!"

Sarah nodded in confirmation. "It wasn't just that he lost contact with most everybody. He was so scared that his family would find out," she explained. "He refused till his dying day to tell them. He's even left me in charge of his estate. That's how much he didn't want them to find out."

"Amazing; you'd think they would have guessed by now," Thierry said pensively, "since he never had a girlfriend or anything."

"I know," Sarah said, "I'm convinced they would have accepted it. I'm glad the subject never came up this afternoon, though. It's just painful, you know. They're his family."

"Well, let us know if we can be of any help with the house, sweetheart," Thierry offered.

"You've got enough on your plate, listening to what you want done before the summer season," Sarah laughed good-naturedly.

"Speaking of plates…" Thierry said as he got up from the table, "we still have desert!"

The next morning, after breakfast, Beatrice and Thierry walked Sarah to the car.

"Thanks, you guys, for a wonderful time," Sarah hugged her friends warmly. "It was so good to be here. I absolutely adore your new place!"

"Are you sure you've had enough breakfast? You hardly ate!" Beatrice complained.

"It was plenty, Bee, thanks," Sarah smiled gratefully and got in the car. "And thanks for the survival kit," she called out, holding a small, richly filled, wicker basket. "You have spoiled me way too much!"

Thierry knocked on the car roof as Sarah slowly pulled out and stared after it. Matthew had always cherished that car.

Sarah opened her window to wave and called out: "Thierry, tell your mother the chowder was *fantabulous*!"

They waved back and smiled as they recognized Matthew's terminology for everything good and tasty.

In the pale sunlight Sarah drove along the changing coast-line she loved so much; big rocky boulders and sandy beaches taking turns. She turned off the stereo and took in the beauty of her home country. Despite all that was wrong in her life, she felt happy to be back where she belonged. Sarah got out at Peggy's Cove and climbed on to the boulders underneath the lighthouse. There she sat at the waterfront, gazing out over the ocean, seeing the waves hit the rocks. Two large seagulls were playing with the sprays of water; it looked like they were daring the water to reach them. Every time they would near the edge of the rock, looking down at the waves. Until a wave broke on the shore and then they hopped off with loud shrieks, flapping their gray wings.

"So, Mr. & Mrs. Seagull, so glad you followed me here," Sarah said softly. And as the sun was setting she felt her loneliness was lifted.

Chapter 31

In the meantime, Abe was showing a few interested buyers around the house every week. It was a large house with a lot of potential in a popular area in Friesland. Abe mostly saw people who wanted a second home for vacationing and sailing the Friesian lakes. The boat landing and direct access to the water were among its many attractions. Abe cleared up as much as he could without making the house look too empty. He knew it wouldn't be long before a good offer would come in. He called Annemarie to inform her of the goings on and she sounded pleased with the progress. She asked how Abe was doing and if he had decided on his future plans.

"There are some things I wish to explore," Abe said thoughtfully, "which I hope to be able to finalize not before long."

"Wow, Abe, that is possibly the most non-information I have ever gotten out of you," Annemarie laughed into the receiver.

"Anyway, hope you are well. Let me know if an offer comes in and let's discuss it. Bye, Abe."

"Bye, Annemarie."

"Say, how did it work out with that American girl?" Annemarie couldn't help herself.

"Canadian, actually," he smiled in spite of himself, "and… I really don't know."

As Abe got off the phone he wondered how it was possible he had once committed to 'till death do us part' with Annemarie. Goes to show how easy it is to make a huge mistake. The good news was: this feeling was mutual.

That evening Abe decided it was high time for a phone call to his brother.

"Hylke," he said, "I need advice from my kid-brother. Have you got a minute?"

"Sure, Abe, good to hear from you!" Hylke said enthusiastically.

"How are you? How was Scotland?"

"No me first: how are Jess and the boys?" Abe insisted.

"Jess is doing very well," Hylke said proudly, "she did land that new job she applied for."

"Wow, that's great!" Abe said warmly. "And Luke and Jason?"

"They're doing fine; in each other's hair sometimes like we used to be, but nothing out of the ordinary," Hylke said casually. "They're doing well in school and their karate careers have quite literally kicked into gear – no pun intended." Hylke laughed.

"I'm happy to hear things are going so well," Abe said sincerely.

"So, how *was* Scotland?" Hylke asked again. "Did you walk it all out of your system?"

"Scotland, what can I say," Abe sounded doubtful. "Scotland was a start to get my life in order again."

"Your life in order; that sounds big, brother!" Hylke realized too late that Abe sounded very serious.

"Well, you know, with everything falling to pieces around me," Abe explained, "I'm wondering if Grou is the place for me for the future."

"Sounds like you got a new plan?" Hylke sounded curious.

"Nope, nothing final," Abe said curtly, "but I am thinking of picking up sailing again and I need to pick your brain, tap into all you still know."

"Okay, what are you considering?" Hylke nowadays called himself 'sailing-impaired', now that he was living in the Colorado mountains.

"You know, I was thinking to try and find dad's and uncle Benne's skûtsje," Abe said enthusiastically.

"Why, what for?" Hylke instantly deflated the happy buzz.

"That's not picking up sailing; that's not just a boat, that's a full ship! Are you getting sentimental at your old age? You just sold that thing a few years ago!"

"I know," Abe sighed deeply, "but I've regretted it ever since."

"But you can't even sail that thing on your own," Hylke said. "You will always need a crew to sail it."

"You guys could come over and sail it with me," Abe suggested meaningfully, "like we used to when we were kids."

"Geez, Abe, that sounds nice, but... hardly worth buying the ship for," Hylke sensed he was totally bursting Abe's bubble. "We could rent one when we come over – including the crew." "Yeah, I guess you're right..." Abe exhaled and Hylke heard the disappointment at the other end.

"Why don't you come and visit us for a while?" Hylke said, feeling uneasy with the situation. "We'd love to have you. Luke was asking about you the other day."

"You know, Hylk, I don't need rescuing or anything," Abe protested.

"I didn't mean to..."

"No, I know – you're right, of course," Abe said. "If I make plans to come over, I'll let you know, okay?"

"Okay, Abe, take care," Hylke hung up wondering what on earth was wrong with his brother. It sounded like Abe had seriously stepped out of character, or else had landed in a total mid-life crisis.

The first offer made on the house really was an offer they couldn't refuse. Abe and Annemarie agreed on it instantly. There was one catch, however. The new owners wanted to move in as soon as possible, so they could get it ready, sail their boat up to Friesland and spend summer there. Abe did not mind. He hadn't wanted to spend much time there anyway. He would put his last furniture in storage. Now he had no choice but to get working on his plans.

Dear Sarah,

Just a quick card to let you know I have been thinking of you. I hope you are well and that going back to Nova Scotia was a good decision, I mean, instead of going back to Scotland.

We have sold the house and I have moved into a small bed-sit; it's a bit snug but it will do for the moment. You will find my current address at the bottom. My cell phone and e-mail have not changed.

I would love to hear from you.

Best wishes,

Abe

Chapter 32

Sarah stared at the postcard: the Hollum beach at Ameland. She put the card on her dresser not knowing what to do with it. The wording on the card proved the awkwardness between them. Best wishes… Right!!

Sarah opened her cell phone and stared intensely at Abe's picture. What was it about him that kept her in doubt? Looking back, most of their interaction had been a disaster. *Forget about him and move on!*
She looked at the card on her dresser and saw the endless ivory beach. That day – right there on that beach – had been magical. In all fairness, Scotland had had its moments, too. "So in essence, Mr. Maggagga," Sarah said out loud, "you and I were good together on any island. Granted; the one bigger than the other. We should have steered clear from the mainland."

A few weeks later, just as Sarah was getting started at the office, John walked into her office with a question about her current projects.
"Have you been able to instruct your team about the progress?" he asked, his voice sounded stressed. "I know you will only be gone for a few days, but I will be at a conference myself."
Sarah nodded 'yes' and wanted to reassure John that everything was prepared for her trip, when something on her screen caught her eye.
In the list of e-mails she saw a subject: 'I love you'.
Oops, that looked like the computer virus they'd had a few years ago. At that time she'd received an e-mail from Matthew's mailbox stating the same subject and she had made the mistake of opening it. That had instantly shut down their entire computer server at the office.

"Looks like we have to have the virus-filter upgraded again," Sarah said to John.

"Upgrade what?" John asked.

Then Sarah noticed the sender: abe@makkinga.com.

"Sorry, John," Sarah sounded distracted, "never mind!"

John studied Sarah for a moment.

"Sorry to keep you," Sarah said, willing her brain to switch back to work-mode. "Yes, I have indeed been talking to the team and we are all on the same page as to what needs to happen in the next few days."

John left Sarah's office only half convinced things were on track.

As soon as John was gone, Sarah immediately opened the e-mail that contained a short text and an attachment.

The e-mail read:

Subject: I love you

Dear Sarah,
I haven't heard from you for some time and I haven't been in touch for a while. I was hoping we could start over again so I have written you an official love letter.

Please, please take into consideration that is has been **forever** since I've written a letter like this, and that I am writing in a foreign language!

Please read it and let me know how you feel.

Love,
Abe
xxx

Sarah grabbed her mug of coffee and debated whether to open the attachment or not. Did she really want to go back into this? She was just getting back on her feet and had tried to get him out of her mind. She had so much to do to prepare for her days away from the office. She had no time now. Curiosity, however, got the better of her and as she clicked on the PDF attachment, she recognized his regular handwriting – he had actually hand-written the letter.

Dear Ms. McFadden,

Allow me to introduce myself: my name is Abe Makkinga and I just turned 40.
I am a stubborn Friesian and a colossal fool when it comes to expressing my feelings. I am even worse when those feelings reach so deeply within me. I am known for my sense of humor, believe it or not, and my creative way of seeing things and looking for solutions.

Dear Sarah,

How lost I feel without you. I am so sorry for the way I acted when you were here. I should have told you of my love for you. I don't know why I couldn't at the time. Blame it on my being too serious and thinking too far ahead. Also, I am not as brave as you.
I wondered if it was fair to express my love to you and feared what it might bring. Our worlds are literally oceans apart. Maybe that is why it was so much easier to be together in Scotland than it was back here.

Meanwhile, I have figured out that the changes in my life, the loss of my beloved father, the ending of my marriage and having no direction for my future hadn't quite gotten a place in my head when I returned to a place that used to be home. Everything was different. Nothing was in sync anymore and the confrontation of it was painful.

The promise of you and not being able to act upon it made our encounter worse because I started to doubt my intuition – something I have never really done before and it scared the hell out of me.

I am now getting my life back together and every day I know that the one thing that is missing, is you. I will never forget the connection we had in Scotland and I know we both had a sense of belonging that I screwed up so badly. Now that my head is clearer, you have taken up an even bigger part of it. My heart you had already conquered before.

Sarah, can we please start over again? Can we get to a point where we can get together and get to know each other better? I want nothing more than to look into your beautiful 'rainbow' eyes and tell you how I feel. And this time, I promise, no more speed skating.

I hope I have been able to convince you that you were right; giving us both space and time was a good decision. I can now only hope that it worked at your end too!

Yours with all my love, Abe, xxx

P.S.: have I told you I love you yet? I do, I love you, I miss you!
P.P.S.: the house is sold and I have moved – I even have pictures on my new walls!

Chapter 33

Sarah stared at her screen. What a wonderful letter; so open, so sincere. She took out her cell phone and stared at his picture again. She knew she wanted nothing more than to see him again, but she was also afraid. The Dutch escapade was still vivid in her memory. What if it didn't work out next time either? What if they were only supposed to be a travel romance?

He said as much himself; it felt good in Scotland – it felt weird in Holland. Trying to forget him, however, hadn't worked out at all. Falling in love had taken her forever, falling out of love would probably take at least as long. He was on her mind a few times each day. For a moment she allowed herself to remember the good times they'd shared. So far she had only relived the disappointment of Friesland. She had tried to break the spell by asking herself if Abe was just a rebound for the loss of Matthew, if only to get her mind off Abe. The more she thought about it, the more she knew it wasn't a real question. What she had felt for Matthew had long lost the spark of being 'in love'.

Sarah decided to wait sending a response. She had dinner plans with Janet and they were going to catch a movie after. Over dinner she couldn't keep her mind from wandering off from time to time. Her heart jumped that Abe had contacted her. He missed her – he *LOVED* her! She didn't feel as brave as he claimed though, because the prospect of seeing him again filled her with fear as much as excitement. What was she going to answer him?

"Are you okay?" Janet asked a few times. Janet looked at her friend and colleague with inquisitive eyes.

"Yes, right as rain. How's your veal?" Sarah changed the subject.

"Oh, it's very good, thanks!" Janet replied bubbly. "I wonder what the sneak preview movie will be this time."

As Sarah drove home she switched on the car stereo. Her own car only played cassette tapes, sometimes adding an unsolicited twang to the song. Matthew's car had a fancy stereo system. The first thing she heard was *'Accepting Me'* on her CD-player.

There is no coincidence in this life, she thought to herself, turning up the volume. She was instantly zapped back in time to the rental car in Scotland, trying not to choke with Abe sitting next to her. With a start Sarah realized that she had first thought of Abe, when she had heard the song, not of Matthew. She would send him a message the next morning. Truth be told, she couldn't *wait* to see him again. Maybe she should suggest another island. How 'bout Newfoundland? ... Oceans apart, but for how long?

Subject: Can't wait!

Dearest Abe,
I cannot begin to tell you how much your letter has touched me. You have been on my mind and the short version is:
I would love to start over again. In all honesty, it also scares me.

Maybe we should find another location to meet up that is not one of our home areas. Can I suggest Newfoundland? ;-))
Can't wait to see you again!
Hugs, kisses, love,
Sarah, xxxxxxxxxxxxxxxxxxxxxxxxx (I win!)

P.S.: I appreciate your promise about the speed skating!
P.P.S.: I am still totally going to get even with you; be afraid, be very afraid…
P.P.P.S.: Have I said that I'm sooo happy you are doing better?
P.P.P.P.S.: Sorry for the short message, I am getting ready to leave the office for a few days – showing the Scottish team around New *improved* Scotland.

As she pressed 'send' she wondered what the next step would be. Where to go; where to meet? Sarah felt a happiness in her heart that she hadn't felt in ages. For once it seemed things were starting to move in the right direction. What hadn't been a very happy year so far could still turn into something special – and she literally felt a buzz at the prospect of seeing Abe again soon.

Chapter 34

"I never knew you could actually miss your daily shot of NS Brew," Sarah said to Janet, early the next morning, "and I'm going to have to miss it again." She poured more coffee in her cup and held up the pot.

"Janet, do you think that bucket is big enough to get you started in the morning?" Sarah laughed as she could only see Janet's brow above the rim of the cup. "That is not a shot of coffee, that's a *downpour.*"

"As if I am the one consuming most of the brew," Janet replied in mock-offense. "You just came back from coffee rehab, no?"

"Yup, my sponsor is somewhat disappointed; says my cold turkey is more of a tepid turkey, but he does think I am on the way to recovery," Sarah laughed.

Janet's lovely round face with her vivid blue eyes, freckles and strawberry blond hair was smiling from ear to ear.

"I'm so happy you are better, Sarah!" she said. Walking back to their offices, Janet added: "I'm sure your team is happy to have you back, too."

"Yeah, sure they are," Sarah said cynically, "I had become impossible to work with, I know."

Janet had always admired Sarah for her openness, however daunting sometimes.

"You know, Sarah," Janet said kindly, "none of us here have had to go through what you have with Matthew," Janet rubbed Sarah's arm briefly. "The question is, will we do any better when facing a similar situation?"

Sarah looked at Janet gratefully. "And I sincerely hope that none of you will have to experience this; it is a life altering experience." Sarah sighed and then nudged Janet. "All right, enough with the serious talk in the morning; back to the grindstone."

"If you insist," Janet pretended to haul her coffee mug to her office.

"I have places to go, people to see!" Sarah called out. Then she added: "I can't wait to take the Scots to PEI, Janet. Wish you were coming."

"That would have been fun, but someone has to hold the fortress!" Janet said soberly.

"You know, it's been quite a while since I've been myself, and it feels good," Sarah entrusted to Janet. "Thanks for being such a great friend."

Janet blew a hand-kiss to Sarah. "You're welcome. You've always been there for me, too!"

"Good morning, John," Sarah tapped on John's office door, "fancy going out to dinner with Jaime and Maggie early this evening? They're arriving end of the afternoon."

"Sure," John did not look up from his computer, "where are we taking them?"

"I was thinking The Dartmouth Boardwalk – give them a typical taste of Nova Scotia." Sarah looked expectantly at John. That got John's attention, the Boardwalk being his favorite place.

"Great idea!" he grinned. "Count me in. How lucky am I that my plans got changed at the last minute."

Sarah walked over to her assistant.

"Evelyn, could you make dinner reservations for this evening for four at The Boardwalk, you know, in Dartmouth? We'll be early, say six-ish? Thanks."

"Sarah, how wunderful to see ya again," Jaime said in his rich Scottish accent.

"Hi Jaime, Maggie, welcome to Nova Scotia," Sarah greeted them with a smile. "Did you have a good flight?"

"Aye, it was grand – landing was a bit bumpy," Maggie said, "but the views over Newfoundland were beautiful."

"Too bad Allan couldn't make it," Sarah said.

"We couldn't plan for the three of us being away from the office, now could we?" Jaime said.

Over dinner Sarah explained about the schedule she had prepared for them to drive to Cape Breton and over to PEI.

"I think you will like the island, Maggie, it is quite different from any other island we have here," Sarah said. "The beaches are somewhat reddish in color. Hopefully the weather will be nice enough."

"I've seen your pictures. What is it that colors the beaches?" Maggie asked, trying to suppress a yawn. "Sorry, jetlag," she smiled apologetically.

John did not pick up on this. "Prince Edward Island is formed on sedimentary bedrock of a red sandstone," his voice in lecture mode, "which is red with rust essentially. And so…"

Sarah interrupted him. "And so building sand castles in summer turns them into real pottery castles, baking in the sun!" She smiled. "I think we need to get you to your hotel to get some sleep."

Maggie smiled back gratefully.

"Oh, I see," John said sheepishly.

The first spring rays of sunshine couldn't have timed their arrival any better. It would be fantastic to be on PEI with the sun and the wind. It wasn't exactly warm, but it would certainly be better than the weather they'd had so far.

Sarah paid the toll at the Confederation Bridge and explained to Jaime and Maggie how the bridge had changed the lives of the people on PEI, to no longer be real 'islanders'.

"On the way back I thought we would take the Northumberland Ferry," Sarah said. "If weather permits, of course."

As they drove onto the island Sarah said that all of PEI was in a nervous frenzy for the upcoming royal visit of Prince William and Katherine.

"They're pulling all the stops to give them a real impression of life on PEI," Sarah said, "including performing the Anne of Green Gables musical and a Mi'kmaq smudging ceremony."

"What on earth is that?" Maggie asked with a chuckle. "Will they be smudged in this red clay you mentioned?"

Sarah laughed as she pictured this. "Can you imagine? No, it is a ceremony where the smoke from burning sweet grass or cedar is being brushed toward the body to cleanse the spirit."

"You'd think they don't need cleansing, wouldn't you?" Maggie snorted, turning to Jaime on the back seat.

Jaime looked out the window. "I only hope they don't burn the Royals," he grinned wickedly.

After about 25 kilometers they stopped for lunch at a small roadside restaurant in Summerside. Since the tourist season hadn't started yet a lot of the places were still boarded up. As they got out of the car Sarah tightened her woolen scarf to block out the chill.

"The name Summerside doesn't really deliver on its promise, does it?" Jaime winked at the women.

"I'll say!" Sarah said shivering.

"Not that we only have 20+ Celsius in Inverness all year long. If only that were true," Maggie said with longing.

"Let's get some lunch in ya, that'll help," Jaime said, opening the door for them. "My treat!"

They found a nice table at the window, overlooking the water-front.

"After lunch it's not too far to the North Cape where I want to show you what we did to preserve the rugged coastline," Sarah said. "We were able to make use of the protection offered by the longest natural offshore rock reef in North America," she explained as she handed out the menus.

"Be prepared for a combination of old and new," Sarah pointed over to where they were heading. "Over there we have the very first lighthouse of PEI, which makes a shrill contrast with the high-tech wind farm." She shrugged: "Still, we can't stop progress, can we? As much as we'd like to sometimes."

That evening they stayed at a picturesque Bed & Breakfast called 'The Anchor Age' - a beautiful symmetrically laid out house in colonial revival style from the late 19th Century - just outside of Alberton, overlooking the Gulf of St. Lawrence. During the project work on PEI Sarah had often stayed there. The house had been designed by and built for a naval shipbuilder. Inside the ornately carved wooden paneling in deep oak and big marble fireplaces gave the house grandeur of another era.

As they were waiting for their room keys Sarah whispered to Maggie in the central hallway: "Can you imagine they offered the place to me for 1 Canadian dollar a number of years ago?" Maggie looked around, admiring what she saw. "You are pulling my leg now, Sarah, maybe both of them!" Maggie laughed.

"No, honestly," Sarah said, "but that was before it was restored." "Gosh," Maggie said, still looking around, "that must have been some restoration."

"Can you picture me – a landlady of a B&B?" Sarah giggled. "I could, actually!" Maggie said with a wide smile. "You could do guided tours, make jams and tell tales. It'd be grrrand!"

The visit to PEI went well. Jaime and Maggie were genuinely impressed with the work that the CAPF had done and asked all the right questions. In the two days they spent on the island Sarah explained about the different challenges the Foundation was facing; the rugged coastlines at the North of PEI; the dunes on the east side that were very heavily damaged by a storm just the year before. Jaime and Maggie recognized the work was never really completed. The long-term approach and government support were of vital importance to preserve the beauty and history of places such as PEI.

At many of the places they visited Sarah wished Abe could be there. *I should have suggested PEI instead of Newfoundland*, Sarah thought to herself. Walking hand in hand along Brackley Beach surely would be the most romantic she could imagine; an endless walk along the endless shore...

They would make so much more of their time together next time. How she hoped it would be soon. The beach at Brackley was deserted, though, and did not offer any such promise.

Upon their return to Halifax the first thing Sarah did was check her e-mails. No messages from Abe, hmmm. Probably because she had mailed him she would be out of the office.

Still, it would have been nice to hear from him after her reply to his letter.

Jaime and Maggie had one more morning to round things off. New steps in their future collaboration were defined and they left very satisfied. John complimented Sarah on how she had handled the visit and all the preparations.

"I'm glad I put you on the project," he said warmly. "No one could have done this better than you. Well done!"

"Thanks!" Sarah blushed slightly. "Hey, you still owe me a celebration with champagne," she teased him.

John stared at her, looking guilty.

"What?" Sarah laughed. "You didn't buy and chill a bottle, or you did and already finished it?"

"Option 3," John said. "I immediately bought one and left it in the car. What can I say… It froze harder than I thought that night…" he had that familiar helpless look in his eyes.

"It exploded in your car?" Sarah asked incredulously.

John nodded speechlessly.

"You don't think that gets you off the hook, do you?" Sarah couldn't help laughing, this was too funny.

"Of course not, as soon as spring starts, I will be able to buy a new bottle, risk-free!" John beamed at her.

"You know, if you buy two bottles we can invite the team, too. We can bring them up to speed who's going to Inverness next time," Sarah suggested.

"Great idea!" John nodded in approval. "I'm sure they'll really enjoy that!"

Chapter 35

As Sarah arrived at Matthew's place in Dartmouth her heart sank. She looked at the house he had designed with such devotion. He'd called it his signature design, showing what he was capable of as an architect. Once inside, she realized that the next few days were going to mean that all of his carefully selected collections were going to be taken apart. His house would never be the same again.

Sarah made her morning coffee in Matthew's fancy machine and sat down on the windowsill to gaze at the view of Halifax harbor, as she had done so often before.

The last time she was here, she already had the hospital bed removed. She was glad about that now. Sarah looked over to 'the big chair with the big ears' near the book wall. That's where he used to sit; contently with a glass of wine, always with a book in his hands. She remembered with a sad smile how very English he had felt, sitting there in his private library.

Matthew's book on Madresfield – the real Brideshead – was still on the coffee table. It was the description of the house and family that Evelyn Waugh had based his Brideshead Revisited novel on. How thrilled Matthew had been to find out that such a family really existed! He had read the book over and over again.

"Madresfield as a house is not nearly as nice as Castle Howard," his voice rang in Sarah's head.

She would always give him the same reply: "But then, no house could ever really live up to Castle Howard, right?"

As his illness progressed he had not registered her teasing anymore and had replied seriously. "Well, both houses had beautiful little chapels," or some other comparison between the two estates.

Sarah regularly checked her cell phone for messages only to be disappointed. No message from Abe. Good grief, the man cost a lot of energy even when he was not around! She decided to dismiss all thoughts of him until she got back, or should she try to call him one last time?
She decided to try to call him and was switched instantly to his voice-mail. His voice-mail was in English. She'd never noticed that before. She did not leave a message - she longed to hear his voice *live*.

An hour later she heard a bleep from deep inside her bag.

> Whatchadoin' Whoyaseein' Whereyagoin'?
> Sorry I couldn't answer the phone; I was at the notary to sign over the house. Computer now disconnected; will try mailing from the Internet café. Abe xxx

Sarah smiled at the first line of the text message; Abe had told her that whenever he called to his brother in the US and his 8-year old nephew Luke answered the phone, this was how they started their conversation.
What the message didn't say, however, was if he had received her e-mail or not. He may not even have seen her last message. *Men!*

Dealing with Matthew's affairs was different than Sarah had imagined. She had braced herself and promised not to study everything she picked up. More and more she felt a deep gratitude for what they had shared together. So many fond memories started popping up in her head that she sometimes smiled to herself, something she hadn't thought possible a month ago. She now knew how unique it was to be able to share this much quality time with such a special friend.

With the music school picking up the violin and everything related to Matthew's classical music collection, the first steps towards breaking up his home were taken.
Sarah decided to leave the rest of the house, especially the

library, intact for as long as possible. It looked so much better with everything still in place. She made appointments with three real estate agents to get a feeling for the value of the house. She would hire the person she thought most fitting for the job. All three realtors were eager to sell the house; it wasn't often that a quality house like this came on the market in such a sought-after waterfront location. Matthew had always loved looking at his 'living picture' as he called the big windows overlooking the harbor.

Sarah intuitively chose the person of whom she expected the most integrity in dealing with the sale of Matthew's house. After all, she would have to hand them a key to show the property to others. Sarah knew she did not want to hear people discussing Matthew's house, comment on it.

She couldn't imagine what it would be like never to be in this, *his*, house again.

She called Paul with the first estimates and explained she had chosen a realtor.

"Wow, Sarah, things are really moving now," he sighed. "We know it has to be done, but it's still strange."

"I know, I was just thinking today, it feels disloyal to Matt to empty out and sell his house."

"Helen asks if you have come across Matthew's Christmas decorations yet," Paul said. "She would like to keep those. The girls always loved their uncle Matt's crazy colorful Christmas tree."

Sarah inhaled sharply; damn… **damn!** The Christmas decorations, she had hoped she could keep some of them; she had such wonderful memories of their Christmas celebrations together.

"I haven't gotten to the attic yet," Sarah exhaled slowly, trying to hide her disappointment. "Of course, I will make sure that all the decorations get to Kemptville. I can imagine the girls loved their uncle Matt's tree. It truly was a sight."

One of the many things Sarah had to do in the house was go through Matthew's clothing. Sarah felt overcome as she entered the immaculate walk-in closet, which still had

200

Matthew's woody aftershave smell. She ran her hand along the sleeves of the blazers. How he had loved this rugged chic look; his English tweeds and brogues. It was funny that he had always been up to speed with the latest in technology; stereo systems, kitchen appliances; you name it, Matthew had it. Not for his wardrobe, though; he wanted classics, which he spent an absolute fortune on. His taste was so specific Sarah wondered whom to please with his clothes. Paul most certainly wouldn't wear any of it. Maybe Marc? But Marc was not quite as slim as Matthew. There was so much clothing, Sarah would try to sell the best pieces online. In trying an international second hand site, she might tap into fans of Matthew's favorite brands. If she did not get any reactions, she'd consider the Salvation Army, or a charity shop.

The hardest part to go through was Matthew's study where he kept all his personal memorabilia. While the rest of the house always looked like a design showroom, Matthew's study was the exception. It looked like a baroque room with a priceless wooden desk. You wouldn't know it, though, for all the stacks and stacks of papers on it. Every piece of furniture in this room had swirls, everywhere there were angels and gold-colored candelabras.

Sarah unlocked the low cabinet that she knew held his diaries. What on earth was she going to do with his diaries? *She* certainly wasn't going to read them and had strict instructions that nobody else was allowed to. She couldn't bring herself to having them destroyed just yet. She would move the cabinet to her apartment and keep it locked until she decided what to do with it. Then there was his computer and his cell phone. She started up his computer and meanwhile charged the battery on his cell phone. Because Matthew was so well organized, it was easy to tell which folders to delete without going through all the details. The folders went by clear names, so the first folder she chucked was "Tim". No need to read through any of that *crap*, Sarah thought bitterly.

Then there was a folder about the Gay community centre, which she also deleted. She knew how much effort Matthew had put in giving guidance to young people struggling the way he had. He had been a member of the board and had written catchy pieces for their newsletter. What a different life he had lived from his family members in Kemptville. They only had had to look up his name online once, and they would have known. However, Matthew knew his family well enough to know they would never really enter the digital era and so he would not be exposed that way.

Whereas the other rooms in the house had nice paintings on the walls, the study walls were completely filled with photographs, postcards, concert tickets and dinner menus – every single item had a memory attached to it.

Chapter 36

"You know," Matthew sighed happily, "already, coming to Vermont is a splendid idea."
"How so?" Sarah laughed, "We just got here!"
"Well, you know what they say in White Christmas, don't you? '*Must be beautiful this time of year, all that snow.*' And were they right or were they right? It truly is picture perfect!" He walked out the door and down the pathway, singing loudly: *"What is Christmas with noo snoow… no White Christmas with nooo snooow."*
"It is now official; you are *crazy*!!" she called after him, laughing.

Sarah stared at the photograph. They had decided to do something sporty for a change – Sarah had opted to take Matthew skiing. He had immediately seen the challenge in this. How silly he had been at times. She looked at the photograph again. There he was, posing with one ski in the air. That was probably the only time he had been able to stand upright on those things. The logo of the Ski school was at the bottom of the photograph.

"So Matt, how did skiing go today?" Sarah asked after the first day in the snow. "Did you learn anything?"
"The beginner's class was just *so* beneath my level," he said coolly. "I know I have only just started, but come on, how hard can it be?" he exclaimed. "I don't think I will be quite good enough to join your class, but let's see tomorrow. I'm quite done with this Idiotenhügel."
"This what?" Sarah snorted.
"Idiotenhügel," Matthew said as though she should have known, "a term used in the land of my ancestors, meaning 'the idiot hill' – bunny slope!" Matthew said in a disgruntled tone.

"A man my age; I looked ridiculous!"

"Where do you pick up this kind of knowledge?" Sarah pushed his shoulder, chuckling.

The next day Matthew had joined a group of youngsters who had bought a ski pass for the day and were going up the mountain. They had decided to follow the black diamond route, way too difficult for the unsuspecting Matthew, of course.

"And still, I was the first one to arrive back at the ski lift, would you believe it?" he boasted as he was telling Sarah that evening.

"Not a word of it!" Sarah said honestly.

"Well, I had fallen a few times already – mighty icy up there," Matthew tried to sound like an expert, "and by the time we get to the level where that little café is, I see that there is a drive way I can take."

"A drive way… skiing, you mean?" Sarah asked, trying to picture it.

"Well, technically I tried to shuffle backwards, but I was scooping up so much snow, I took off my skis."

"You had better be joking! *You took off your skis?*" Sarah yelled at him. "Has nobody explained to you that that is the last thing you do on icy snow?" She sighed deeply; Matthew and his schemes.

"Whatever, Miss Olympian 1932," Matthew said, totally unimpressed. "Anyway, I see two women crying in each other's arms," he got up and posed how he had found them, "I don't want to anymore, I'm too scared," he boohoo'd in imitation. "And you know what? … They'd already called a cab. After a few minutes a mini-van arrives, that can take at least 5 people." Sarah meanwhile couldn't help laughing. He'd survived it, obviously.

"So I said to the damsels in distress I would share their cab if they didn't mind, which they didn't. And, hey presto, we zip down the mountain, skis on the back rack of the mini-van. It was easy-peasy!"

Sarah looked up from the photograph. She remembered how the next day he had traded in his skis for cross-country skis - which wasn't a huge success either.

"You can't even mount a mole hill on those things!" Matthew told her that evening. "I mean, they're not even connected at the back!" He made it sound like he had been given faulty material again.

"Like that time with the canoe, huh, in Keji Park?" Sarah was laughing so loud, her sides were aching.

"I am going to do the shopping mall tour tomorrow," he informed her soberly, "you know, sponsor the economy of the great US of A."

There was no great sportsman lost in Matthew, Sarah thought. The shopping spree, though, had gone exceptionally well.

On his memory-wall you could see Matthew collected the wonders of the world. Posing in front of the Taj Mahal, where he went with a former classmate, or walking the Chinese Wall. He had never, ever, expected he would be in a position to visit them all. But with his business going so well, he could afford to go anywhere he liked. And so he did.

Sarah took down the "VACANCIES" sign that Matthew had taken from the window of a B&B they'd stayed at on Lansdowne Road in Bath.

"My dear girl, I'm so happy that we have been able to combine this trip to England with my new-found love, Roald Dahl," Matthew sighed.

"Here we are again, in Bath in a house that looks just like the one where 'The Landlady' was filmed," he looked around appreciatively. "How *do* we do it?"

"Yes, well, that was an eerie story of his, I thought," Sarah said as she unpacked her bag.

"Hopefully we will get out of here in one piece," Matthew whispered softly in her ear. "You know this landlady of ours, what's her name, looked sort of strange, did you notice?"

"Stop it!" She pushed him away. "You're giving me the creeps." Sarah remembered that evening in Bath Matthew had ordered the Blue Stilton cheese platter with port wine.

"Have you finished reading Uncle Oswald?" he asked her, as if he was checking if she'd done her homework. "Wow, this Uncle Oswald knew about the finer things in life. His favorite was Blue Stilton with Port. So it has to be good."

They tried it and agreed Uncle Oswald turned out to be a good advisor. It was one of the few evenings that she had ever seen Matthew tipsy. He had tried just a tad too much of the Uncle Oswald combo.

Sarah made a promise to herself to stop looking at everything so closely. This way clearing up would take forever.

Sarah carefully put all the postcards he had received from friends and family in different stacks, to give them back to the senders. The dinner menus of the fancy restaurants they'd been to, the photos of their gala balls at Dal-U and their trips together she would give to Paul and Mary. They would love hearing their silly stories.

Chapter 37

Subject: Miss You!

Darling Sarah,
Live from a charming Internet café: Words cannot describe how happy I was to read your reply to my letter. What can I say, besides: let's go steady, or is that too old-fashioned these days?
Newfoundland sounds really nice, but cold, no?
Anyway, I am taking care of the last things with my house, and redecorating my new place. Meanwhile I am slowly starting to look at new career possibilities, but nothing has jumped out at me so far.

My brother is traveling to Portugal for his work and I will be meeting up with him – I haven't seen him forever!
He will be there in a week, after that you and I can make plans!! Can't wait to see you again!
With all my love, yours, Abe, xxxxxxxxxxxxxxxxxxxxx

P.S.: since I cannot go online every minute of every day, I'm sorry if my replies take a while! If there's anything urgent, send me a text message! Please know I am not forgetting about you in the meantime! ;-)) xxx

Finally he had written to her. Sarah's heart jumped for joy that they would be making plans soon. Not long now before they would pick up where they left off. She wondered where it was exactly that they left off, but that approach was too unromantic. She'd just have to be patient; not her strongest point.

Sarah decided to type in a reply immediately. At least he would know she'd seen his message next time he got online.

She had to share her excitement with someone and instantly called Nicky.

"Hey, Nicks, it's me." Sarah's voice immediately gave away her excitement.

"Hi, sis, you sound chipper!" Nicky said.

"Nicky, I have just heard from Abe – we are making plans to see each other soon!" Sarah sighed. "I am so happy about this!"

"Oh, Mouse, that sounds great!" Nicky said. "This alternative quest may not have been such a bad decision after all." She smiled into the telephone. "I mean, dead McFaddens will be dead McFaddens forever, but a real live hunky Dutchman doesn't come along every day."

"I don't know what to do in the meantime." Sarah sounded more frantic now. "He's going to see his brother next week in Portugal and after that he says we'll make plans."

"Is that his brother from Colorado?" Nicky asked.

"Yes, he's only got one brother." Sarah paused. "Nicky, I'm so scared that next time it will not work out."

"Sweetheart, he's already explained why it was hard for him. Goodness me, Sarah, seeing you storm into his house at your normal tornado-speed, it's a miracle he has recovered at all. Takes a strong man to deal with you, you know."

"All right, enough with the correcting your kid sis," Sarah said. "I guess you're right, though. I must have really flipped him by just waltzing in. I can be so stupid sometimes."

"Don't worry, I'm sure it's going to be great. He's seen you at your most, shall we say, *pro-active*, and he still wants to see more of you. Things can only get better from here," Nicky put sister's mind at ease.

"Enough about me and what may become of Abe and me. How are you doing?" Sarah asked.

"Oh, nothing out of the ordinary; busy at work and at school. Nothing overly exciting."

"I wish I had a 'nothing out of the ordinary' like you do with your family," Sarah said with envy. "Okay, Nicks, I'm going to mail Maddy with the news; she keeps asking how things are progressing with 'Kevin'. I wonder if Mr. Costner will ever understand how he is deeply loved by at least one person on this planet."

"Somehow," Nicky said with irony, "I'm quite sure that 'Mr. Costner' is well aware of this."

Re: Subject: I Miss You TOO!

You know, Sarah, your English is not too good either:
"leapfrogging across the ocean!"
Is it the leap that does the frogging; or the frog that does the leaping?
Is it the oink that does the pigging; or the pig that does the oinking?
Abe, xxx ()()()()()()()

Chapter 38

"Hey, Hylke, it really is good to see you again!" Abe gave his brother a hug. "How was your trip?"

"Hi, the trip was comfortable and work at the NATO-base was routine," Hylke smiled thinking about it. "The boys just love to hear that their dad is on a 'secret mission' for the government. I am quite a hit at home since they now think of me as a James Bond kind of figure."

Hylke looked over at his brother.

"You look well, Abe; this love-thing must be agreeing with you." He nudged his brother gently and laughed at the face Abe made at him.

"This is no love-thing; this is the real deal!" Abe protested with a wide grin.

"Well, I'm glad to hear it and I'm looking forward to spending some time with you," Hylke tapped his brother's chest with his fist. "Let me just give Jess a call, which is good now with the time difference and then we'll grab a bite to eat, okay?"

"Give Jess and the boys my love!" Abe called after him.

"Okidoke!"

Abe decided to give Sarah a call to hear her voice.

"Hey, there, sleepyhead!" he said as he heard her croaky voice.

"Abe, I can't believe it's you!" Sarah was instantly awake. "How *are* you?"

"I'm fine, sweetheart," his voice sounded soft, "just wanted to let you know that Hylke and I have arrived safely in Portugal."

"That's great – I love to hear you say 'sweetheart', by the way," she said lazily.

"Then you won't mind hearing me say that I really, really, miss you," Abe added longingly: "I wish I were holding your hand and I could look at your lovely face."

"Oh, Abe, let's agree to see each other soon," Sarah couldn't keep the impatience out of her voice. "Have you given it any more thought?"

"I sure have, I have looked up Newfoundland," he said.

Sarah interrupted him: "And?"

"Definitely too cold!" Abe laughed.

"You ninny, what do you mean: too cold? You should've asked me to come to Portugal!" Sarah said sulkily. "I could have met your brother; I'd have liked that."

"Neh, as soon as you see my brother, you will trade me in," Abe teased her. "I can't take any chances. Not that he'd have you, of course!"

She heard the smile in his voice.

"Oh well, plenty more fish in the sea for me, Mr. Maggagga," Sarah said haughtily.

"Okay, that settles it; nothing near the sea then," Abe's laugh echoed down the line. "Oh, got to go, Hylke is done calling home. We're going to have lunch. Bye, Sarah, *I love you*."

"Bye, Abe, I love and miss you."

"See you soon!" Abe said softly.

"Yes, on the Bahamas?" Sarah suggested, "You, ninny!"

"Too hot!" Abe hung up, still sniggering.

In the days after Abe's call Sarah received a few short text messages from him to say what a great time he was having with his brother and he wished she could have been there. She tried to call him just before her birthday, to say she would be turning 39 and would be entering her 40th year, but couldn't get through. She couldn't remember having mentioned that May 19th was her birthday.

"Shall we leave out the 'happy birthday to you' this time?" Sarah asked as the whole family gathered in the big garden at her mother's house. "It doesn't feel like a birthday today."

To turn 39, the age Matthew had never reached, was heart-wrenching. She had started to feel really down on the eve of her birthday and the thought had not left her the entire day. She was grateful that everybody was there; Tracy, Nicky and Jack and the boys – who were growing into young men, Marc and Deirdre, Maddy only on Skype, unfortunately. She had so hoped to talk to Abe.

Sarah had received very sweet cards from Paul & Helen and one from Mary with a bunch of red roses. Those dear people, thinking of her on a day like this. It must be hard on them, too, seeing the world go on.

Beatrice and Thierry couldn't leave the inn, but had sent her a silver bead with hearts for her bracelet.

To our darling Sarah,
May this bead remind you of the friendship we will share forever. The two hearts signify our hearts being with you always.
We're thinking of you on this special and sad day.
Love, Thierry & Bee, xxxxx

How great these two always were to her. Sarah wondered if she had given them enough attention of late. She had been so preoccupied. They had been such great friends for such a long time already.

"Have you heard from Abe?" Marc asked her as he put his arm around her.

"No, I heard from him when he arrived in Portugal, but I don't exactly know how long he is going to stay there; silly of me not to ask," Sarah said, deep in thought.

"You mean, he hasn't called you on your *birthday*?" Marc was starting to get some doubts about this Dutchman who claimed to like his sister so much.

"No, I did try to call him," Sarah said quickly. "I honestly don't think I told him today's my birthday. I also don't know when his birthday is exactly, I only know he recently turned 40, I think before we met." She was starting to get defensive with all these questions about Abe, partly because she wished she could answer them herself.

They went out to dinner to one of Sarah's favorite restaurants. She normally enjoyed the lively atmosphere, but now thought it was loud and crowded. Somehow she found it difficult to relax.

Over the next days Sarah tried to call Abe a few more times, but there was no answer. She would get his voicemailsaying he couldn't be reached. Her e-mail had gone unanswered for quite a while now. She decided to send him a text message instead.

> Dearest Abe, I have been trying to call you a number of times. I am also not getting a reply to my e-mail. I am getting worried about you. Are you still in Portugal? Please reply a.s.a.p. Love you, Sarah, xxx

Bleep!

Sarah heard after a few minutes and sighed with relief. Her relief was unjustified though; all the message said was:

> **The following message to receiver: Makkinga, Abe, could not be delivered:**
> Dearest Abe, I have been trying to call you a number of times. I am also not getting a reply to my e-mail. I am getting worried about you. Are you still in Portugal? Please reply a.s.a.p. Love you, Sarah, xxx

Sarah muttered under her breath: "For crying out loud, Abe Makkinga, why can't you be reached?" She tried to calm herself and looked through her e-mails to see how long it had been since she had sent her last message. How thoughtless of him not to reply. Or maybe his phone was out of order?

Chapter 39

"You know what you need?" Janet said to her in the office a few days later. "You need to get over this Abe dude. What is he playing at, anyway? He pulls you close and then he lets go again," Janet gestured with her hands. "He's done that a few times now. If you ask me, I think he has commitment issues." Sarah swallowed her instant response: '*Well, nobody asked you!*' Instead of taking her foul mood out on Janet, she nodded over her coffee.

"Me, I am considering going back online to start some Internet dating," Janet stated brightly. "I mean, it can't hurt now, can it? It's been ages since my divorce and I'm about ready to prove that not all men are..." Janet stopped talking as she saw the expression on Sarah's face. "Oh Sarah, don't mind me; I'm babbling as usual."

Slowly Sarah looked up from her coffee.

"Janet, when you're right, you're right," she smiled thinly. "I'm just not ready for filling out my own advertising. I have never done that before. Besides, it's just too soon after losing Matt and, shall we say, 'misplacing' Abe?"

Janet couldn't help laughing. From what she had heard of him, this Abe was quite a tall article to misplace.

"You know," Janet said with a concerned look, "it sounds like you should be more careful with your men; you go around losing and misplacing them. At the rate you're going, no wonder none of them work out!" she said innocently.

Sarah gave Janet a surprised look and went limp with laughter. You had to admire Janet for having the talent to make things so literal and so practical. Janet was also one of those people who could get away with this. Any other person, Sarah would have bitten their head off.

"Oh, Janet, I wish we could have a glass of wine together after work," Sarah said, still hiccupping. "For the next few days, however, I am going to be moving into Matthew's house. I can get so much more work done if I stay there."

"Wow, that sounds heavy!" Janet went back to being serious.

"Yes it will be," Sarah sighed. "On the weekend, his brother Paul is coming with a truck to pick up some of Matt's things. The realtor is getting a lot of requests for viewings, so at some point this house is going to get sold and needs to be emptied."

Just before Sarah left for Dartmouth, she received a letter from Abe. Sarah read it with extremely mixed feelings. She had gone back and forth too often now.

My dearest Sarah,

With this letter, I am sending you all my love from Horta, Portugal. I hope it does not take too long for this message to be delivered.

We are enjoying ourselves massively by gawking at the many gigantic ships in the Horta harbor here. Hylke was called back for work for a few more days, during which I have hiked along the coast.

The weather is not as nice as we had expected. Portugal always sounds so lovely and warm to us Dutch, but no such luck — it's clouded and foggy. I thought it would be nice to send you another old-fashioned letter, instead of an e-mail. E-mail is so flighty and I don't feel comfortable typing my messages of love from loud and impersonal Internet cafés. Letters to me have much more value.

We are having really nice long talks, Hylke and me. Hylke was saying how much he admires our parents for the way they have raised us; now that he is raising two boys of his own with Jessica. Jessica was brought up Catholic and we were raised pretty much without a religion, but with very strong values. I never really thought about this, but it made me proud to realize this.

I have told Hylke all about you and what we have been through together. He agrees with you, you should have come to Portugal so you two could have met up. I hope the day will soon come that you can meet my small family. I also cannot wait to meet yours, Sarah, you speak of them so lovingly. Let me tell you once again, that what I feel for you is real. Thinking back to our time in Scotland and also to the better moments in Friesland; I have never felt this way before. I wish to be near you as soon as I can, get to know so much more about you. I love you — see you soon?

Abe xxxxxxxxx

Yeah, indeed; what she felt for him was real, too! She put the letter down on her dining table and decided not to reply. She had more important things to take care of now. Abe was in no hurry to meet her. She was *certainly* in no hurry to get back to him.

Chapter 40

A few days later, Janet stormed into her office with a smile from ear to ear.

"Sarah, Sarah," she said, out of breath, "I have been asked on a blind date for lunch this afternoon!" her excitement abundantly clear.

"How did you do that so quickly?" Sarah responded puzzled more than happy. "We only talked about it a few days back?"

"Well, not everybody is willing to sit and wait five weeks to hear from a guy like you are!" Janet teased. "This is the Internet age, you know," she said, "things don't go by stage coach anymore."

Sarah thought back to Abe's handwritten letter and couldn't help smiling – exactly what she had told him!

"Yes, I know all that," Sarah said impatiently, "but I mean, what do you really know about this man?"

"I know absolutely nothing, which is why I need your help!" Janet cried in exasperation.

"My help?" Sarah looked surprised. "I'm not going with you, if that's what you mean! You know I don't believe in this Internet stuff. People can tell you whatever they like."

"Sarah, you only need to come with me to the restaurant," Janet pleaded. "You can sit at another table where you can see me. If the guy shows up and is nice I will give you a sign so you leave after you finished your lunch."

"What if he's a freak?" Sarah shuddered visibly.

"That's where you come in!" Janet said. "If he is a freak, I will signal to you to call me on my cell, upon which I can leave with the excuse of an emergency."

"I don't know about this…" Sarah said doubtfully. "What are you planning to do; hold up signs? CALL ME – LEAVE US," Sarah raised her hands in turn mimicking holding up the sign cards. "I don't know, Janet, he just might notice!" She chuckled.

"Please do this for me, Sarah, he sounds really, really nice, this one…" Janet was now to the point of begging. "Please! I will pay for your lunch!"

"All right, but only because you're paying," she winked at Janet. "And don't think I'm going to enjoy this," Sarah couldn't keep from adding. "Tell me, what are the signals?"

They waited at the restaurant for what seemed like forever. Sarah had meanwhile ordered lunch for herself. Janet's blind date was not in a hurry to get there, apparently. Sarah frequently looked over at Janet's table and every time Janet was still sitting there on her own.

She texted Janet, who had her phone on the table as agreed.

> My poor misguided Janet, can it be that there is a slight possibility that maybe you have been somewhat stood up??

Janet picked up her phone and gave her a dorky smile and stuck out her tongue at Sarah.

Bleep!

> Whatchadoin' Whoyaseein' Whereyagoin'?
> Did you receive my letter from Horta? I miss you, love,
> Abe xxx

WHAT?!? Sarah stared at her phone. She decided to immediately reply to him.

> Hi Abe, Sorry, I am on a blind date at the moment. Gotta Go! Sarah

So what if it wasn't completely true?? It was true enough! She continued eating in silence with an angry stare and looked over at Janet's table; nope, still no blind date by the looks of it.

Sarah turned around to signal to Janet she was going back to the office. Just at that moment, someone passed Sarah's table and blocked her view. Janet disappeared out of sight. Sarah moved over to look over at Janet as the person blocking her view moved back. *What the...*
"Blind date, huh?" Sarah heard someone say and her fork with the last bite of salad stopped midway. *No way!*
She looked up and looked straight into the eyes of the man she had been cursing for the past weeks.
"Abe… what... how...?" Sarah stammered, completely dumbfounded.
Abe bent over and kissed her softly. He sat down opposite her at the table. Sarah literally gasped for air, totally speechless.
"It's nice to be surprised by spontaneous plans, isn't it?" Abe beamed at her.
Sarah stared into his eyes in disbelief. The finalists in the tug of war in her head were 'ecstatic happiness' and 'total anger'; they fought and it remained a tie.
"I never imagined there was anything to silence you!" Abe's eyes were twinkling.

A second later Janet walked over to their table.
"Enjoy your lunch, Sarah!" she rubbed friend's shoulder briefly. She was about to walk out the door, when it dawned on Sarah.
"You *knew* about this?" Sarah turned around to the door and gaped at her.
"Yes indeed, since early this morning, I confess, I did!" Janet looked over to Abe, who winked at her.
"You mean to tell me you were in on this and did not tell me?" Her level of irritation unmistakable.
"Didn't I mention this to you this morning?" Janet asked innocently. "The blind date was divided; the blind part was for me – the date part was for you."

Abe laughed at Janet's creative explanation.

Sarah abruptly turned back to Abe. "You think this is quite funny do you?"

"I do, actually!" Abe made no attempt to hide his pleasure.

As Janet walked out the door, she called over her shoulder to Sarah: "Don't hurry back to the office, John knows you might not be coming back!"

Janet waved briefly at Abe, before she left and called out: "Nice to meet you Abe; enjoy!"

"Oh Sarah, do say something!" Abe had ordered a cup of coffee for himself. "I have been planning to come and see you. And you did say, close to Nova Scotia," Abe said simply, "I couldn't really get much closer, could I?" He was teasing her, only aggravating the situation. "Maybe I should have brought your e-mail as proof?"

Abe smiled widely at Sarah as he waved a hand in the air, remembering Sarah standing at his own front door in Friesland. The irony did not land with Sarah and she did not reply. In Sarah's head she only heard Janet say that John also knew about this. The whole office was probably enjoying this scene with input from Janet. How embarrassing!

"I came to see you at your apartment, but did not find you there for two days in a row, so I called your office," Abe tried to explain. "I asked for your assistant, but she was out. I was then put through to Janet, who put two and two together. Or rather, one and one."

"I am staying in Matt's house at the moment," was all the information Sarah could muster.

"Oh, right," Abe said, "I'm sorry Sarah; we do seem to have incredibly poor timing."

Sarah briefly nodded.

"Tell you what," Abe broke another silence, "I'm staying at a small hotel – do you know the Lambeth Inn?" Sarah nodded again.

"If and when you're ready to meet with me," Abe said with a shy smile, "give me a call. My cell is working again."

He got up from the table, caressed her cheek and walked out.

Sarah sat there with her last bite of salad still in front of her, completely overwhelmed and undecided about what to do.

Chapter 41

As soon as the phone rang Abe almost dove toward the table to pick it up.

"Abe, it's me." *Darn, wasn't her*.

"How did it go with Sarah?" Hylke asked excitedly. He obviously expected a whopper of a success story.

"Geez, Hylke, I really don't know." Abe raked through his thick gray hair with his hand.

"What do you mean '*you don't know*'?" Hylke said in disbelief. "Haven't you seen her yet?"

"I have only seen her briefly this afternoon and she really didn't look too happy to see me," Abe said in bitter disappointment.

"Imagine that! After all the trouble you've taken to go and see her!" Hylke swallowed the rest of his opinion on the matter.

"I know," Abe sounded worried. "In retrospect, I do think I should have warned her in advance. Anyway, can't be helped now. I have left her my contact details. What do I do if she doesn't call?"

"Oh, I'm sure she'll call," Hylke said reassuringly. "She wanted to get together as much as you did, didn't she?"

"Yes, well at least I thought so..." Abe wasn't so sure anymore.

"Let me know if you hear anything, Abe." Hylke said in a deflated tone.

"Will do… And Hylke?" Abe paused to get his brother's attention, "thanks again for the great time."

Abe couldn't see Hylke's smile on the other side of the line, but heard him say: "We should definitely get together more often, I had a ball."

Abe waited at the hotel the rest of the afternoon and evening, but there was no call from Sarah. Wow, he must have really blown it and he didn't understand what had changed so dramatically. The next morning Abe decided to play tourist and went to the Cable Wharf to see if he could catch a harbor tour.

He might as well see something of Halifax now that he was here. He checked his cell phone – yep, still working; nope, no messages.

As he boarded the ferry for the tour he wondered how long he would stay in Halifax waiting for a message from Sarah. What if she didn't call? What if her feelings for him had changed and he had come all this way for nothing? He pushed the thought from his mind and walked over to the railing.

"It's a good time of year to be in Nova Scotia," a lady standing next to Abe at the railing was saying to him.

"Yes, indeed, it is very nice. The sun is surprisingly warm, actually," Abe said in a friendly voice.

"So, where are you from?" she asked him.

"From Holland," Abe replied.

"Oh, *Holland*, I love Holland!" the lady exclaimed happily. "I have been a few times and absolutely *adored* it!"

"Really?" Abe was getting prepared for a standard tulip and windmill conversation, but much to his surprise the lady replied: "Yes, my father fought in Europe in the second World War, and we went to see the family that took care of him after his platoon marched into Holland."

"That's amazing," Abe said gently. "We Dutch owe so much to the allied forces liberating us."

"Well, the hospitality that we receive when we're over there is just so warm," the lady chatted on. "My father passed away a couple of years ago, but we've decided to stay in touch between the families. They live in a town called Eeeduh, spelled E-D-E."

"That is a nice part of Holland, Ede." Abe smiled kindly at her.

"I especially love going to that Open Air Museum," she was saying, "all these quaint little houses and I just love that little cheese factory."

"The Open Air Museum, wow," Abe was obviously enjoying the conversation, "I can't remember when I've been there. We used to go on a bus trip from school."

"So what brings you to Halifax, business?" she asked, studying him openly.

"Yes, here on business and now I get to dink off to do some

sightseeing," he winked cheekily at her. "I will be leaving in a few days," Abe said without conviction, trying to hide the question marks he had for himself.

"Well, one tip I can give you," the lady said, "is to go see the Titanic graves at Fairview Cemetery - the graves form the shape of a ship – and there is the grave of Jack Dawson, you know, from the movie. I can also advise the Maritime Museum where the maiden voyage of the Titanic is explained and many artifacts are on display."

Abe thanked the lady and couldn't help but smile at the irony; the history of a sinking ship seemed very well suited for his situation and mood right now.

After the tour Abe went to have lunch at the Wharf. It really was a great place. Abe enjoyed the atmosphere of the city; it was very friendly and laid-back. He looked around at the traditional wooden houses. Great photography material for after lunch, Abe decided.

Bleep!

> Whatchadoin' Whoyaseein' Whereyagoin'?
> Can we make plans for tonight? Sarah

Abe answered directly:

> Havin' lunch / Seein' whales / No plans for tonight for the moment!
> I'd love to see you, Abe

Bleep!

> Really whales? Sorry I'm missing that.
> Pick you up at the Lambeth at 7pm; dress casual. Sarah xxx

Ah, the kisses were back; surely that must be a good sign!

Abe smiled into his mug of coffee. They would see each other tonight and go on a proper date. He had so much to tell her.

> Yes, Ma'am – ready at 7pm sharp, can only dress casual, didn't bring anything fancy. Abe, xxx

Sarah arrived early at the Lambeth. She was nervous at the prospect of seeing him again. The tug of war in her heart was eventually won by the excitement of seeing his face. He had come all this way to see her. That was big, surely? Right?

"Hi Abe," Sarah's voice sounded shy and she really did not know how to compose herself. She started to say "Sorry..."
"No need to say sorry," Abe meant it. "I'm just happy to see you."
Sarah wanted nothing more than to jump at him, shake him and ask: *'what took you so long?'* but decided against it. She desperately wanted to know, but what if she couldn't live with the answer? The information would have to come from him.
"So, what are the plans for the evening?" Abe asked.
"I was thinking of taking you out to dinner," Sarah suggested, "and we could have a stroll around Halifax, if you like."
"Sounds great!" Abe replied with enthusiasm. "I like what I've seen of it so far."
Sarah did not reply instantly.
"I'm taking you to a little Italian restaurant," she said, "sort of like the one we went to in Glasgow."
"Wonderful," Abe smiled at her but Sarah did not look up, "I could do with a large basket of garlic bread, how 'bout you?"
Sarah turned around to Abe and gave him a light kiss. "See, that won't taste half as good after the garlic bread!" She smiled at him. Abe was taken by surprise by this and took her hand.
"Have I said I am really happy to see you in one piece?" Sarah asked him as they walked to the restaurant. Abe did not take the bait, however.
"I'm happy if you're happy," was all he said.

Chapter 42

Over dinner initially they didn't get beyond small talk and what had been going on with Abe's house and Sarah's job.

"Are you sorry the house is sold?" Sarah asked.

"Nope, I think you have seen that I didn't feel very much at home there anymore," Abe replied, struggling how to address the situation back in Friesland.

"So, what's been happening with you?" Abe asked.

"Oh, the visit from the Scottish team was really good," was all Sarah said.

"I'm glad for you," Abe said.

Another long and uncomfortable silence fell between them.

"So, shall I order the wine this time, Mr. Marlboro Man?" Sarah asked with a shy smile.

"As long as it's not too oaky, please!" Abe looked at Sarah to gage her reaction. She did not pick up on his remark.

Over coffee Abe decided to address his questions head on. He decided they had now been playing 'hide and seek' long enough.

"You said you are staying at Matthew's house?" Abe said. "I never really fully understood what the situation was between you and Matthew..."

Sarah was caught off guard by this and swallowed hard, trying to avoid Abe's eyes. She remembered his kind blue-gray eyes; they had haunted her over the past weeks. Now she saw how friendly and inviting they really were. She also saw that he got a nice deep suntan in Portugal, which made his eyes an even brighter blue.

"I am staying at his house, because I am taking care of his estate," was all the information Sarah volunteered.

"That's the practical side of things," Abe kept looking at her, "that's not really what I meant."

"What can I say, Abe," Sarah sighed deeply, "the situation with Matthew was extremely complicated."

"Complicated, how?" Abe felt like he was interrogating her, but he had to know.

"Complicated because we were very close," Sarah said breathlessly.

"To be honest, Sarah, that doesn't sound too complicated to me."

"I loved Matthew pretty much from the moment we met!" Sarah blurted out. She paused before she added softly: "For all intents and purposes he was the love of my life."

"Did he love you?" Abe almost whispered the question. He sensed he needed to tread carefully. Sarah looked as though she was about to start crying.

"He did love me as an important part of his life, but not as his life partner," she said.

"And you were in love with him all that time," Abe concluded.

"No, not really 'in love' with him," Sarah swallowed. "There was just a very deep sense of belonging there; he and I did everything together."

"Oh," Abe only partly understood.

"Matthew was gay, Abe," Sarah finally said.

"I already wondered about that," Abe replied simply. "You know, that is nothing to be ashamed of," he said sincerely.

"Maybe in Holland that is how it is seen," Sarah said defensively. "In Matthew's case he did feel very guilty and ashamed. He never told his family and only a number of people here in Halifax really knew."

"That must have been very difficult for him," Abe said, nodding in understanding.

"It's just that his parents were, his mother still is a devoted Catholic," Sarah sighed. "Matt told me his father used to say the most horrible things about gay people, never realizing his own son was gay."

"Geez, that does sound painful," Abe admitted as he saw the gravity of this.

"Whenever the topic of homosexuality was discussed on TV or something, Matt's father would shout it was forbidden in the bible."

"Of course, there are very old cultures where same-sex relations were quite common, such as in ancient Greece," Abe said patiently.

"You know, people underestimate how difficult it was for Matthew to be different," Sarah said sadly. "If he'd had a choice to be a 'normal' heterosexual man, he would have taken it in a heartbeat. I have seen up close how big the struggle is. He did not accept himself for a long time, if ever, really."

"Well, at least he had you," Abe almost whispered the words, realizing how deep the mourning for Sarah must be.

"I was one of the few people he ever really trusted with his secret," Sarah said with a combination of pride and loneliness. "He and I had such a special bond." She paused for a moment. "He was my better half and I was his... Though some part of me has always known that if Matthew would find the love of his life, things would be very different. I knew that my commitment towards him was deeper... I guess that's why I fled from Friesland."

Abe did not reply.

"It's strange I accepted this imbalance with Matthew," Sarah nervously turned the ring on her hand. "Normally I firmly believe that relationships need to be give and take – you can't only make withdrawals from the human bank accounts we have, you have to deposit too."

"How long had you known Matthew?" Abe asked, taking her hand.

"Since University, so more than half my life."

"Such a young life, still," Abe said.

"And yet, so scarred already."

"A very sweet Canadian girl once said to me," Abe looked her in the eyes, "that the loss of a beloved one turns into feelings of gratitude, given enough time."

She smiled through her tears: "She must have been a very smart Canadian girl!"

"Did you want to walk around some more?" Abe asked as they walked out of the restaurant. The Friday evening had brought many people to down-town Halifax.

"No, that's okay, thanks." Sarah looked exhausted. "If you don't mind I'll just pick up the car at the Lambeth and then drive to Matt's house. I took the day off tomorrow. Matthew's brother, Paul, will be meeting me there early in the morning to collect a number of things."

With a pang she remembered that all of Matthew's beautiful Christmas ornaments would be going too.

"It must be confrontational for you to deal with all of his affairs," Abe spoke softly.

Sarah nodded; glad he was trying to understand.

"Abe, this was a really lovely evening. Thank you so much for listening to me. I am happy to see you again. How long will you be able to stay in Nova Scotia?"

She looked up at him, wondering what he would say next.

"I have an open return," Abe said casually, "so I am in no hurry. You said we would need some time, so time we've got plenty of."

"Thanks, Abe, let's make plans for tomorrow afternoon," Sarah said.

"Oh, tomorrow afternoon? I have already made plans," he said seriously. "I was advised to go to the Maritime Museum and the Titanic Cemetery."

"Who advised you that?" Sarah looked up in surprise.

"Oh, some wonderful girl I met on the harbor tour today," he remembered with a smile. "I decided to join the 'getting in touch with the locals' program."

"Is she taking you?" Sarah felt a hint of jealousy.

"No, Sarah, she was a lovely 'golden' girl of about 60 years old," he laughed.

"Oh, you wretched man, you!" She pounded his chest with her fists.

Abe looked down with a smile and took both her hands.

"So, yes, let's plan something for tomorrow afternoon. I'd like that." He pulled her close and held her for a few moments.

Sarah felt that with Abe around, she would feel very safe.

The problem was, you never knew if and when he would be around.

Chapter 43

"Hi Abe, it's me," Sarah called Abe the next day. "Paul is just putting the last pieces into the truck, so I'm ready to make plans," she smiled as she said it. "This gives us more time than I had expected."

"Hi sweetheart, what would you suggest?" Abe asked.

"Well, I'm still in Dartmouth, but I was thinking: why don't we take a drive along the South Shore," she suggested. "There are some spectacular views along what's called 'The Lighthouse Route'. I'm sure you will like it."

"Sounds terrific!"

"Okay, I'll pick you up in about an hour. Dress code is: extremely casual."

"I have brought just the thing. See you soon."

"Abe?"

"Yes, Sarah?"

"I'm *sooo* happy you came to Nova Scotia," she shrieked into the phone.

"Me too... Now, go get started," he instructed playfully. "I love the audio sound, but would prefer the live image to go with it!"

"Okay, see you later," Sarah said with a happy smile.

"Okay, rainbow eyes... I'll let you go."

Sarah turned from the window in the Matthew's living room to find her tote bag and saw Paul standing behind her.

"Hey, Paul, did you get everything in the truck?" she asked.

"Sarah," his voice sounded strange.

"Yes?" Sarah kept looking around for her bag and her car keys.

"Sarah!" Paul said louder to catch Sarah's attention.

"Yes," Sarah looked over at him.

"Who's Tim?" Paul asked in a thickened voice, holding up a package.

"What?" Sarah instantly focused on Matthew's brother. She did not recognize what he was holding.

"**Who... is... Tim?**" Paul asked, his anger obviously rising.

"Tim was a friend of Matthew's, from the quartet," Sarah inhaled sharply.

"Really?" he asked cynically. "A friend?"

Sarah's breath caught in her throat.

"What do you have there, Paul?" she asked carefully.

"How stupid do you think we are?" Paul glared at Sarah with contempt.

"I don't think…"

"Peasants from the country, the hinterlands, huh?" Paul interrupted her, clearly livid.

Sarah turned around at a loss for a response, mumbling an excuse and fled to the kitchen.

Abe, sorry, something's come up, I need to reschedule till tomorrow!
Sorry, sorry!
Sarah

Bleep!

Sarah, are you okay? Call me!
Abe, xxx

Sarah did not answer Abe. She had to get back to the living room. She looked at Paul, gazing out at the harbor. She could not find the right words.

"Paul," she tried, "Matthew didn't…"

"Is this the reason he shut us out completely?" Paul stared at Sarah hatefully.

"What do you mean, Paul?" Sarah honestly did not understand.

"All this time…" he said angrily. "Who else knew?"

"Only a few people," Sarah stopped, not wanting to give away what Matthew had kept to himself for so long.

Paul sank onto Matthew's couch and covered his face in his hands.

Sarah sat down next to him.

"You know, Paul," she said softly, "Matthew has always wanted to protect you and your parents."

"Oh, please, spare me the…" Paul swallowed hard.

"No, Paul," she continued bravely, "it's true. He always said he feared he would not be accepted for who he was."

"Helen and I have suspected it for a long time," Paul said, staring at the harbor through the window. "We always thought he would tell us if he met someone."

"You know, Matthew truly and honestly loved Tim – loved him for years and years."

"But why didn't he tell us, me?" Paul choked.

"Tim was not a free man, Tim was already in a committed relationship when Matthew and he met," she explained, hoping Paul would understand. "And even if that was not the case, I wonder if Matt would have dared to tell your parents."

"Who else knew?" Paul pushed again.

"A few friends here in Halifax," Sarah said, not sounding too convincing.

"So, everybody but his family, huh?" Paul concluded. "How stupid you must all think we are!" He bit at her again.

"Matthew never called any of you stupid. He just refused to burden you and your family with his struggle," Sarah studied Paul's defeated demeanor. "Do you think your mother knows?" she asked carefully.

"I honestly don't know," he sighed deeply, "I don't know…"

"What will happen if she finds out?" Sarah sounded worried.

"I think my mother will be less of a problem than my father; why did he not tell us after Dad passed away?" He wiped his nose with the back of his hand.

"Matt did always say that your father would not have accepted him for who he was…"

Paul nodded in understanding and paused. Finally, he said: "Matt was right."

"Do you think we need to tell your mother?" She fervently hoped that would not be necessary. Otherwise Matthew's struggle for most of his life would have been pointless.

Paul whispered: "I don't think we should. God, this is so messed up! My own brother! Why did he not talk to me?" Paul slowly put the package on the table marked:
'Letters – TIM'.
"You know, Paul, he himself never really accepted being gay and out of love for all of you, he did not confront you with it." Paul dropped his head at the word 'gay'. Now it was out in the open, he couldn't bear it. He nodded briefly as if to find the courage to get up, picked up his keys, looked at Sarah with intense sadness and turned to walk out the door.
Sarah wept after Paul left. All this time, Matthew had fought this, and now that he could not defend or explain himself anymore, his secret was brutally uncovered.

Bleep!

> Hi Abe, sorry, I'm too overcome to talk. I'll tell you tomorrow. Sarah, xxx

Chapter 44

"Hey, Sarah," Abe said as he saw her at the reception desk, waiting. He studied her closely.

"Hi Abe…"

"Are you all right? What happened yesterday?"

"I'll tell you about it in the car, okay?" Sarah looked up at Abe. He saw her reddened eyes and knew something was seriously wrong.

As they got in the car, Sarah sighed. "Sorry about yesterday."

"What happened?" Abe asked again.

"Matthew's brother, Paul, found out what Matthew had been hiding from his family all this time. He found some very personal letters."

"Oh, no!"

"This is so sad," she said, staring through the windshield. "His whole life Matthew tried to hide it. His brother and sister-in-law suspected it all along; they just knew."

"How did his brother respond?"

"He was absolutely furious," she said pensively, "and deeply hurt that Matt hadn't talked to him."

"I can imagine," Abe nodded, "he only had one brother."

"Anyway, we don't think Matthew's mother knows," Sarah added with some relief.

"Well, maybe she knows and never voiced it either," Abe said.

"I didn't mean to cancel yesterday," she said and took Abe's hand.

"I wish I could show you all the picturesque little places along the coast," Sarah said as she started the car, "but I have a surprise for you this evening, that won't work if we stop at each place."

"A surprise?" Abe asked curiously, "I thought you and I were all 'surprised out' for at least the next five years."

"No this is no biggy; it's a mild surprise," she said with a smile, patting his hand reassuringly. "Only about 2 on the Richter scale. One I do think you will like this time. At least your ex-wife is not expected there."

Abe burst out laughing, remembering the sight of Sarah, soaking in her shoes holding up the card, and Annemarie and Erik looking at him with bemusement.

"So let's take a drive along the South Shore; so many lovely places, Chester, Mahone Bay, Lunenburg. We'll take a driving tour now, so you can see how pretty it all is, and we'll really visit them some other time."

"Okay, can't wait!"

"And then let's take a walk on Louis Head Beach," Sarah injected the next part of the plan. "I know a great restaurant where we can have lunch. Do you like lobster?"

"Absolutely *love* lobster," he said brightly. "We don't get to taste it in Holland unless we spend an absolute fortune."

"You know here even the fast food places do lobster burgers?" She chuckled.

"No way!" Abe stared at her in disbelief.

"Way!"

"This town, Liverpool, is where you will find my favorite lighthouse in all of Nova Scotia – the Fort Point Lighthouse," Sarah said as she turned off the road into an almost empty parking lot. "Isn't it just the prettiest little white thing you've ever seen?" She pointed over as she got out of the car. "Its shape is all boxy and has little extended roofs on all sides, and the light sticks out at the front."

"I now understand why you looked at the Hollum lighthouse in surprise." Abe put his hand over his eyes. "It must be at least more than twice as high as this one."

He followed Sarah to the other side of the lighthouse where they chose a bench on the waterfront.

"Don't you just love it?" She asked dreamily. "I could sit here all day listening to the waves crashing on to the boulders."

"I could indeed sit here all day with you," Abe put his arm around her and nudged her neck.

"But, no time like the present; we have to keep moving!" Sarah pecked his cheek, jumped up and walked back to the car. Abe raised his hands in surrender. "I'm about to go on strike here, with this heavy schedule you burden me with!" he complained with a sigh.

Their walk along the white sandy beach at Louis Head was as romantic as their walk on Ameland. There was one main difference with Ameland.
"Good Lord! This water is *freezing*!" Abe cried out after he had run in up to his knees.
"I told you not to go in, unless you wanted to dive up your own lobster."
"You never warned me it would be this cold! And at my age – I could have been *killed*!" Abe was obviously enjoying his shenanigans.
"I had never taken you for a wimp, but now I know the truth," she shook her head discontentedly. "Just in time too."
"A wimp, huh?"
"An OLD wimp at that!" Sarah said with a deep frown, "that's twice as bad!"
"To think I came all this way to be called an *old wimp*." He raised his hands in despair. "There is no kindness left in this world, I swear."
"Okay, Wimpy, let's walk back to the car – I'm taking you to lunch in Lockeport," she grabbed his hand and pulled him forward. "Come on, let's get you that lobster burger!"

"After lunch, I will take you to where the surprise is," Sarah teased him, clearly enjoying she was now in the driver seat.
"Woman, you are hurrying me around this island like there is no tomorrow," Abe said, faking tiredness. "I feel like a tourist with only one day to see all of Nova Scotia."
"I'll have you know, that I am trying to give you an impression of my home country," she said earnestly.
"But I didn't come all this way only for Nova Scotia, did I?" he said.
"Hey, I didn't exactly come for Friesland, remember?" She

could laugh about it now.

"I will be better as soon as my that my feet will start defrosting."

Sarah was starting to understand that Abe often shouldn't be taken too seriously, which made a nice change. She loved being with him, but something in the back of her mind still wondered about him.

"Next stop: Shelburne!" Sarah got in the car and waited for Abe to get in.

"What's in Shelburne?" he asked.

"Well, not literally in Shelburne, but you'll see," Sarah said mysteriously.

Chapter 45

On the drive south to Shelburne Sarah noticed Abe had gone quiet. Sarah looked to her side a few times but he did not seem to notice. He only stared out of the window.

"Not long now before we get to the surprise," she said to him.

"Okay," Abe said, with surprisingly little enthusiasm.

They drove past another marvelous lighthouse, where Sarah pulled over into the parking lot of a small hotel.

"Sarah, can I ask..." Abe started, but stopped mid-sentence as he saw two people storming out. Sarah quickly got out of the car.

"Sarah, how great to see you again so soon!!" Thierry and Beatrice hugged her warmly.

"Guys, can I introduce you to Abe?" Sarah pointed to a bewildered Abe in the car.

She walked to the other side of the car and knocked on the window. She raised her voice: "Abe, these are my good friends Thierry and Beatrice." She turned perkily towards her friends and said in a voice, sweeter than maple syrup: "He's a bit shy... He's at that age…"

"Welcome to the Bee&Tree Inn," Beatrice said with a hospitable smile, as Abe got out and shook hands with Thierry and Beatrice. "Pleasure to meet you," he said politely.

Sarah was surprised at his look. No kidding, there it was again; that shy, almost guarded, look.

"So this is Bee and this is Tree," Sarah said pointing at Beatrice and Thierry.

As they walked over to the Inn, Abe held Sarah back for a moment.

"This is the surprise, right?" Abe asked her furtively.

"Yep, this is it," she said reassuringly. "You said you wanted to meet my family and my friends. I thought we'd start with my best friends. What did you think, I'd kidnap you to a hotel and then what?" Sarah asked.

Abe relaxed visibly and followed her in. Sarah looked around at him totally puzzled. What a strange man.

"Abe, what a surprise to turn up in Nova Scotia!" Beatrice was saying. "You thought you'd get even with Sarah, did you?" She smiled warmly at him.

"I can see that you are well informed, Beatrice," Abe winked at Sarah.

"Oh, call me Bee, please," Beatrice said.

Abe beamed at Beatrice. "Our Queen in Holland is called Beatrice – well Beatrix; we'll have to call her Queen Bee!"

Beatrice laughed. "I'm sure she'd appreciate it!"

"Can I pour you a drink, Abe?" Thierry asked.

"I don't know, Sarah," he looked over to her, "shall I drive this evening?"

"I will drive back, don't worry – if we take the highway we will be back quicker," she said hastily.

Beatrice and Thierry had offered to give them a room, or rooms, so they could stay. With Friesland in mind, however, Sarah did not want to create another awkward situation and had declined the offer.

"In that case, Thierry, I would like a beer," Abe said gratefully. "Sarah's been dragging me around your island at the speed of light."

Beatrice chuckled at his silliness.

"I'll join you, we don't have any guests tonight, it being early season," Thierry said.

"I would very much like to see your place," Abe said looking around. "Sarah told me you just bought it."

"Gladly! Let me show you around," Thierry handed him a beer and led the way. "Bee, can you look at dinner in about ten minutes?"

"Sure, will do, honey!" Beatrice said.

"Thanks, Toots!"

As soon as the men walked out, Beatrice almost cried out at her friend: "My God, Sarah, he is stunning!"

"Yeah, I guess, but sometimes I really don't understand him," Sarah said in despair. "Must be a cultural thing."

"Well, his English sure sounds very good," Beatrice said, "so you'd think that you could clarify any misunderstanding between the two of you."

"So how are things going over here?" Sarah decided to change the subject.

"Would you believe it?" Beatrice said proudly. "We have our first bookings in for the summer and we have been approached by a tour operator who wants to discuss making us a stop for a fly-drive along the Lighthouse Route."

"Bee, that's fantastic!" She was sincerely happy for them. "See, I told you!"

"Yes, maybe being hoteliers is not as much of a stretch as I thought it would be," Beatrice sighed. "Thierry has always firmly believed we could do it."

"I'm sorry I did not bring a bottle of bubbles; this calls for a celebration!" Sarah said.

"I'm sure we have something bubbly to crack open," Beatrice said inspecting the food. "Good idea – also to celebrate Abe and you getting together."

"Well, let's not propose a toast to that just yet," Sarah said anxiously. "I don't know, something keeps bugging me about the man."

"Personally, I think you're seeing ghosts." Beatrice knew Sarah a little too well. "Just because nobody can keep up with your level of keeping contact, doesn't mean there's something wrong with them."

"Yeah, maybe you're right." Sarah didn't sound too convinced. "Besides, you have about the patience of a kitten with a new ball of yarn," Beatrice challenged Sarah with a bright smile.

"Thierry, this is amazing!" Abe was impressed with the tour. "What a great property and the location is fantastic!"

"Well, we hope it will work out; the first signs are kind of promising," Thierry said. "We really wanted to get out of the city and we love the coastline. I have wanted to do something like this for some time, but Bee wasn't too sure."

"I think this will be a very popular spot by the time people pick up on it," Abe said sounding convinced. "Have you considered how to advertise online?"

"We are now talking to an old friend who builds websites as a hobby," Thierry said.

"I used to be in that line of business with my former company," Abe said. "If I can help you with some search engine optimization or anything, let me know." Abe offered.

"I might just take you up on that offer." Thierry sounded pleasantly surprised.

"So Thierry, are you a sportsman, like sailing for instance?" Abe asked.

"I used to be a fanatic basketball player, back in Sidney Mines. Now..." Thierry looked down holding his belly with both his hands, "I'm sort of out of practice."

"Sarah is a basketball player too, isn't she?" Abe asked.

"Oh yeah! She played in Halifax in the girls' league before she started university," Thierry nodded fiercely. "Her team even made it to the national championships."

"Wow, she didn't tell me that part, well not yet anyway," Abe smiled. "We still have a lot of catching up to do."

"Sarah's a great girl, Abe; very much worth getting to know better." Thierry clapped Abe on the shoulder briefly. "So, Abe, are you a sailor? We have a great Yacht Club out here in Shelburne. It is a fantastic marina – and actually Shelburne is one of the best natural harbors in the world."

"Really?" Abe said.

They walked back in to catch up with the 'womenfolk' as Thierry called them. In the kitchen Sarah and Beatrice were preparing a large salad.

"Thierry, would you mind starting the barbecue?" Beatrice asked. "This meat needs to broil for quite a bit before it's done."

"Sure, Bee, I'll get on it straight away." And off he was again.

"Cheers, you guys – here's to a happy and healthy future here in your new hotel!" Sarah proposed the toast to her best friends. "Chin, Chin!"

"Cheers!"

"Proost!" said Abe.

"Is that how you'd say that in Dutch 'Proast'?" Sarah asked.

"Yep, remember it well – I hope for you to need it often." He winked at Thierry and Beatrice, who laughed at his cheekiness. Sarah only managed a thin smile.

"Sarah, Thierry tells me that Abe would like to go see the Shelburne Yacht Club at some point," Beatrice said as they sat down at the terrace table. "Can't we convince you to stay the night so you can take him there tomorrow?"

Sarah gave Beatrice an intense glare; they'd already discussed this. She looked over at Abe, who was talking to Thierry and seemed not to have heard. Sarah's initial feeling of another plot subsided, and she exhaled oh so slowly.

"So Abe," Beatrice raised her voice enough to catch the men's attention. "I was just saying to Sarah, if you would like to visit the marina out in Shelburne, we can offer you and Sarah a place for the night so you can go tomorrow? They do an excellent Saturday lunch buffet there." Beatrice smiled brightly at Abe. Sarah was outraged by Beatrice's behavior and looked about ready to hit her.

Abe shrugged and said: "Sure, it would be nice to see it at some point, but we can do it some other time."

"Thank you, Abe," Sarah muttered under her breath.

Having had champagne and a few drinks, Abe and Sarah eventually did decide to stay – in separate rooms at Sarah's explicit request. Beatrice walked into Sarah's room with a t-shirt to sleep in.

"I don't understand you, Sarah!" Beatrice confronted her. "Thierry and I both think he is great. We don't see anything secretive about him at all."

"I don't know, Bee," Sarah sighed. Was she really imagining things?

The next morning as they got up, Abe knocked on Sarah's door.

"Good morning, this is your wake-up call," he said happily.

Sarah opened the door and looked up at Abe. She stood on her toes and kissed him. "Good morning, this is your wake-up kiss."

"Hmmm, I could do with a couple more of those..." Abe said softly as he wanted to wrap her in his arms.

Sarah pushed him playfully and said: "Breakfast awaits!"

Abe took her hand and they walked downstairs.

Beatrice saw and tried to catch Thierry's attention. "Psst, Tree… look!" she whispered as she nodded towards the stairs. Thierry looked over and saw the two coming down, hand in hand. Thierry whispered back: "If this hotel business doesn't work out," he sniggered softly, "we can always go into match-making, or dating services."

Thierry and Beatrice served a breakfast with great variety. "Can we help you?" Abe asked.

"Nope, do sit down, we need the practice for when we have real guests," Thierry said, smiling.

"Not that you are not real guests, of course," Beatrice said apologetically.

"Say Sarah, I was thinking – if you're going to Shelburne today, Abe might also enjoy the Dory Shop Museum," Thierry mentioned as he put home-made marmalade on the table.

"What's that?" Abe asked.

"You know, you're right, Thierry," Sarah replied. She turned to Abe and said: "The Dory Shop is where they used to make wooden fishing boats, a thriving business at the end of the 19th century."

Thierry added: "They are flat-bottomed boats used to stack onto schooners to be able to spread fisherman along the sea. In the museum you can see how these dories were made."

"I am a big fan of handcrafted boats," Abe said. "I really would enjoy seeing that. Great tip, Thierry, thanks!"

Chapter 46

"What would you like to do first? The Dory Shop or the Yacht Club?" Sarah asked as they drove towards Shelburne the next day.

"Why don't we… do the Dory Shop now, have lunch in town, maybe walk around? We can do the marina in the afternoon," Abe suggested.

"Good plan!" Sarah sounded pleased. "I could do without the lunch buffet at the marina, you? I imagine a long row of elderly people waiting in line for a cheap lunch in a nice area." Sarah snorted.

"Well, I'm just glad we're not labeling people, or anything," he teased.

Sarah tried to give him an angry look, but laughed as she heard how right he was. "Sorry! I guess I'm doing it again, huh?"

They spent a long time at the Dory Shop and Museum. There were only a few people there; the summer season would start in a few weeks. It gave Abe the possibility to really understand in detail what was unique about this type of ship. He enjoyed every minute of it, especially hearing about the way there were built.

Outside, Sarah took Abe's hand as they walked into town. She explained that the historic waterfront of Shelburne had been used as a film location for 'The Scarlet Letter'.

"I don't think I have heard of it," Abe admitted.

"It's a story by Nathanial Hawthorne and this version was with Demi Moore and Robert Duvall," Sarah explained. "Shelburne starred as 17th Century Boston."

"I wouldn't mind watching *Demi some Moore*," Abe chuckled at his own joke. "I guess, we'll have to watch it sometime."

After lunch they drove over to the marina. Sarah sensed that Abe was excited about going. Men and their boats are obviously just as bad as men and their cars, Sarah concluded. She couldn't quite understand why men would stupidly gape at another man's fancy car or boat.

At the marina Abe and Sarah walked along the endless rows of ships, while Abe was admiring different systems for tilting the mast, automatic rolling of the jib. To use Matthew's phrase, Sarah thought, *'that is **most un**interesting'*.
They got to a part of the marina where older, wooden ships were docked. Abe looked admiringly at an old schooner that was just sailing in.
"Man, Sarah, look at the rigging on that ship, that schooner, over there!" he exclaimed.
"Yes, I have to admit, that one looks beautiful." In her head Sarah only heard the words *'sweet lines'* from the movie Message in a Bottle. Robin Wright Penn knowing nothing about ships and still wanting to impress Kevin Costner.
"How about this one?!" Abe broke through her reverie as he pointed towards another wooden ship.
"This one's nice too." Sarah did enjoy looking at the older boats more than the sparkly new ones they'd seen over at the other end.
"Say, if you like older boats, we should go see the Blue Nose over up in Lunenburg. I bet you will get a kick out of seeing that!" Sarah tried.
"I bet you this one flies, look at the sharp lines on that thing." Abe was obviously enthused. Sarah flipped as she saw him step across the railing onto the deck of the ship.
"Abe! *What do you think you're doing?"* Sarah hissed at him and looked around furtively to see if anyone noticed them. "You can't just step on!"
"Sarah, come and see this back deck here! It would seat 10 people easily!" He peeked inside and yelled: "The interior looks nice too!" Abe walked back over to the front of the ship.
"Don't get yourself all worked up," he said with a bright smile, "the sign at the front says '***For Sale***'! It is common practice that you can walk on and in."
"I don't *believe* you're doing this," Sarah was mortified, "what are you, planning to buy a ship?"

"Come on! Come and have a look; she's a beauty!" Abe took Sarah's hand as she looked around again. He sounded so excited he was talking really loud. Nobody was around to see them, so Sarah gingerly stepped across the low side of the railing and walked onto the deck.

"Can you please not talk so loud?" Sarah pleaded.

"Have a look at this, Sarah!" Abe was peeking in. "I bet this ship is at least 50 years old."

"Just a quick peek and then promise me we'll get off, **please**!" Sarah said whilst she kept looking around.

"Okay, just a quick look inside, see how much space is inside." Abe opened the little doors and slid back a hatch. "Wow, it is very spacious inside, Sarah, you *have* to see this!"

"Doesn't anyone lock their boats anymore?" Sarah muttered.

As Sarah walked to the other side of the ship, ducking so she wouldn't be seen from the other side of the marina, Abe went down the steps of the boat.

"Abe, you are trespassing! You know that! I'm getting off this thing!!" Sarah was furious.

"Sarah, please humor me for ten more seconds," Abe tried to convince her. "Have a look inside!"

Sarah looked through the open hatch into the cabin and her breath stopped. She saw it immediately, but was having difficulty processing the information.

"Abe, I don't understand!" Sarah stammered. "Are those the pictures of your parents?" She would have recognized those pictures anywhere – his 'movie star' mother and his 'rock-star' father - but what were they doing here?

"You like?" Abe asked expectantly.

"What..." Sarah was at a loss for words.

"Step inside, sweetheart, welcome to what's been my home for the past two months! See, I told you I had pictures on my walls," he said as he proudly pointed around.

"Do you mean to say you bought this ship already?" Sarah asked.

"Yes, I bought it back in Holland," Abe said.

"Then why is it for sale again?" Sarah was exasperated.

"It's not," Abe smiled, "but I had to say something to get you on board, didn't I?"

"But how..."

"I sailed her from Holland to Portugal with a good friend of mine, Bert."

"Portugal?" Sarah was having a hard time to catch up. "You mean to tell me you *sailed* to Portugal?"

"Yes, we were a bit rusty at first, but soon got the hang of it again." Abe laughed at the memory of it.

"And..." Sarah looked at him questioningly but couldn't say it.

Abe nodded. "Yep, and then I sailed from the Azores, Portugal, to here with my brother Hylke. He said 'hi' by the way and was sorry not to meet you here. He wanted to give us some space."

"But how long..." Sarah tried to picture it as it was slowly sinking in.

"Long enough to get you ticked off at not hearing from me, I guess."

Sarah took Abe's hand to walk down the small steps.

"Abe, this is unbelievable," she said, clearly overwhelmed. "You did all this… for me?" Had he really gone through all this trouble just to be with her?

"The closer we got to Shelburne the more nervous I got," Abe said. "I was waiting for a good moment to tell you."

"I honestly don't know what to say…"

"I thought, Sarah, if we can have a relaxed time getting to know each other, we can really make it work." Abe looked at her with such tender love in his eyes. "That way we can both have our own space."

Sarah walked up to Abe and put her arms around him.

"You crazy Dutchman; you're supposed to be flying, not sailing," she sniffed.

Abe turned around in her arms and passionately kissed her like the sailor he had become; back from months at sea.

"One thing you should know," he said, "the Flying Dutchman was a ship – a ghost ship. It never made it into a harbor and was doomed to fly over the seas."

"So glad you made it into this harbor," Sarah whispered.

"Sarah, I would do just about anything for you," he took her face in his hands. "I hope you know that."

"I've been so worried about you," she said in an accusatory tone.

"I know; I'm sorry about that, really." Abe did look like he felt remorse over this. "But you would have called me crazy and not let me do this. I had to do this of my own accord. Besides, we were never in *real* danger, just some storms and a lot of fog and some growlers, that's all."

"Oh, Abe…" Sarah looked at him affectionately.

That evening they made love for the first time, with a sense of urgency that both of them felt. In the big cabin, which Abe had decorated in simple off white colors, he showed her how much he loved and wanted her. Then their lovemaking became gentler, softer and playful.

Sarah finally understood that Abe had been true to his word all this time. He would do *anything* for her.

The next morning as she woke up she turned around and looked at him, still sleeping. His face was the nicest she had ever seen; such gentle features. The little creases around his sunburned nose as he lay there. '*Sweet lines*' she thought again, giving those words a whole new meaning. Even with his eyes closed it felt like he smiled at her lovingly. She softly stroked his thick gray hair, which woke him up. His eyes, those eyes... He took her in his arms and grinned contentedly.

"Sarah, sweet Sarah... You're all I've got…" Abe said softly.

"I mean, I want you to have all I have, share with you."

Sarah looked at him as if she considered this. "So, what you're saying is, I am *all* you've got and I can have *all* you have; which is basically 'me'. I already had 'me', Mr. Maggagga," Sarah stuck her nose in the air, "you're going to have to do a **whole** lot better than that!"

"Woman, I hope you know that no one can beat you at this word game," Abe sighed deeply. "You make fun of a poor Dutchman's disabilities," he said as he wrapped her closer in his arms.

"All right," he whispered, "I will throw myself into the bargain

too, but I hope you know what you're in for…"
Sarah just smiled; she knew *exactly* what she was in for and it was *all* she ever wanted.

The End

Epilogue

As Christmas was drawing closer, Abe sensed Sarah was growing more and more quiet. She didn't have to say it; it had always been her favorite time with Matthew.

A week before Christmas Sarah came home from work. As she opened the front door to her apartment, she stopped on the doorstep. In her living room she saw her Christmas tree, completely decorated with the hundreds of wooden figurines she had collected over the years.

"Abe?" Sarah walked over to the small kitchen where she heard the radio. Abe was preparing for dinner, doing his 'special magic' as he called it. Sarah called it 'world-war-III', after Abe had attacked the kitchen.

"I almost forgot how beautiful my Christmas tree is – and how prominently present in my small apartment," Sarah smiled shyly.

"Do you know how many of those decorations you own?" Abe embraced her and kissed the top of her head.

"How did you do all of that?" Sarah asked.

"Nicky and later Marc!" Abe said simply. "We had a great time!"

"You guys are the greatest!" Sarah sighed happily.

Abe took Sarah by the hand and led her back to the living room. There was a big gift-wrapped box underneath the tree, that Sarah hadn't spotted. She looked at Abe, who innocently raised his hands.

The label on the box said:

FOR SARAH - OPEN WELL BEFORE CHRISTMAS!

Sarah looked at it more closely. It exclaimed *HANDLE WITH EXTREME CARE* on all sides of the package.

Sarah absolutely loved presents. It must have shown on her face, because Abe said: "I think it really cannot wait much longer, do you? I mean, it being well before Christmas already."

Sarah displayed an even wider smile. "Oooh, this is exciting.

I wonder what it is."

"Well, sit down and open it!" Abe enjoyed her childlike enthusiasm.

"I will, I will. Come sit with me and we'll open it together." Sarah patted on the couch next to her.

"Open the card first," Abe said.

"Okay," Sarah said, taking the card from the box.

Dear Sarah,

In this time of togetherness, we wanted you to have a special reminder of Matthew. Matthew explained to us that these were your favorites from his collection. Thanks for all you have done for Matthew and for us.
Stay in touch Sarah, love from us all,

Merry Christmas to you and to Abe,

Mary, Paul & Helen

Sarah gave the card to Abe and stared at the box.
After she carefully undid the ribbon, she whispered to Abe:
"I can't."

"Sarah, this is one of those moments that you will feel grateful for all you have shared together," Abe took her shivering hand. "Matthew's family is right; you deserve whatever that box contains."

"I think I know what it contains…" Sarah tears were unstoppable. She slowly opened the box and inside were Matthew's most precious glass Christmas ornaments.

"He remembered…" she only said and cried as she picked up the beautiful pieces wrapped in paper; the violin Matthew had bought in Vienna; the humming bird with its colorful tail; the baroque chairs from York. "It's just too much…" she turned around looking at Abe.

"I know, sweetheart, I know." Abe stroked her hair in comfort.

"How did the box get here?" Sarah asked.

"Paul brought it over especially," Abe said calmly.

Abe picked up the keys to Sarah's car. "You know we will need to hurry, don't you?"

"Hurry? Where?" She looked up at Abe, trying to swallow.

"Well, we're going to have to get another tree, especially for Matthew's decorations!" Abe made it sound like this was common knowledge.

"Abe, I can't go out looking like this!" Sarah pointed at her face, all blotted and red.

"Don't worry," Abe said with a dismissive hand gesture, "we'll just say you had too much eggnog or something. No one will notice it in the dark anyway. Question is: where do we go to get a tree this close to Christmas?"

"I don't know, there's this one place close to my Mom's house." Sarah shrugged, trying to clean up her face. "They usually have some left with a few green twigs and double the price."

Abe grabbed her hand and pulled her out the door. "We're just going to have to keep looking till we find the right one, Sarah!" Sarah pulled him back. "I love you for doing this..." and kissed him gently.

"Hmmm, salty kisses, my favorite!" Abe smiled down on her.

And with that a new Sarah & Abe Christmas tradition was born; decorating the *'Matthew Tree'*.

* * *

Acknowledgements

Writing this, my first book, has been a fun challenge. I would not have been able to finish it, without the help of the very special people surrounding me.

First, I want to thank my amazing husband. You have already been the greatest happiness of my life for more than half of it, and we still have so much more to come. I love you so much and cannot thank you enough for all the cycling, skiing and skating you have done to give me peace to write. I know that it has been hard on you that my mind wondered off and the bed lamp was doing overtime in the middle of many a night. The refills of tea in my 'Emma'-mug are what got me through in the end.

I cannot give enough credit to my exceptional proofreaders, who have undertaken to read the first drafts of **All I've Got** and have given me such fantastic input that the book has improved dramatically over time. I know it must have been hard to give me brutal feedback when it was needed. Killing someone else's darlings is difficult, but sometimes really necessary, and I cannot tell you how much it has meant to me. Thank you for your time, effort, patience and trust. I could not have done it without you!

To my father and my dearest friend; how much I miss having you around – I cannot begin to tell you. I do feel that you have been with me all this time I wrote **All I've Got** and I know you will be with me, forever.

That concludes the acknowledgements of what has been achieved up till now. There are also some people that I would like to thank in advance, taking the liberty of looking into a bright future for my first novel:

Thank you, Kate, for playing the part of Sarah so beautifully in the Hollywood movie.

Thanks, Matt, for playing Matthew, just the way Matthew deserved to be played.

And Jack, portraying the character of the big brother – Marc - so well.

Last but not least: John – the Abe that we all look for in our lives.

I am looking forward to all the award ceremonies to honor your brilliant work; you deserve all of that!

Emma